"ARE YOU HERE TO GIVE ME ANOTHER KISS, MISS DELAMERE?"

Staverton smiled as he opened the door of the coach, but the lady did not offer a smile in return. She was situated on the far side of the roomy conveyance, gowned so differently from the day before that he wondered if it was the same young woman after all. Her elegant demeanor was as confusing as her expression. There was a hardness in her green eyes that took him aback. Had she been a man, he would have known himself to have been challenged.

"Do step into my coach, my lord. The early morning air chills me."

Staverton obliged her willingly, for he was beginning to be intrigued. She held a small muff over her right hand, an odd article in itself for a day that would prove to be quite warm by nuncheon.

"Thank you, Molly," she said, apparently directing her remarks to a serving person visible over his shoulder. "You may hand his lordship's baggage to one of the footmen. Yes, thank you, Shaw—do close the door."

Staverton turned sharply and saw that the maid was indeed delivering his luggage to one of Miss Delamere's servants. "What the devil?" he cried. When he glanced back at Miss Delamere, he discovered that she held a pistol in the hand once hidden by the muff. "Are you abducting me?"

BOOK YOUR PLACE ON OUR WEBSITE AND MAKE THE READING CONNECTION!

We've created a customized website just for our very special readers, where you can get the inside scoop on everything that's going on with Zebra, Pinnacle and Kensington books.

When you come online, you'll have the exciting opportunity to:

- View covers of upcoming books
- Read sample chapters
- Learn about our future publishing schedule (listed by publication month *and author*)
- Find out when your favorite authors will be visiting a city near you
- Search for and order backlist books from our online catalog
- Check out author bios and background information
- Send e-mail to your favorite authors
- Meet the Kensington staff online
- Join us in weekly chats with authors, readers and other guests
- Get writing guidelines
- AND MUCH MORE!

**Visit our website at
http://www.kensingtonbooks.com**

MY LADY VALIANT

VALERIE KING

ZEBRA BOOKS
Kensington Publishing Corp.

http://www.kensingtonbooks.com

ZEBRA BOOKS are published by

Kensington Publishing Corp.
850 Third Avenue
New York, NY 10022

All Kensington titles, imprints, and distributed lines are available at special quantity discounts for bulk purchases for sales
promotion, premiums, fund-raising, educational or institu-
tional use.

Special book excerpts or customized printings can also be created to fit specific needs. For details, write or phone the office
of the Kensington Special Sales Manager: Kensington Publishing Corp., 850 Third Avenue, New York, NY 10022. Attn:
Special Sales Department, Phone: 1-800-221-2647.

Pinnacle and the P logo Reg. U.S. Pat. & TM Off.

First Printing: February 2002
10 9 8 7 6 5 4 3 2 1

Printed in the United States of America

ONE

Berkshire, England, 1811

I shall force the Earl of Staverton to marry my cousin!

This thought, so novel, so perfect in form, struck Anne Delamere with all the intensity of a lightning bolt from heaven. Just how she would compel one of the wealthiest men in England to marry a vicar's daughter from Berkshire, she hadn't the least notion. However, she was a young woman of ability, in possession of an unshakable confidence, and she was certain she could achieve any object to which she set her mind.

Besides, if she had to, she would simply kidnap Lord Staverton. With her dear cousin in tow, she would cart them both off to Gretna Green, and see them married, *over the anvil,* before the cat could lick her ear.

Presently, she was walking along a winding lane which led almost directly from the village of Sulhurst to her home. Her cousin Cassaundra's house was a mile in the opposite direction, on the far side of the village. She had spent the morning there gathering raspberries from her cousin's vines, while dear Cassie had followed her down along the thick waterfall of plants, all the while weeping and at times even sobbing.

She had recounted in detail her recent and terribly unhappy experience in Brighton as the object of Staverton's false pursuit. Her tale of woe, therefore, had been accompanied by innumerable heartfelt sobs so that Anne's tender heart had been aroused to a place of wrath. All she could think of presently was the proper means of retribution for Staverton's faithless conduct toward Cassaundra.

The source of her cousin's misery was a familiar one to Anne. For years, she had heard of the wretched exploits of the Earl of Staverton from any number of cousins and more distant relations scattered about the kingdom, for hers was a large family. Apparently, his lordship enjoyed nothing more than tormenting the hearts of innocent young ladies of quality.

While sojourning in Brighton for the summer with her mother, Cassie had most unfortuitously fallen under Staverton's wicked spell. According to her cousin, the earl had sought out her company at every turn, flirting outrageously with her and making her hopeful of a happy outcome. By Cassie's report, he had expressed a profound interest in her, clearly preferring her society above all the other ladies present during the summer season.

"He even hinted at his desire to wed me," Cassie had sobbed. "I do not understand him at all!"

"Nor I," Anne agreed, carefully avoiding the thorns on the raspberry vines as she worked steadfastly at filling her basket. She wore gloves and was bent over the task at something of an awkward angle in order to keep any of the berries yet on the vine from staining her embroidered, white muslin gown. "So tell me, did he actually speak of marriage?"

"Well, no, not precisely," Cassie admitted with a frown. "But he kissed me, which is very nearly the same thing."

Anne had been so stunned by this revelation that she stood upright and turned to face her cousin, her mouth agape. *"The Infidel* kissed you?" she asked, astonished. For several years now, Anne had been in the habit of calling Staverton by a nickname she had given him upon first hearing of his antics a full five years past. She had delighted in the fact that the truly wretched name had stuck and that he was referred to by that appellation in every part of the kingdom. She continued, "If he kissed you, you had every right to be hopeful of an offer of marriage. There can be no two opinions on that score."

"The next day," Cassie had explained further, "instead of offering for me, he gave me a horrible setdown, saying that rather than setting my cap at men of rank I ought to be improving my mind."

"As though you would ever do such a thing!" Anne had returned warmly.

"Well, I might be tempted to open a book on occasion if I truly felt it was at all useful."

"I did not mean that!" Anne cried, laughing. "I mean, you would never *set your cap* at any man!"

"Oh. Oh, yes, of course I would not." Cassie chewed on her lower lip.

"What a vile, vile man he is. He misled you wretchedly, as he has a dozen others, and then tried to tell you it was all your fault that he felt inclined to flirt with you. I am more and more persuaded someone ought to set about bringing him down a peg or two. I wish I was acquainted with him, then I should be happy to do the job myself." She paused for a moment, finding herself perplexed on one point in particular. "Only, tell me, Cassie, how was it that even though you knew of his horrid reputation, you still allowed yourself to be taken in as though you were a chit just out of the schoolroom instead of an experienced lady of three and twenty?"

Cassie had appeared stricken by these accusing words and dabbed at her nose with a very damp kerchief. "I know it must seem as though I am at fault, but if just once you were to lay eyes on this gentleman yourself, you would comprehend perfectly how it was I was led astray. He is so very handsome, and while at Brighton I was actually introduced to him, which had never before occurred in London. We conversed for a few minutes and, well, I tumbled violently in love. I know you cannot understand how it happened, but so it did."

"One brief conversation and you fell in love?" Anne was completely mystified, for nothing of the sort had ever happened to her.

Cassie nodded and sniffed a little more. "I was never more surprised, but he has the most unusual gray eyes and is perfectly capable with scarcely a glance or two of attracting the notice of any female he chooses. I wish I had not been humbugged by his attentions, but I was as foolish as any lady who ever crossed the threshold of a drawing room. Oh, Anne, I do so love him. I do, I do. I doubt I shall ever be able to love another."

She fell to sobbing once more and Anne found herself reluctant to press her cousin further about how it had come about she had been bamboozled by such a man as Staverton.

At this juncture, she had changed the subject slightly, hoping to give comfort. "Have you seen Harry since you returned? Papa told me he has purchased a new team recently." Prior to this most unfortunate trip to Brighton, Cassie had been enjoying the courtship of Harry Chamberlayne, a local baronet's son. It was believed by everyone in the neighborhood that a marriage would soon be forthcoming.

Cassie blew her nose. "H-he came to Brighton and offered for me but I refused him, I was that lost in Staverton's attentions. He has not come to call since I returned. I doubt he will, and for that I would never blame him."

Anne felt angry all over again, that Staverton, in trifling with Cassie's heart, had disrupted what had previously been accounted by all an excellent match.

"I will say again," Anne had said, plopping the berries a little too harshly into the basket, "that the Infidel deserves to suffer some truly horrible punishment. I only wish we could petition the gods, as they were used to do in ancient

Greece, and beg Nemesis to attach herself to Staverton's footfalls. I have little doubt she would know precisely how to persecute him for his arrogance and cruelty!"

"If only such a thing were possible," Cassie had murmured, still weeping.

When Anne had quit her cousin's house, the basket of raspberries dangling from her arm, her mind had soon become filled with a dozen ways she might effectually become Staverton's nemesis herself. Her chiefest thought was that somehow she must find a way of forcing his lordship to do his duty by Cassaundra, and to marry her as was only right and good.

So it was, that as she strolled along the dusty lane, she became convinced that Staverton must somehow be forced to wed her cousin.

Her decision made, the task before her became easier somehow. She simply needed to find some means of bringing about the most necessary marriage. She found herself smiling. She was never so happy as when she was searching out an answer to a troublesome problem, particularly if the answer involved an adventure of some sort. Surely, a trip to Gretna Green could be accounted a very fine adventure, indeed!

The mid-August day was very dry and mounds of a fine, powdery dust had built up near the hedges. Anne stopped to remove her sandals and stockings in order that she might feel the dust between her toes as she completed the remainder of her journey to Sweetwater Lodge. Loosening the ribbons of her straw bonnet, she resumed walking and turned her mind to the happy prospect of solving a most perplexing dilemma.

If Staverton thought he could do injury to her kinswoman without the smallest repercussion, he was much mistaken, for it seemed to her that she had been chosen for just this purpose, to right this terrible wrong. She giggled, thinking someone ought to warn the earl that he had become the object of her vengeance.

She was about to cross the lane, when the sounds of a rapidly approaching carriage met her ears. The shouts of a man encouraging his horses along at a spanking pace rose into the air. She was curious as to who might be traveling such a rarely used cart track, and waited to see if perhaps Harry was out trying the paces of his new team.

A moment later, a dusty curricle emerged from around the bend in the road, producing not the aspect of Harry, but that of a complete stranger. His face was the color of beets from driving his team hard under the hot August sun, and his expression was twisted with distress. His dark, stringy brown hair hung almost to his shoulders, and his features were narrow and thin. His nose pinched at the tip and his chin pointed, and his complexion was swarthy beneath the ruby sheen. His eyes were almost black in color.

As she met his gaze, she instinctively took a step backward. Something was amiss. He was traveling at breakneck speed and did not slow in the least, even though it was obvious to a sapskull that the lane was full of dangerous twists and turns.

His gaze became fixed to hers and he narrowed his eyes. To her utter astonishment and horror, she watched him give the reins a hard jerk. His team responded, heading directly in her path. With but a second to spare in avoiding the menacing hooves of the sweating horses, she threw herself away from the team at the edge of what was a prickly hedge. The basket flipped out of her hands, the raspberries flew everywhere, and she landed with a thud on her chest, nearly losing her wind.

The curricle rushed by with but inches between herself and disaster. She found herself covered with the powdery summer dust, which quickly billowed high in the air.

She sat up choking and sputtering. Dozens of raspberries were smashed against the front of her gown, some even splattered onto her face. She groaned at the terrible stains now pressed into the gauzy white muslin. She was just struggling to her feet, secretly cursing the vicious driver, when she realized another curricle had just rounded the far bend, apparently in pursuit, and was suddenly upon her.

Fearing that this driver, too, intended to harm her, she once more leaped in the direction of the pile of crushed raspberries.

"Hell and damnation!" rent the air.

More dust billowed around her as the gentleman drew his horses up sharply. She sat up and covered her face, coughing and sputtering as she had done a half minute earlier. Before she knew what was happening, she felt herself lifted into the air by a pair of strong arms. She uncovered her face and found that the stranger was carrying her to his curricle. Did the man intend to abduct her?

Panic flooded her and she began to struggle. He held her tightly, however, unwilling to let her go.

"Gently, my dear, gently," he soothed. "I'll get you to a surgeon as quickly as possible. This is all my fault. Pray, be still! You are badly injured and your struggling will only worsen your suffering. Please allow me to attend to you!"

The gentleman's voice, commanding yet concerned, caused her to lean her head back that she might look at him. The sight that greeted her eyes bereft her entirely of speech. The man holding her was extremely handsome, like no one she had ever seen before. The lines of his face were angled powerfully. His eyes were an unusual, forbidding gray, his hair was as black as a raven's wing and his cheekbones appeared almost chiseled. The whole effect made her think of a well-crafted sailing vessel fitted for the roughest seas. The image this created in her mind made her feel entirely undone by his mere appearance. So unusual was the experience for her that she could only stare at him, her mouth agape.

She realized he was speaking and that his voice held within its core a resonant quality that afflicted her stomach in the strangest, inexplicable manner. She felt almost nauseous. "The man who did this to you is a reprehensible creature. He shall pay for hurting you, I promise you that much. Are you in terrible pain?"

Anne shook her head numbly. "I think I scraped my knee," she offered.

"What?" He seemed disbelieving.

"My knee hurts a little," she explained further. "I think I scraped it when I fell—the second time."

"My poor child. You are delirious. I must get you to the village."

"Why?" she asked sensibly.

"You are dangerously hurt!" he exclaimed. "Only look, though I fear in commanding you to do so, you will likely swoon."

He nodded his head toward her stomach. She glanced down and saw the raspberry stains. Somehow he had mistaken the color of the fruit, muddied as it was with the dirt from the lane, as blood. This struck her as so amusing that she began to laugh and could not stop.

"I fear you are brainsick!" he cried. "Come. I will drive as quickly as I am able."

He tried to lift her onto the seat of his curricle, which was rather far off the ground, but she planted her bare feet on the rim of the wheel and thereby prevented him from sliding her onto the seat.

"No, no!" was all she could manage. Her laughter had become almost hysterical so that she was unable to find the words to tell him she wasn't hurt.

"Do try and climb aboard. We must hurry!"

"No!" she cried again, wiping at her eyes.

"Do take your feet off the wheel!" he cried sharply.

The harder he tried to maneuver her onto the seat, however, the harder she laughed and resisted at the same time. Finally, she managed, "Sir, I am not hurt. I assure you. Please, put me down."

At that, he ceased in his efforts to guide her onto the curricle's seat, but he did not set her on her feet just yet. He glanced at her as she began wiping at her cheeks.

"My dear," he began softly, "your face is cut in several places and your gown is covered in blood."

She wanted to explain, but the soft seriousness of his expression set her off again.

"You must be suffering a fit of delirium," he cried, and once more began trying to get her into the curricle.

At that, she felt it necessary to explain between chuckles. "Not a fit . . . of delirium," she said, again planting her feet on the wheel. "Rather, a fit . . . of raspberries."

She whipped her arm toward the hedge, pointing in the direction of the half-hidden basket. Already, several sparrows had collected about the wicker container, pecking at the unexpected bounty. Her bonnet lay nearby, as well.

"Good God!" he exclaimed. "Are you telling me you are covered in raspberries and not blood?"

She nodded.

"Undone by a basket of fruit!" he cried. He looked at her gown and began to smile. "Well, then, I cannot tell you how utterly relieved I am. You can have no idea."

"You were very kind to have meant to take me to the surgeon, only who was that fellow who tried to run me down? Oh, and you may settle me on my feet now."

"You are barefoot," he stated, lowering her gently to the ground.

"I could not resist because the dust that collects about the lanes this time of year tends to feel like powder in places." When he appeared not to take her meaning, she added, "I am partial to the sensation of the very fine dust between my toes."

"Oh, I see."

"Only, do but tell me who it was who sent me flying into the hedge."

At that, the gentleman's expression shifted, so completely,

that it was as if a dark cloud had suddenly obliterated the sun. "I daresay he achieved his end, though I suppose it is a good thing after all. He knew I would stop if I thought you injured. Only, thank God you are not. By now, he will have . . . that is, he will have won our race. As you can see, he is hardly a gentleman."

"Well, I have no opinion of such a bad sport!" she cried, indignantly.

"Nor do I."

"Regardless, I am sorry the berries gave you the wrong notion." She suddenly felt overwhelmed by the man before her. She had to look up to meet his gaze and she was not precisely a short female. His shoulders were quite broad— no need for buckram wadding there!—and his entire demeanor spoke of athleticism and power. She had no way of knowing his interests, but if she were to guess by the sheer size of his muscular frame, he excelled in all the manly sports—boxing, fencing, riding to hounds, and driving.

Presently, he stood with his hands on his hips, glancing up the lane in the direction of the village. "I suppose I have lost him now," he murmured. "At least for the time being."

"Perhaps he stopped for a tankard at the inn. It is some of the best in the county. Such a man, I daresay, will want to gloat over his victory."

He turned to her at that and smiled. What a brilliant smile! Her heart suddenly constricted to the size of a chestnut and a euphoric sensation teased her brain. He might have been undone by the raspberries, but she felt certain she had just been undone by his smile.

"You, on the other hand, have been an excellent sport about all this, and for that I am grateful, Miss—?"

"Delamere," she responded. "Of Sweetwater Lodge." Perhaps he meant to stay for a time in Sulhurst. Armed now with her direction, perhaps he would call on her.

His expression became knowing suddenly in a manner

that she did not precisely comprehend. "I must go," he said, "but allow me this one favor."

She was about to say, "what favor," when she found herself suddenly enveloped in a Herculean embrace. He did not beg permission, but swept his lips over hers in a commanding fashion.

Anne had never been kissed before, and she had certainly never been hugged so tightly. She was three and twenty and a perfect innocent, but for the life of her, in this moment, she did not feel either innocent or inexperienced. She felt as though she had been made for just this—being kissed by a man whose mere smile could pluck her heartstrings and who had intended, when he believed she was dangerously wounded, to have saved her life.

She was stunned by the pleasure she took from his embrace. Her heart hammered so loudly in her ears that she wondered if he could hear the thumping as well; and when had her arms become slung about his neck, and when had she leaned into him so wickedly?

She did not want the moment to end. She wanted to stay transfixed forever to this very spot, the stranger's embrace the only protection between herself and the earth's continual demands.

At long last, he leaned back. His own expression seemed a reflection of how she felt. He appeared surprised, even a little doubtful, as though he could not believe what he had just done.

Her gaze drifted to his neckcloth. "Oh, dear," she murmured, seeing that the raspberries had now worked their mischief on his clothing. "It is ruined. Your coat as well, no doubt."

"Don't fret. It was worth every second of that delightful kiss. I would call on you and hopefully repeat so delightful an experience, however, though I intend to pass the night at the Grey Castle Inn, I am leaving for Bath *in the morning.*"

He bowed swiftly and with equal speed mounted his curricle. "Good-bye, Miss Delamere."

"And whom have I kissed?" she asked, taking a step toward his vehicle. More than anything, she wanted a name to accompany this most blessed event in her life, not only because she had every intention of chancing upon him at the inn this evening, but because she knew to a certainty that this was the man she would one day marry.

He smiled rather crookedly. "Though I have little doubt you already know who I am, I shall speak my name aloud merely because you've been such a good sport today. You may tell your friends that this afternoon you kissed none other than the earl of Staverton."

With that, he tipped his hat and set his team in motion.

Anne stared after him until not only he, his horses and his curricle had disappeared down the lane, but the dust his brisk departure occasioned had fallen back to earth as well. Her mind felt stuck in a very deep abyss from which she was having great difficulty retrieving it.

Finally, her thoughts began to make sense of what she had just learned: brutally handsome, the kiss of a lifetime, intense gray eyes—just as Cassie had told her—and a belief she had met her ideal.

Good God, Staverton!

"It can't be," she murmured into the empty air. "I have kissed the Infidel!"

TWO

I have kissed the Infidel.

That evening, Anne took up her place adjacent to her father at the dining table and smoothed out the peach silk of her gown in quick, agitated strokes. She had spent the entire afternoon struggling to comprehend the horrible truth that she had kissed the very man who had cut up her cousin's peace entirely and who was, in her estimation, the scourge of all English maidenly hearts. How had it happened?

"Are you all right, my dear?" her father asked, his brow slightly puckered. His brown eyes evinced a compassion that had been a great source of strength to her over the years, particularly from the time of her mother's death when she had been but a child of eight. "You seem distressed."

"I am perfectly well, thank you," she responded crisply.

He raised a brow but said nothing more as he gestured to his footman to fill their glasses with a rich, dark claret.

Anne knew her father was not bamboozled in the least but she was grateful he did not pursue the subject. The truth was, she was not at all well. Indeed, she felt badly infected, as though a disease had entered her through the portal of the kiss she had shared with Staverton, and she hadn't the least notion how to effect a cure. She had but to think of how utterly entrancing the kiss had been and she began to tremble just as though she was afflicted with the ague. As much as she despised Staverton, she could not help but believe that were she to be held in his arms once more, she might allow him to kiss her again. How was this possible?

For the entire duration of her adult life, even her schoolroom years under the tutelage of a frequently love-struck governess, she had never once known the prick of Cupid's golden-tipped arrow. The closest she had come to being enamored of anyone was of a stable boy who had worked at the manor some few years past, but when he tried to kiss her she had felt nothing short of disgust. He might have had a magical way with horses, but she did not think it a strong enough reason to oblige him with a kiss.

So it was, when Staverton kissed her and she had responded in what she had to admit was a truly wanton fashion, she could only shake her head at the mysteries which had been at work today. Had Cupid finally descended from his mansion in Olympus to prick her at last?

Lord in heaven, she hoped not! What greater irony could there be than for Staverton, the Infidel, to be the only man on earth who could possibly charm her? Of course, the mere mention of irony somehow told her the gods were at work. They were a rather unfair lot, the gods and goddesses, interested more in their own amusement and vengeance than in easing the lives of mortals.

She pondered Staverton once more, and recalled his parting words to her, spoken so arrogantly, *you may tell your friends that this afternoon you kissed none other than the earl of Staverton.* She realized suddenly that he was probably expecting her to find some excuse to come to the inn tonight. The more she ruminated over the last part of their discourse, the more she was certain of it, for he had made such a point of the matter, having emphasized, *I am leaving for Bath in the morning.*

As Anne unfolded her napkin and laid it decorously across her lap, her father disturbed her hapless reveries.

"My dear, you seem out-of-reason cross this evening. Have I offended you in some manner?"

She saw in his soft smile, the twinkle in his eye, and the absent way he scratched at his balding pate that he thought no such thing, but rather that he was concerned about her. She loved him so very much and he was such an agreeable companion, that she could not help but laugh. "You know very well you have not offended me. Indeed, how could you have when you were buried in your study all day? If I recall, I saw you but once, at nuncheon, when you appeared for a brief moment like a shooting star, took an entire plate of sandwiches from the table, bid me enjoy my correspondence, and disappeared back into your sanctuary."

"A shooting star, eh? I must say I like the image very much. However, I feel it my fatherly duty to ask what it is that seems to be troubling you, for it has been a long time since I saw your brow this riddled with thunder."

Anne chuckled and took several thin slices of roast chicken from the platter the footman had extended to her. "Like thunder, eh?" she queried, mimicking him.

He chuckled. "Yes, like thunder. So tell me, my pet, what has disturbed you?"

"As it happens, I paid a call upon your niece, Cassaundra, earlier this morning. She was in tears, and the source of her unhappiness has become my deepest concern."

"Oh, dear, oh, dear," he murmured, a new twinkle in his eye. "You are not thinking of meddling again, are you?"

"Meddling?" she cried indignantly. "Of course not. Something much stronger than a little mild interference is required in this case. No, I should think the task which needs to be performed might be better termed a mission, of sorts."

"A mission!" he cried. "Now I have palpitations." He worked at the chicken on his plate.

"I should like to see you in the grip of palpitations," she retorted, laughing.

"I say, Anne, tell me this—why was the laundrywoman

wailing earlier? I vow I heard her through three flights of stairs. Does this have anything to do with your mission?"

Anne grimaced. "Only as a rather odd coincidence. As it happened, I took a bad tumble today, in the lane. The raspberries I picked flew everywhere, but it would seem I landed on most of them, which of course is why we shall be having plum pudding for dessert instead of pie."

"Very inconsiderate of you to have stumbled, Anne. I wanted pie with my dinner."

"I know, dearest," she murmured appreciatively. "I do beg your pardon. I time my stumbles ill."

"I take it as a sign, however. You should neither meddle nor execute a mission. You should stay home, as I do, and read books, or if you like, accompany me to Cornwall next month for I intend to explore parts of the peninsula for evidence of King Arthur's existence."

To this she lifted her brow. "Intriguing," she murmured. "Almost you persuade me. However, I am pledged to do what I can for poor Cassie. She was horridly distraught, Papa. You would not have been unmoved had you seen her yourself today."

He appeared attentive, or at least tried to. She knew him well, however, and was not surprised when he said, "I do love Cook's chicken. Always a delightful flavor of lemon."

When her father began speaking of the food on his plate, it was a subtle hint that he felt he had conversed enough and meant to concentrate on his meal, which was just as well. Anne had much to contemplate, not least of which was just how much rope would be required to bind Staverton properly.

Regardless of her confusion about the kiss she had shared with the earl, there was one aspect of the whole dilemma that was perfectly clear to her—Staverton deserved to be punished. He had used so badly any number of ladies over the years, that however handsome he was, he had a reckoning to pay and she meant to ensure he discharged his debt properly. She had no doubt were his career not interrupted at this juncture, at the place where he had trounced Cassie's heart, he would continue arrogantly misusing an entire host of young ladies yet to cross his path, just as he had misused the Misses Patney, Marsh and Whitehaven.

Anne was acquainted with each of these ladies and knew their histories well. Indeed, after learning of the nature of Georgina Patney's encounter with Staverton, she had created the earl's nickname, calling him the Infidel for the first time.

Georgina, now Lady Wespall, had tumbled in love with Staverton five years ago, meeting him during her first London season. Georgina had told her the sad history herself, that Staverton had singled her out to the degree that even the most exalted of the High Sticklers were congratulating her on her conquest, when he suddenly quit her court without, according to Georgina, the smallest explanation. The humiliation and heartache she had endured was beyond description and had been the reason Anne had created Staverton's sobriquet in the first place. In her opinion, any man who would so use an innocent young lady deserved such an epithet. She had since married well, a baronet in Lincolnshire who was Anne's cousin, Sir Charles Wespall.

Prudence Marsh, a distant cousin of Anne's, was the second lady to suffer at the earl's hand. Little more than a year later, she met him during a holiday at the Lake District in the northern county of Cumbria. She had become trapped with Staverton in a covered boat dock, on the far side of Grasmere Lake, when a terrible wind had swept suddenly down from the north, blowing the waves to ungovernable heights for their small sailboat to manage.

Previously, the earl had courted her in a marked fashion for which he had since become renowned. When the wind subsided several hours later, not only did he fail to offer for her, but he quit Lakeland shortly after as though chased by a pack of hounds. Prudence, devastated by his desertion, had been disconsolate for months. A stream of anguished letters had made their way to Anne's door, revealing a deeply broken heart.

When the greater part of Prudence's grief had passed, she took up residence in a lovely cottage, deep in the Cotswolds, where she still resided. Her more recent letters indicated a genuine contentment—but at what a price. An unnecessary price, in Anne's opinion. Prudence had become a spinster because Staverton was a wholly unprincipled man.

Finally, Molly Whitehaven of Bath, who Anne knew personally from having attended Miss Mimm's Academy with her, actually spent an entire night with the earl. While taking a curricle ride about the country lanes, an unusually heavy rain had descended unexpectedly on the west country. They had found shelter in a deserted cottage and spent the night together in the face of the horrific downpour, which had sent many a rivulet flooding its banks. In the morning, however, he absolutely refused to marry her! Surely a man of honor, *a gentleman,* would have offered for her instantly, for he had all but ruined her reputation, besides the fact that Molly was desperately in love with him. Of course, her friend was made of stern stuff, and the following year, she brought the duke of Scarsfell up to scratch. Still, Staverton ought to have wed her, there could be no two opinions on that head!

These were perhaps the worst of the examples which came to mind. However, there were dozens more, of young hopeful ladies, who, once having been caught by Staverton's charm and godlike aspect, were eventually thrust aside like last year's fashions.

The list of grievances against the monstrous earl of Staverton, therefore, was long and bitter, which only made it more the wonder that she, herself, had succumbed to the Infidel. Granted, she had not known his identity when he had kissed her, but even now she could feel the tug of his charms on her untried heart. She finally understood, truly, what each of these ladies had suffered.

Once having returned home this morning, Anne had

found her thoughts consumed by the incredible encounter she'd so recently had with Lord Staverton. It all seemed so *Greek* in its portentousness. Certainly, if nothing more, her original notion of forcing the arrogant earl to marry her cousin had become so fixed in her mind, so necessary to put the world right, that she had thought of little else since. At nuncheon, her father had been mistaken when he had spoken of her "correspondence." As it happened, she was making lists, an absolute requirement for anyone embarking on so difficult a task as kidnapping a peer of the realm.

"The rope must be narrow, I think," she murmured, forgetting for a moment she was still dining with her father.

"Eh?"

"Nothing to signify, Papa," she responded, patting his hand.

Even now, she slid peas and potatoes onto the back of her fork, pressed them with her knife into the tines, and mentally reviewed all the various aspects of tomorrow's extraordinary task. She would need a fair length of rope, that was certain, as well as her pistols. How happy she was suddenly that her papa had taught her not only how to fire a weapon with a striking degree of accuracy, but how to clean and care for her firearms as well. She strongly suspected such a large man would not be brought easily to the altar without such aid as gunpowder could afford.

"Papa," she said, breaking the silence.

"Yes, my dear?"

"Did you, that is, when did you discover you were truly in love with my mother?"

"This is a most singular question," he mused, actually setting his fork down and turning to stare at her. "I cannot remember your having asked before, which leads me to wonder, why do you pose the question now? Does it have anything to do with the raspberries?"

She knew she had colored faintly for she felt a slight burning on her cheeks. "It might," she responded. No use prevaricating. Her father might be something of a recluse but that did not diminish his perceptive abilities.

"I see," he mused. "Well, then, I shall tell you. You know I met your mother in Tunbridge Wells—"

"Yes, that much I know." She took a bite of roast chicken.

"She was walking down the Pantilles in one direction and I the other. My gaze fell on her, our eyes met and held, and before I had walked two paces, I found myself tumbling in love, deeply and irrevocably. I cannot explain it, but I knew she was the woman I would one day marry."

The horror these words had upon Anne could not be expressed except in a sudden and violent choking as a piece of a chicken refused to go neatly down her throat. She immediately sipped her claret and swallowed hard. Her eyes watered and she coughed until her sides ached.

"My dear! My dear! Are you all right?"

Between sputterings, she assured him she was perfectly well.

"Remind me never to tell you about love again."

She laughed and choked a little more. She had the strongest impulse to tell him what had really happened today, and that for the barest moment, before learning of Staverton's identity, she had believed she had met the very man she would marry.

When a fine ham had been brought to her side, she stabbed a slice with her fork and pulled it indecorously from the serving platter onto her plate. "Papa," she said, "you would not worry overly much were I to disappear for a sennight, or perhaps two, would you?"

Mr. Delamere did not blink for a long moment, a certain sign that he had both heard what she'd said and was a trifle bemused by it. Being a stoic creature, and not easily ruffled by even the most turbulent of circumstances, he showed little signs of astonishment, but sat back in his chair and appeared to give her query a great deal of thought. Finally, after several minutes had elapsed, he took a sip of his claret, then said, "My dear, you are three and twenty. You may go into the world with my blessing. If you should chance to lose your fortune, remember, you can always live in the poorhouse and I will send you books on occasion."

With that, Anne smiled. She leaped from her chair, rounded the corner of the table and planted a kiss on her father's cheek. "I love you so much, Papa. However, I beg you will excuse me for I have something of a very serious nature I must attend to, even now. I will take the housekeeping money which you may remove from my account at the bank if needs be. I do not know when I shall return but I shall be gone by morning's light."

"Will you not tell me anything of this adventure upon which I perceive you are about to embark?"

She was to the doorway by the time he asked his question. She turned and smiled brightly. "I mean to kidnap a husband for Cassie, of course!"

"Oh, dear," he murmured resignedly. Mr. Delamere watched his daughter disappear through the doorway and smiled, if ruefully. He pitied the poor soul upon whom he had, in essence, unleashed his pride and joy. He loved his daughter, but he feared she was a great deal like her dear, departed mother, more than she would ever admit. His wife had been impulsive, daring, a little wild, heavenly to kiss and the greatest pleasure of his life.

He sighed heavily. He had missed his wife terribly over the years, yet he could not regret the accident which had deprived him of her companionship. After all, the very qualities which had robbed him of her company had also been the same aspects of her joyful countenance he had treasured the most.

He therefore wished his daughter well, all the while knowing, with something of a tender ache in his heart, that never again would his relationship with his beloved Anne be the same. For a long time now, he had watched her trying out her wings, uncertain of leaving the nest. Tonight, it would seem, she was going. Instinctively, he knew she was going forever, particularly since she had all but told him she had at last tumbled in love.

Lord Staverton sat in the parlor of the Grey Castle Inn and felt his impatience mount. He had been so certain the lady he had kissed, a Miss Delamere of Sweetwater Lodge, would come to him, that the hour had advanced to nine o'clock without his once doubting his conviction. Only now, as the clock slipped toward the ten hour mark, did he begin to question that she would ever arrive. He sipped his brandy and glared at the empty grate: cold, unfeeling, uncompanionable grate.

Why the deuce hadn't she come? He had told her who he was. He had kissed her thoroughly. He had even played the rescuing prince; still, the doorway remained empty. Where was Miss Delamere?

When he had kissed her in the lane leading to Sulhurst, he had felt a wonderful response in her and had known by the fairly besotted expression on her face that she was already half in love with him. So, why had she not come to the Grey Castle when he had so much as told her he would be awaiting her?

He rose to his feet, snifter in hand, and began a brisk pace of the small chamber. Four strides and he was staring out the window at the cobbled inn yard. Darkness and silence returned to him. Sulhurst was more hamlet than village and the Grey Castle was just far enough off the Bath Road to be an infrequented posting inn. The quiet of the place was almost as irritating as the absence of the female he had desired to keep him company this evening.

Damn and blast!

At the very least, he had wanted to know more of a lady who walked barefoot in the powdery dust and who, when he had thought her covered in blood, had laughed so heartily at his error. No swooning, no maidenly protestations, no artifice, no simperings. She was a country novelty and he had wanted to kiss her again. So where the deuce was she?

He was still staring out the window when the image of her face shot into his mind. Good God! She was the most beautiful female he had ever seen, a diamond of the first water. Her complexion was a milky sunset, her eyes the color of fine emeralds, her golden hair a reflection of the sun, and her lovely face a delightful combination of every elegant renaissance feature he had witnessed in the portraits of England's great houses.

Yet, with all this true beauty, she was oddly connected to the dusty lane she had been traversing, in country fashion, with her bare feet enjoying the earth and a wicker basket full of plump raspberries slung over her arm. She was a sublime, remarkable creature who had somehow managed to preserve her life in the face of the other driver's vicious intent.

Thoughts of her, of her many unique qualities, forced him to become aware that the desire to see her again was unusual. Over the years, the frequently dishonorable aspects of females in general had hardened him to womankind. Somewhere along the way, he had become a confirmed bachelor. Somehow, he had forsaken the possibility of any female ever meeting his two primary requirements, which were, in his estimation, not such harsh dictums: she must be honorable and she must truly love him. Was this so very much to ask? His experience indicated somehow it was.

Yet, there had been something about Miss Delamere in her barefootedness, her laughter in the face of a frightening event, and her beauty, that had given rise to former desires, of a wife, a family, of children filling his ancestral home.

Was it possible she was a lady who could both love and behave honorably? Because he meant to leave early in the morning, however, he doubted he would ever know the scope or design of her character.

He tossed off the rest of his brandy and crossed the plank

floor angrily to refill his glass. What was he doing in Sulhurst? He need not have spent the night here. He could have continued on his way and found a better inn at Theale or Thatcham down the road.

He had lied to Miss Delamere when he spoke of having lost a race to the gentleman who nearly ran her down with his curricle. What she would never know was that the man who had tried to hurt her was a Monsieur Bertaud of Calais, a French spy, in fact, who had in his possession documents, which, if they ever found their way to the hands of Napoleon, would endanger Wellington's army in Spain.

As a spy for England, Staverton had been assigned the difficult task of following Bertaud, and at some point in his pursuit, replacing the documents with false ones.

When the clock struck eleven, he knew for a certainty his prize had eluded him. He drained his glass of brandy, then headed for bed. Sleep did not find him right away, however. For some reason he could not explain, his thoughts were crisscrossed with images of a golden-haired beauty who had not come to him. He felt strangely as though something precious had slipped through his grasp.

THREE

At seven o'clock in the morning, Staverton bid one of the inn's serving girls to enter his chamber. She bore, per his request, a pot of strong coffee and a plate of toast, as well as a pleasant "good morning" on her lips. He scarcely noticed her greeting, offering a perfunctory smile in response as he waved her to settle the tray on a table by the door. He was fully dressed and packed for the journey ahead, his thoughts fixed entirely to the task at hand, of making certain he neither followed Bertaud, one of Napoleon's most dangerous spies, too closely nor lagged so far behind that he lost him. Either would mean disaster for the mission he had yet to complete.

He poured himself a strong cup of coffee, debating whether or not to hire someone to precede him from village to village, in order to keep a more certain, calculated watch on Bertaud as he made his way to Bristol in the west. His own position had been compromised—Bertaud now knew he was being followed.

The government's spy network had already informed him that it was their belief Bertaud would not be leaving England for at least five days, perhaps even a sennight, that he was heading to Bristol, where he would await the arrival of a smuggler's ship. Blundering upon him in Reading as he had, indicated the accuracy of this information. Had Bertaud meant to leave England quickly, he would be on a ship even now.

The incident with Miss Delamere in the lane had been an absolute godsend. He had been in pursuit of Bertaud not because he meant to capture him, but because the circumstances demanded he behave in a manner that would not arouse the spy's suspicions. Failing to give chase would have undoubtedly done just that.

Staverton's orders were not to capture Bertaud, but to switch the documents the spy was presently carrying with him. A mishap had occurred in London, where the carefully prepared but false documents intended for Bertaud had been left behind and the true ones planted by mistake. In Brighton, just a few days ago, Bertaud had succeeded in stealing the documents before they could be properly exchanged. Now it was up to Staverton to somehow retrieve the packet Bertaud had in his possession and replace it with the one containing the false documents, all without the spy knowing what was going forward. Should Napoleon's marshals serving on the Peninsula come into possession of them, a great deal of Wellington's position and strength would be compromised.

When he had come upon Miss Delamere in the lane, apparently wounded, he had been horrified by the spectacle of what had seemed like a disastrous and bloody injury. Yet, he was not surprised, for Bertaud would not hesitate to maim or even kill an English maid if it suited his objectives. The knowledge that Miss Delamere had been uninjured had relieved him beyond words. At the same time, as soon as he discovered she had not been hurt, he had thanked the gods for sending so simple an excuse for ending his pursuit of the spy.

Now, as he prepared to take up the game once more, his thoughts were only for Bertaud. Miss Delamere's lack of apparent interest in him was completely forgotten. England's welfare had taken full possession of him once more.

He finished what remained of his coffee in a single gulp. Time to be going.

A scratching on the door disrupted his thoughts. "Come," he called out.

The same maid who had brought his coffee proffered a note. He took it, frowning. What the devil was this?

He unfolded the missive, reading the signature first. *Anne Delamere.* He smiled broadly. Better late than never, he mused with a chuckle. Scanning the brief message, he discovered to his surprise that Miss Delamere was, even now, in the inn yard, in her coach, awaiting him. She had something of import she must tell him before he departed and would he please oblige her by attending her at her coach's door. She would have come to him last night to converse with him, but alas, her father was something of a tyrant and she had found no opportunity until the early morning hours to escape his watchful eye.

So that explained why she had not come to him the night before. Of course. How unfortunate, however, that he could not remain in Sulhurst a little longer. The tone of her missive indicated she had been most anxious to see him again—and why shouldn't she be when he had kissed her so thoroughly yesterday?

He left his room briskly, his booted feet happy to be hurrying to a lady in a waiting coach. Did he have time for a stolen kiss or two? Of course. Always.

When he reached the inn yard, the state of her coach surprised him on more than one count. The vehicle was quite one of the most elegant equipages he had ever seen, indicating the family had no small degree of wealth. The body of the vehicle was black and maroon, highly polished, coachman driven and attended by two footmen, all three servants of which wore a rather plain, dark blue livery. What was more, a number of trunks strapped to the coach suggested the lady was on a journey of her own. He frowned slightly. Did she suppose the brief encounter of the day before had led her to believe he would whisk her away in a scandalous elopement? Good God, she could not be such a ninnyhammer as that!

Though he was reluctant to believe she could think anything so ridiculous, his past experience with any number of foolish young ladies made it wholly possible she had arrived at just such a conclusion.

Well, if she had decided an elopement was in the offing, then the forthcoming encounter with her would prove most amusing, to be sure. He smiled. Several kisses and then he would tell her he never meant to see her again. She would express her extreme sense of ill usage and beg to know whether the kiss they had shared on the day before had meant so little to him. Had he no heart, no honor? Tears were likely to follow, as well as false fumblings with a kerchief.

When he reached the coach, he opened the door. "Are you here to give me another kiss before I depart, Miss Delamere?" he asked, smiling.

The lady did not offer a smile in return. She was situated on the far side of the roomy conveyance, gowned so differently from the day before that he wondered if it was the same young woman after all. He felt confused as much by her elegant demeanor as by her expression. There was a hardness in her green eyes that took him aback. Had she been a man, he would have known himself to be challenged.

"Do step into my coach, my lord. The early morning air chills me."

He obliged her willingly, for he was beginning to be intrigued. She held a small muff over her right hand, an odd article in itself for a day that would prove to be quite warm by nuncheon. With her left hand, however, she slowly removed the muff.

"Thank you, Molly," she said, apparently directing her remarks to a serving person visible over his shoulder. The coach rocked gently as one of the footmen hopped off the back of the coach. "You may hand his lordship's baggage to one of the footmen. Yes, thank you, Shaw, and do close the door."

Staverton turned sharply and saw that the same maid who had brought him his coffee, as well as Miss Delamere's missive, had, by prearrangement, secured his luggage and was even now delivering it to one of Miss Delamere's servants.

"What the devil?" he cried. He shot a glance back at Anne, and to his great shock discovered that she held a pistol, primed and ready, in her left hand where the muff had been.

"Pray, do not fret, my lord. I have discharged your bill already. Oh, and do not think for a moment that I am unacquainted with weaponry. I have a precision of aim equaled only by my father." Here, she smiled faintly. "Although, I believe one would have to be a poor marksman, indeed, to miss one's target at this range."

He stared at her, realizing he had blundered seriously, *again,* for the second time in the space of two days. He had stumbled into Bertaud at Reading, and now this! Good God, how could he have ever permitted a mere woman to have tricked him as Miss Delamere had in this moment? Was she in league, then, with Bertaud?

He could not imagine this being true, but then, many strange things had occurred since he first made himself of use to his country as a spy.

"Are you abducting me?" he asked.

She nodded. "I see you do not lack for intelligence."

He glanced at the very fine pistol she held in her hand. She may have boasted of knowing how to use it, but he doubted this was true. He had never known a lady, any lady, to be interested in anything other than her gowns, her needlework, the latest gossip, and whether she would dance every dance at a ball. Regardless of his opinion of the fairer sex, in the close confines of the coach, just as she said, it would not matter whether she was an excellent shot or not.

"What do you desire of me?" he asked. "For what reason could you possibly want to abduct me? I cannot believe you require a ransom since your coach and your gown speak otherwise of your circumstances."

"Again, your perceptions are correct."

"Why then? Is it Bertaud?"

The quick frown on her forehead told him she did not know of such a man.

"Who?"

"Never mind. Only tell me what you want."

A cold smile touched her lips. "To right a dreadful wrong. You wounded my cousin severely, Lord Staverton, and I intend to see that you do what is right by her and marry her."

"You want me to marry your cousin?" he asked, astonished. Who the devil was her cousin?

"Precisely," she responded.

"You do not want me for yourself?" he asked. He saw the barest flicker of emotion pass through her eyes. So brief was it, however, that he wasn't certain whether his question had hit the mark or whether she was merely disgusted. Good God! He had never before had a woman express disgust toward him, at least not after he had kissed her.

"No," she responded definitively. "I have no interest in you."

He regarded her for a moment. His attention was caught suddenly by her elegance. She looked quite different from the barefoot country maid of yesterday. Presently, she was very English, gowned fashionably in a dark green traveling gown of a fine-patterned silk, high-necked and edged with a ruff of lace. Her bonnet was of a matching fabric, of a slightly poke style, and trimmed with Brussels lace. She was a blend of forces, he thought—her incomparable beauty, her country liveliness of yesterday and today's cool elegance. Apparently, she was a woman of various parts, and he found himself even more intrigued.

Who was Anne Delamere? Why had he never before met her in London? He had the strangest most sudden desire to pull her into his arms again and feel all that beauty and self-assurance cradled against his chest. He felt in some mysterious way completely undone by the lady aiming a pistol at him, a sensation he had never before experienced. Always the ladies he met in the elegant salons of the *haute ton* made no secret of their intentions in their quick smiles and fluttering fans. They were predators, hurrying to his side with artifice and cunning, hoping to engage his interest in order to capture a handle to their names.

Apparently not so the young woman before him, however, except perhaps on behalf of her cousin.

"Who, then, is this lady you intend for me to wed?" he asked, thinking the encounter, though intriguing, could not be more absurd.

"Cassaundra Bradley."

Now he understood. "I see," he murmured. He had singled out Miss Bradley recently in Brighton because she had so clearly set her cap at him. He had merely delivered a lesson richly deserved.

"You met her, and used her quite ill, at Brighton this summer. You do remember her, do you not, my lord?" Her tone was coarsely facetious.

"Of course I remember her. She pursued me day and night for weeks. I gave her what was only her due—a flirtation, a setdown, and the ending of her hopes."

She pursed her lips together and narrowed her eyes. "Why, how very magnanimous of you," she returned sarcastically. "Though I daresay you are twisting the truth a trifle, for I believe it was you who pursued her."

"I suppose it could have appeared that way, but not in truth."

"I have no doubt we shall disagree on the nature of truth this morning. For now, however, pray seat yourself with your back to me. If you struggle, I warn you I will fire the pistol without the smallest qualm of conscience. You have enjoyed your final flirtation, Lord Staverton, and you must now prepare to marry the last of the hearts you have so cruelly used and broken. My cousin is a dear young woman, with one of the sweetest natures in all of Berkshire. She will make you an excellent wife, yet how much better had you discovered as much for yourself these past several weeks, instead of treating her so shabbily. Pray, put your hands together in fists. Yes, that will do nicely."

He felt the loop surround his wrists and he flexed his muscles that he might eventually be able to work his hands out of the rope. Even so, he was astonished at how tightly the lady was able, with one hand, to draw the knot. She was not, apparently, without some experience. He winced. She wound the rope several mores times about his wrists. When he felt her other hand working the ropes as well, he knew she had settled the pistol on her lap and that he had a chance to escape. Once again, however, her carelessness could easily discharge the pistol, which could mean the end of his life. He waited, therefore, stunned by how she had managed to capture and bind him so cleanly, as though she had practiced doing so for ages.

He could not help but ask, "You seem quite expert. Are you much in the habit of kidnapping men of rank and forcing their nuptials?"

"You may sit back now."

When he did, she shifted at the same moment to the forward seat, her pistol aimed at his heart. "I will trust you not to use your boots against me and to behave the gentleman, for I warn you, my servants are utterly devoted to me and will not hesitate to come to my aid."

He was suddenly all out of patience. "I beg you to consider what you are about, Miss Delamere," he snapped. "I should not like to see you hang at Tyburn Tree." He would have revenge on this ridiculous chit who told him he was to behave the gentleman while she was committing a crime worthy of hanging.

"That is a risk I am willing to take," she stated without flinching, "for the pleasure of seeing you do, just once, that which is right."

"That which is right!" he cried. "How would you know

what that is unless you have marched about in my boots for a time and seen just how cleverly your cousin arranged to be everywhere I happened to be. You seem to believe her innocent of any wrongdoing, that all cruelty was on my side, but I tell you, never for a moment did I believe she loved me."

The lady opposite him stiffened. "You are wrong, my lord," she stated, her voice quivering. "Had you seen her yesterday you would be in no doubt of her sentiments, but I will not quibble with you about any of these things. You are to wed her, and that, my lord, is that!"

Lord Staverton had never been so furious in his life. He felt that in some incredible way, fate had reached down to him for the sole purpose of slapping him hard across the face. This was, in his mind, the culmination of his entire courting career, that a lady, indignant he had snubbed her cousin, was actually kidnapping him for the purpose of forcing him into an unwanted marriage. He shook his head in disbelief. This was what he had been attempting to avoid his entire life—a loveless marriage. Yet, here he was, apparently bound for the altar to be joined in matrimony to a woman he could not esteem and whom he truly believed did not love him.

"You cannot mean to do this thing!" he cried at last. "It is ridiculous in the extreme."

"Ridiculous or not, consider it done," she responded pleasantly.

When he saw she meant to signal for her coachman to set his team in motion, he cried, "Please, wait! There is something you must know."

She lifted a single brow. "Yes? And what might that be?"

Staverton was not in the least certain of the wisdom of his present intention, but given the tightness of his bindings, the pistol still primed and leveled at his chest, and the obvious willingness of two footmen and a coachman to do whatever their mistress required of them, he felt he had no choice.

"The man who nearly ran you down yesterday—" he began, lowering his voice. Good God. Was this in any manner what he ought to do, to tell her he was a spy for the British government? Did he truly have a choice? After all, he could escape at some point, particularly since he had nearly worked loose of the rope, but how much precious time would he lose in waiting for the right moment to part from her? He could not afford to allow the French spy to leave England in possession of the particular documents he had stolen three days ago from the Brighton Pavilion.

"Speak, my lord," she commanded. "Unless you can give some extraordinary reason as to why we cannot fetch my cousin and begin our journey to Gretna Green, then I shall give my coachman the order now."

"I was not in a race with that man yesterday, the one who tried to hurt you. I told you it was a race, but that was a lie."

"I don't see how this is pertinent."

"I was pursuing him on a matter of extreme import to the Crown, indeed, to England." His voice was low, almost a whisper. "The man you saw, who tried to run you down, was none other than a French spy."

A gentle frown split her brow. "I beg your pardon? A French spy? And you expect me to believe this? Lord Staverton, I begin to think there is something critically wrong with your mind that you must make up such a Banbury tale merely to avoid being married."

"Please listen, Miss Delamere," he said, leaning forward intently. "We were not in a race. I had made a tactical error yesterday at Reading. I blundered into the spy, supposing he must have already passed through the market town. I had been assigned to follow him at a distance and at an appropriate moment to engage in a particular mission for the government."

"What mission?" she asked.

Staverton paused for a long moment, searching her eyes carefully. Finally, he said, "To exchange documents in his possession with ones I am presently carrying."

She stared at him in some astonishment, even disbelief.

He continued. "When Bertaud recognized me, for he has long since known who I am, I had to give chase in order that he might think I had always intended to capture him and turn him over to the government. To appear as though that was not my intention would have aroused suspicion. The documents he'd stolen, destined no doubt for Paris, could affect the outcome of the war."

"Good God," she muttered, her shoulders drooping slightly.

"You believe me then?"

"I am not certain." She settled the pistol on her lap. "Are you saying, then, that you, yourself, are a spy?"

"Of sorts, only here in England. I perform services for the Crown when called upon. This was one of them. I do not do the truly hard work overseas, being utterly inept at languages. My French is abominable or I would have enjoyed functioning as secretary to the foreign ambassador's office. I cannot believe I am telling you these things except that time is of the utmost. I cannot let Bertaud outdistance me. I fear were we to delay much longer I might lose him entirely."

Never in her wildest dreams would Anne have imagined hearing these pronouncements from Staverton's lips. A hundred, a thousand other things, all proffered in the hopes of preventing an elopement, but not this! Still, what if he was attempting to bamboozle her? "I wish to see the documents," she stated at last. She must have proof or she would always wonder if he had made up the story merely to distract her, particularly if at some point he escaped her.

"We do not have time."

"Nonsense. If I find you are telling the truth, you can hire an extra team for your curricle and make up these lost minutes quite easily."

"Very well!" he snapped. "Summon your man."

Anne called to her footman who once more jumped down from his post behind the coach again rocking softly.

"Yes, miss?" he queried.

"Shaw, I beg you will fetch one of his lordship's portmanteaus. He will tell you which."

Lord Staverton directed the footman to the smallest of the three.

"I hope you mean to untie me. I would rather rifle through my own baggage, if it pleases you."

"Yes, of course," she said. When he turned around, she removed the bonds quickly.

Once Staverton had the proper portmanteau in hand, he made haste to retrieve a leather packet, which he untied and handed to Anne.

Again, she lay the pistol carefully on her lap, facing the muzzle toward him. She slid the documents out of the packet and began to read. "Goodness," she murmured after a moment, "I can only suppose these are genuine since I cannot for the life of me think why you would carry around forgeries in the expectation that one day you might need them in order to avert an elopement."

"You have spoken truly," he said, smiling faintly.

She handed the packet back to him. "I knew there was something wrong with him," she said, eyeing him keenly. "I met his gaze just as he turned the bend in the lane yesterday. His eyes had taken on a strange expression and a moment more he jerked his team purposely toward me. He could have slain me, but I believe he achieved his true objective—to keep you from pursuing him."

"That is my belief, as well. Where my mission was concerned you were sent as an angel in that moment, for I needed badly an excuse to leave off the chase."

Anne felt as though her life had just been turned upside down. She had planned a simple kidnapping, that was all. She had never meant to interrupt a British spy's pursuit of a French spy. She still could not credit it was true, yet by all the evidence before her, it was.

"I must let you go," she said, shaking her head in some

bewilderment. "But the moment your task is completed, you must return to me. Do you understand?"

At that, he laughed. "I will never return," he cried. "Only a nodcock would be so foolish."

"Of course, you are right," she agreed readily. "There is only one thing to be done, therefore."

Suddenly, he leaned forward and, because he was no longer bound, he simply took the pistol from her, emptied the pan of its contents, and tossed the firearm on the floor.

Anne lifted a brow, then laughed outright. She called to her footman again. "Shaw, come *directly!*"

Staverton attempted to leave the coach, but found a pistol pressed against his stomach by none other than Miss Delamere's footman. "Ye'll have to return to the coach, m'lord, until Miss Anne says ye may leave."

Staverton drew back inside and slid onto the seat. "Too devoted to you by half," he complained, laughing. "However did you earn such loyalty?"

She smiled at that. "By treating them all like princes. You would have been much the wiser to have shown even half as much courtesy to my cousin instead of using her to somehow avenge your aggravated pride. If I do not much mistake the matter, Lord Staverton, you are so used to being pursued for your rank and your fortune that you have forgotten that the creatures who pursue you are merely mortal." She gave a brisk nod. "You will not like it above half, but I have decided I will go with you. We shall take my coach and Monsieur Bertaud will be none the wiser. Besides, with three servants in attendance, you will be much more comfortable than were you to travel alone."

He had intended to set up a caterwaul at this juncture, but her words gave him pause. She was right, Bertaud would have no idea he was now traveling in a fine coach with a beautiful lady.

"You do not have a maid with you?" he inquired.

"No. I have always found that the inns along the way can

supply me with the help I need for dressing my hair, whereas my coach and portmanteaus are a different matter entirely."

"I was referring to a proper chaperon if we are to travel together, or have you forgotten the proprieties?"

"I have forgotten nothing," she stated. "The truth is, I don't give a fig for that, at least not for myself since I have no interest in marrying you, or anyone for that matter. You see, I am quite wealthy. My father's estate is not entailed and my mother was an heiress. I mean to have adventures." Her eyes danced. "And it would seem this shall be my first!" She called to her coachman and directed him to take the road to Bath.

"Aye, miss!" the coachman called without even a murmur of dissent. A moment more, and the fine, well-sprung equipage was moving out of the inn yard.

"Do you have a particular route you wish to take?" she inquired. "That is, do you know where Monsieur Bertaud is headed?"

"To Bristol. The old Bath road will serve, though I might wish to take the diversion through the Saversnake Forest, but we probably will not reach the Wiltshire border until tomorrow."

"Very well," she responded, smiling. She seemed inordinately content. She retrieved the pistol from the floor and checked its parts. When she was satisfied with the state of the pistol ball within, she returned the firearm to an inlaid case which held a matching pistol.

Staverton wondered at the creature before him. He had watched her examine and handle the weapon with an experienced eye and his respect for her increased, even if he thought her a trifle shatterbrained. What sort of female goes about abducting peers with all the appearance of one who has sat down to partake of a cup of tea? She could not have all her wits about her, yet there was an intelligence in how quickly she analyzed the situation before her, particularly in demanding to see the documents in question.

He could not make her out. She meant to travel with him, a maiden, night and day, sharing the road with a stranger. She seemed to understand that she would be ruined in doing so, but she did not seem to care. Certainly, she must be addled.

On the other hand, when would he ever enjoy such a perfect opportunity to punish womankind so completely? Miss Delamere may protest that she was uninterested in matrimony, but let her discover how badly her reputation would be ruined and she would demand he wed her.

He smiled to himself. All he would ever have to say to either her or her father was that she had kidnapped him. That word alone would send chills down any thinking man's spine. Kidnapping was one of the most serious offenses in the kingdom. Now that he considered his situation, he found he could relax. He would be traveling incognito, he had three servants to increase his comfort, a wealthy lady to pay the shot, and the means by which he might ruin Miss Delamere's reputation forever.

What a fine morning this had turned out to be after all!

FOUR

As the coach rumbled onto the highway, Anne found herself utterly bemused by Staverton. How could a man, so unrepentantly cruel to the ladies upon whom he deigned to cast his eye, also be in possession of sufficient pluck to act as a spy, to place his very existence in danger with every mission he was given to accomplish? She wound the rope about her fingers in a slow, methodical manner, attempting to reconcile in her mind the earl's seemingly incongruous parts.

To further disrupt her tidy opinions of him, he made an unquestionably dashing figure in a dark blue coat of superfine, a waistcoat of matching fabric, a neatly tied neckcloth, pale breeches and gleaming top boots. He was in nearly every respect the stuff of heroic legends, even to the degree that the angled, almost molded features of his face seemed to belong more to Olympus than England.

"You know, Staverton, you could easily have made a fuss in Sulhurst and brought the local constable to your aid." She smiled faintly. "Indeed, for a moment I rather thought that was what you were going to do."

"I was."

"So, why did you not?"

His expression grew quite shrewd, if cold. "I was pressed for time and I am no fool. You presented me with an alternative that suited my needs even more fully than my own curricle and pair, and I might as well be comfortable as not, just as you suggested. Besides, I did not see how I had anything to lose in acquiescing to your schemes. If you must know, only this morning I was considering hiring a man to aid me along the way. Your offer was providential, to say the least."

"Except that at the end of this journey you will have to marry my cousin, or do you think you shall escape me?" She settled the rope on the seat next to her. She realized she was fascinated by him, by his occupation, and in this moment, by his obvious disdain for her.

He crossed his arms over his chest and held her gaze purposefully. "A great deal may happen on such a journey as this."

"I see what it is," she stated. "You do not believe I am either serious or dedicated in my purpose."

He laughed outright. "Tell me, Miss Delamere, just how do you intend to force a marriage between myself and your cousin? You can hardly drag both of us to the altar and expect a man of the cloth to perform the ceremony when at least one of the party will be protesting strongly, or have you not considered as much?"

Anne lifted her chin slightly. The truth was she had contemplated this particular aspect of the kidnapping and had already concluded that she hadn't the slightest notion just how she was to bring a willing Staverton before the proper cleric to speak his vows. However, the notion of the august earl arguing at the altar was a delightful image to ponder. "Just as you have said, my lord," she responded happily. "A lot may happen on such a journey as ours. Perhaps you will experience a profound change of heart and willingly wed my cousin."

Once more, he burst out laughing. "Not likely, my dear."

Anne shrugged. "Change of heart, or no, somehow the business will be managed. Within at least a fortnight's time, I predict you will have a bride, like it or not."

He narrowed his eyes. "I prefer not to dwell overly much

on the future. Right now, I am thinking only of the man I am pursuing."

"Just as you should," Anne said. She watched him for a long moment, her mind pondering yet again all that he was. She decided he was right in this instance. With such a mission as he had before him, he should not be thinking of his forthcoming nuptials, whatever the circumstances. She turned the subject sharply. "If we travel through the night we can be in Bath by tomorrow evening, sooner if you wish for it. I have no doubt my coachman would enjoy handling a third pair."

"You would do that?" he asked, obviously astonished.

"Whyever not?" she queried. "My coach is built for speed and I have no particular fear of traveling at a breakneck pace, if that is what concerns you. In truth, I would delight in it."

"You do realize that, in the event of an accident, the faster the equipage is moving the greater the risk of injury, even death."

"Yes, of course I do," she responded earnestly, leaning forward in her seat. "However, my coachman is both skilled and experienced. I have every confidence he could manage six horses over the worst of terrain or in the midst of the most tempestuous weather. He has been handling the ribbons since he was a lad. You need not be concerned on that score. Besides—"

"Enough!" he cried, chuckling. "You have persuaded me. And I am much obliged to you. However, the business at hand cannot be concluded so swiftly. We do not, as it happens, need to be rushing headlong to Bath. Our spy is to board a sailing vessel at Bristol sometime later in the week. I am convinced he is not in the least anxious to reach Somerset, which was why I did not hesitate to break my journey at Sulhurst."

"He means to tarry along the way?" she asked, surprised. "I should think he would hurry to Bristol and board any ship that would have him."

"Some would undoubtedly do so," he responded, balancing himself as the coach hit a rut. "Not this man. Because of the war, only smuggling vessels head to France. Bertaud will wait for the agreed upon ship. Besides, if I do not miss my mark, now that he knows I am following him, he will attempt to disrupt my pursuit, if nothing more than for the sport of it."

"Indeed?" Anne murmured, stunned. She recalled the strange look in Bertaud's eye yesterday when he turned his horses toward her at the very last moment. She had known even then it was no accident. "Do you believe he means to do you harm?"

Staverton removed a small enameled box from the pocket of his coat and took a pinch of snuff. "I am in no doubt of it," he responded. "I suspect he will not be content until I am left for dead on some country lane, my throat cut, my very lifeblood draining into the dirt."

He scrutinized her every expression and gesture in this moment to see how his words might have affected her. He had meant to shock her, to punish her a little for the kidnapping. However, beyond a faint rising of color on her cheeks and the glitter in her green eyes, she truly did not seem overset by his remarks. He frowned. Perhaps she was addled, just as he had suspected earlier. "Have you nothing to say?" he asked.

She met his gaze in an open and forthright manner. "No. You meant to give me a shock and you failed."

"You do not feel in the least faint?"

"Did you expect me to, at the mere mention of the word *lifeblood?* Is that how you perceive me, my lord?"

"No," he responded, searching her face. "However, I did think you might at least confess a palpitation or two."

She chuckled. "I am not such a poor creature. In truth, what is it you have said to me other than what Bertaud *intends?* What he intends and what will follow I have little doubt will be two different things entirely. Why borrow trouble?"

At that, he could only shake his head. "You are an oddity, Miss Delamere."

He watched her sigh with some satisfaction. "Yes, I know I am, but I do not care even the smallest whit for what you or anyone else might think of me. I hope to have adventures and I must say, my lord, this is a far better adventure than any I ever imagined, and in my day I have imagined quite a few."

His lips twitched. "You, being as ancient as you are," he teased. He thought she could scarcely be much above twenty.

At that, she laughed. "I suppose it must sound ridiculous to you, but you are a man. What can you know of how cloistered a lady's life is generally? All I had were my airdreams, at least for the most part. I mean, I did ride my horse as far as Reading on occasion, and once to Mortimer, which is on the Hampshire border. Alas, the land is tilled and hedged and all the highwaymen are gone. The closest I really came to excitement was chancing upon a party of gypsies to the northwest, but they were a rather happy lot and did not even try to steal from me."

"How ungenerous of them!" he exclaimed, entering wholly into the spirit of her complaints.

"Indeed, I thought as much. I gave each of the children a shilling anyway."

"Just as you should. Did they test the coins?"

"Of course, biting them."

"That is something. One does not always have one's charity examined so forcibly."

"Yes, but I had much rather have had a pistol held to my throat."

"What lady would not?"

"Precisely. Now you begin to understand me." She appeared contemplative for a moment, then continued, "There is an enormous disparity between pretending that something is happening and experiencing an event when it does happen.

What occurred yesterday in the lane as well as our journey today, both are quite beyond all expectation. I only hope I can be of some use to you where Bertaud is concerned."

"Somehow I expect you will be," he said sincerely. Staverton found himself charmed despite his intention of remaining indifferent. He had meant to sustain the hostility he felt toward her, but already he was conversing with her as old friends might. He had even teased her a little. "And now, I suggest we decide just what our relationship must be, Miss Delamere, during the course of our time together."

"First," she said, "you must call me Anne. It will not do for you to keep addressing me so formally."

"Unless I was your guardian," he suggested.

"On no account," she said. "You are far too young and I too old. It would appear very odd."

"Do you have an idea of your own?" he asked.

"What do you think of posing as brother and sister at the various inns along the way?"

"Brother and sister? On no account, for I am convinced the moment we settled on this relationship, we would chance upon someone or other intimately connected to my family, or yours, who would know at once we were shamming it."

"Then we would be in the basket, indeed," she mused. "Besides, we do not even look alike. Who would believe us?"

"There is that," he said, smiling. "My hair is black and yours a beautiful wheat color. It would be rare siblings, indeed, that exhibited such a contrast."

"Well, we can hardly claim to be mere acquaintances, for how then could we be traveling together without benefit of a chaperon? What a scandal that would be, not to mention that we would be turned away from the finer inns, and whatever this journey might be, I do intend to sleep well when we must take to our beds at the end of the day."

Her mode of expression was so arch, so full of enthusiasm, that he found himself amused. "Your point is well taken," he said. "Might I suggest, therefore, that we become *cousins?*

Nearly the entire *beau monde* is connected in one way or another. A relationship as cousins would go unquestioned."

"Yes," she agreed. "And you may say you are escorting me to Bath. I have an aunt who resides there, one of my father's numerous sisters."

"Very well," he said. "It would seem that I finally caved to enormous familial pressure, and consented to take my extremely irritating cousin to visit her aunt in Bath."

The lady across from him laughed. "Must I be *extremely irritating?*"

"Why, yes, I do believe so. After all, you kidnapped me. I think your character should bear one or two unattractive qualities."

Anne smiled. "You know, you do not seem like such a bad fellow as I imagined, and I can see why Cassie loves you as she does. You have a wonderful sense of the ridiculous."

Staverton smiled ruefully. "Was that a compliment?" he asked. "For I vow I am not quite certain."

Her lashes fluttered in the prettiest manner possible and he could see the faintest bloom on her cheeks. "There, you see—you are being absurd again."

He watched her closely. Had she been any other lady, he would have suspected her of flirting with him, but he knew already she would do no such thing. There was no artifice in Anne Delamere.

She drew in a deep breath and addressed the matter at hand. "So we are to be cousins, then?"

"Yes."

"Well, *cousin,* will you tell me of our spy? If I am to be of any use to you, I should like to know more of him."

"Of course."

Staverton debated just what he ought to tell her. After all, it wasn't as though she was asking him for instructions as to how to go about shodding a horse, but rather about matters that ultimately involved the future of England. On the other hand, there was something about her that invited confidence. He felt certain she could be trusted with at least some of the secrets pertinent to Jean Bertaud. Besides, he might cross her path and she would do well to know as much as possible about their enemy.

"We believe Monsieur Bertaud has been operating in England since nearly the beginning of the war. He would have been in his mid-twenties when he began his career. You have seen him. He is nearly forty now. His longevity as a spy speaks strongly as much for his cunning as for his intelligence.

"Over the past several years, I have been assigned to him on numerous occasions, but I have never actually faced him in battle, as it were. Yesterday, in Reading, was the first time I ever gave chase. My previous missions involved following him and observing his activities. Much of the work of a spy is rather dull, you see, unless of course one bungles it as I did in stumbling upon Bertaud in the middle of Reading's High Street. I hope to avoid future contact with him, but yesterday's disaster may have already made that an impossibility."

"I am wondering," she mused. "Do you presently believe he might have secreted himself between Sulhurst and Theale in order to watch for you? Do you think it possible he knows where you are even now?"

"I sincerely doubt it," he responded, smiling once more. "For he cannot possibly be aware that I was abducted by a deranged young female and forced to travel with her in a quite opulent traveling coach."

"No, he could not," Anne agreed cheerfully.

She turned around in her seat to catch her bearings. "Ah, we are nearly arrived at Theale. What do you intend to do?"

Staverton leaned sideways and glanced out the window. The village was quite small but well-trafficked since the Bath coaches traditionally stopped at the local inn to provide their passengers with cakes and ale. "I should like to inquire at The Crown to see if a man of Bertaud's description has passed through."

"I would be happy to perform the office. Given what you have told me, there is a possibility he might be waiting for you."

"I believe you have the right of it," he said, turning to watch her closely. "Unless you desire one of your servants to inquire about him. After all, Bertaud might recognize you."

"Even if he did, what is the likelihood he would connect my presence in the inn to you? No, I think the matter ought to remain between you and me, at least for the present."

"As you wish," he said. Her complexion was heightened and her lovely green eyes were aglow. Even a nodcock could see that she was anticipating with no small degree of pleasure her first steps into the world of subterfuge.

"What do you think of the notion that I tell the publican I am meeting my brother, then offer a description of Bertaud?"

He chuckled. "I begin to think you might just have a talent for spying, Miss Dela—that is, *Anne.*"

"Why, thank you, Staverton," she returned archly. "Now tell me, was Bertaud's curricle burgundy with black markings?"

Staverton was surprised. "You are right, but how on earth you can remember such a thing when the last time you saw his carriage he was bearing down on you, I shall never comprehend!"

"And this seems remarkable to you?" she asked, her brow furrowed slightly.

"Quite."

"I . . . I do not know," she responded, apparently bemused. "Except that I tend to recall the details of things, regardless of the circumstances."

"Then, describe Bertaud to me," he commanded, desiring to test her. "Let us see the scope of your memory."

Anne was not in the least shaken by his proffered challenge. Indeed, a certain spirit of excitement rose within her and her senses sharpened. Closing her eyes, she took herself to the lane of the day before. She felt the sun on her arms and her neck, where it had crept beneath her bonnet. She heard the sounds of the carriage approaching, the call of Bertaud to his horses, the skill with which he maneuvered the turn that brought him fully into view.

"His hair was brown," she began. "Yes, a very dark brown and rather shaggy, hanging as it did from beneath his black hat clear to his shoulders. The day was hot and I recall that some of his hair stuck wetly to his forehead. His eyes were the color of coal, fierce in expression, certainly devoid of any compassion. He wore a Belcher neckcloth, red spotted, which I must say is not very wise for a spy. Much better a plain white stock and cravat. He appeared to me to be a tall man, though not nearly so tall as yourself, and his shoulders had a slouched appearance. He could benefit from a little buckram wadding in his coats in future. He was lean, his features narrow and thin." She touched her face by way of demonstration. "His cheeks seemed rather sunken. His nose was hawkish and pinched at the tip, his chin pointed, yet as I describe him I must say I recall thinking he was not unattractive. Oh, now that I think on it, there must have been a scar across his right eyebrow because the clean line of his brow was broken."

When she fell silent, Staverton, who had once again crossed his arms over his chest, stared at her with an inscrutable expression. At that moment, the coach began to slow as it entered the village of Theale. "Nothing else?" he asked, facetiously. "The name of his tailor, perhaps?"

Anne could not help but smile. "Perhaps I will remember more later."

He shook his head. "And you saw all this in a matter of seconds, for I know from having rounded the same bend in that lane yesterday, I was upon you in perhaps three beats of my heart."

Three beats of my heart.

These words had a sudden and quite strange effect upon

Anne. Her thoughts curled backward once more to the events in the lane, only this time she was not thinking of Bertaud, but solely of Staverton. Her heartbeat quickened as she recalled being caught up in the earl's powerful arms, of how desperately he tried to save her when he thought her injured, and how warm his lips had been upon her own.

She shifted her gaze away from his. For some reason she could not explain, her heart had begun to ache.

"Yes, you were on me rather quickly," she agreed, pretending to scrutinize the various cottages and shops of the village. The coach had begun to slow on approaching The Crown. She felt overwhelmed suddenly, at how drastically the nature of their journey had changed since the inn yard of the Grey Castle Inn. Was she truly going to seek out a French spy?

"We have arrived," she said, taking a deep breath as the coach pulled into the inn yard. When the vehicle drew to a stop, she tucked her muff next to the coiled rope and moved toward the door. In doing so, she inadvertently bumped Staverton's legs, which caused her to stumble. He quickly placed a hand on her waist and steadied her. "Careful," he murmured.

She looked down at him and met his gaze. How right Cassie had been. He was inutterably handsome. She smiled faintly. "I shan't be but a few minutes," she said.

The footman opened the door for her and let down the steps. A moment more and she was crossing the inn yard, still bustling with passengers from the Royal Mail, which had arrived a few minutes earlier.

Entering the inn, she made her way to the threshold of the breakfast parlor, which was stuffed full of patrons enjoying, just as Staverton had said, cakes and ale, and a fair amount of coffee and tea as well.

Glancing from one visage to the next, she soon discovered that her quarry was not within. She inquired of the innkeeper about her *brother,* but he shook his head, saying, "I've not seen such a man as ye've described, miss, and there's ought but a few customers I don't see in the course o' the day."

"Thank you. Perhaps he was confused about where we were to meet." He offered her tea, but she refused and returned to the coach. The horses were sufficiently fresh to make the next leg of the journey to Woolhampton, and so it was, she ordered the coachman on.

Once settled again on the seat opposite Staverton, she reported what the landlord of The Crown Inn had told her.

"Woolhampton is barely a village," he said. "I would not expect a man of Bertaud's stamp to break his journey there. He probably rested the night at Thatcham, perhaps even Newbury. Yes, I should think Newbury a logical choice for him since it is a market town. He could easily hide in such a large place."

"Particularly since the town has several inns."

Anne's stomach growled in a most unladylike manner. "I am sorry." She giggled. "I did not have breakfast, as you may imagine, since I was entirely preoccupied with *other matters*."

He grimaced and narrowed his eyes.

"However," she continued, "once in the inn, the smell of the cakes, bread and cinnamon was so sharply in the air that my appetite has been thoroughly awakened. If I do not find Bertaud in Woolhampton, would you mind if we breakfasted there?"

"Not in the least," he said. "Having responded so swiftly, yet so unwisely, to your missive this morning, I was unable to finish consuming my toast before we embarked on this delightful journey."

Anne could see that though he was attempting to prick her with his words, he was hardly serious. She answered in kind. "I do beg your pardon for that," she said, adopting a falsely sincere expression. "No one likes to be hurried away from a meal."

He chuckled and directed his gaze out the window. Anne was pleased to see that though their journey had begun in complete animosity, every mile brought a greater ease of discourse. She was beginning to understand him.

As the coach lumbered its way toward Woolhampton on the Bath road, Staverton grew thoughtful. Presently, Miss Delamere—*Anne*—seemed to have fallen silent and was staring out the window, though what her thoughts might be he could not imagine. He was grateful, however, for the opportunity to contemplate his circumstances. His gaze slid to the rope coiled next to her small muff. He recalled how tightly she had bound him. Who was this rather brazen female who not only had abducted him, but who took to spying apparently as easily as a fish to water?

When she had stumbled slightly, and he had steadied her with a hand on her waist, he had for that moment forgotten that she was his abductor. Instead, she was simply the country miss, who, though elegantly gowned today in her green silk with a lovely bonnet to match, he had met and kissed in the lane beyond Sulhurst. He had experienced in that brief moment, as she looked down into his face and smiled so sweetly, a profound desire to prevent her from leaving the coach, at least not without settling his lips on hers again.

As the coach wheels ground through the macadamized road, he found his gaze seeking her face time and time again, in part because she was apparently lost in thought and oblivious to his presence. She was terribly pretty and still as composed as the moment he had first entered her coach, entirely unruffled. Not half bad for a lady who had just committed her first act as a spy at the village of Theale.

A new thought intruded so happily into his mind, that he could not keep from smiling. Since they were to travel together for perhaps as long as a sennight, he might have another opportunity, should he play his cards right, to kiss her again.

"Why do you smile in that manner?" she asked in her arch fashion.

"I refuse to tell you. I daresay you would fly into the boughs if you knew my thoughts."

"I promise you I would not. I am not much given to taking a pet, only tell me."

At that, he met her gaze squarely. "Very well. I was thinking how much I hope to kiss you again before our journey concludes."

However angry he expected her to be, she simply was not. Instead, she appeared stunned, her lips parting as she watched him closely. A faint blush rose on her cheeks. "I fear I cannot allow you to continue in such false hopes," she said quietly. "As far as I am concerned, you are betrothed to my cousin, Cassaundra, and I should think it a gross betrayal of my affections for her were I to do anything so improper. Though I do not like to mention it, ever since I learned of your identity I have been very unhappy at having been kissed by you."

He leaned forward slightly. "You were not so unhappy at the time."

"No, I was not," she confessed, sighing. "Perhaps it was the extraordinary nature of the moment, of finding myself in your arms, or perhaps just the beauty of the day. Really, the entire experience was quite singular, particularly since you were the first man I had ever kissed."

"No," he stopped her. "Not the first. That is not possible."

"Yes, I fear it is true. I am woefully inexperienced in matters of the heart, you see, though I was once half in love with a stable boy some years ago. When he attempted to kiss me, however, I puckered up my face in disgust, which was very bad of me because I had fancied myself in love with him and I believe he had a *tendre* for me, as well. He left Berkshire shortly after."

"You did not kiss me yesterday as though you lacked experience."

"As to that," she responded ingenuously, "I do not have an explanation for you. What I do know, and what is more to the point, had I known who you were I would never have permitted you to kiss me."

He did not know which facet of her remarks surprised him more, that she had never been kissed prior to yesterday or her present insistence she would never have allowed the kiss. "You think so poorly of me, then?" he asked, bewildered. "But why? You hardly know me."

"The manner in which you used my cousin so very badly must be my primary reason. However, there have been so many you have injured over the years, that had Cassie's heart not been so deeply wounded I would still not have wished for you to kiss me."

The subject she had just brought forward irritated him intensely. How could a mere Anne Delamere, who had never been through the rigors of a London season, possibly comprehend what he had endured as the object of so much calculated, even cold-blooded, interest for the past decade? Nothing could convince him, for instance, that had he been a third or fourth son of a mere country gentleman, Cassaundra Bradley would have looked twice at him, nonetheless pursued him so doggedly as she had.

"The truth is," he stated, his temper rising, "you can have no notion of what you speak. Had you been in Brighton and witnessed for yourself what actually occurred between your cousin and myself, I might allow you even a small attempt at convincing me that my conduct had been less than gentlemanly. You were not there, however, so I cannot allow you to be correct in your opinions. You will not find me in the least sympathetic toward Miss Bradley, or any of the ladies to whom you are referring."

She appeared rather dumbfounded by his speech, as well she might. "I can see that I have distressed you."

Whether she was in the least repentant, he could not say, but he felt obliged to continue. "Am I to believe you were hoping I would suddenly become aware of how flawed I am and beg your forgiveness?"

"No, not at all," she responded lightly. "You merely asked why I thought so poorly of you and I was attempting to explain the basis for my opinion, nothing more."

"May I ask what right you have to sit in judgment on me when it was you who held a pistol to my chest just a few hours past and bound me with a rope? How dare you pretend for even a moment that you have such a right."

"I can see that you are perturbed," she said, smiling.

"Yes, I am!" he barked.

The fact that she bit back her laughter as she turned to stare out the window further exacerbated his discontent.

"I do not know what you find so amusing," he stated crisply. "Pray, do not spare my feelings. Tell me why you smile."

"No. I have every certainty you will fly into the boughs if I do."

This reference to what he had said earlier aggravated him further. "I promise you, I will not," he growled. He could feel his brow pinched almost to the bridge of his nose.

"So you say," she said, turning to meet his gaze squarely.

"Indeed, I promise you, I will not," he snapped. "Only, tell me why you smile."

"Because in this moment, you remind me of a satyr."

"A satyr!" he cried, dumbfounded. "How can you say anything so ludicrous?"

"You pressed me, my lord," she responded, still smiling.

"So, what you are saying is, that in this moment, I appear part human, part goat?"

"No," she responded chuckling. "Your expression only. I have seen satyrs depicted in paintings and you put me in mind of them. Your brows arch when you are angry and have this flying aspect." She gestured in little sweeps at the temple. "I expect little horns to emerge any moment. Or perhaps it is your gray eyes, fairly bursting into flames. Satyrs were demons, you know."

A great deal of his hostility dissipated upon these absurd

comments, particularly since he could see there was no venom in her manner, and besides, she was smiling in a completely adorable manner. "How can anyone's eyes appear to burst into flames? You are being ridiculous."

"So I am," she admitted. "Staverton, I did not mean to offend you so deeply."

"You did not offend me," he retorted abruptly. "Well, perhaps you did, but unfairly. I am persuaded you have misjudged me."

"Perhaps I have," she said soothingly. "I do know one thing for certain, I am far too hungry to continue such a discussion."

"As am I," he stated, knowing full well he was barely concealing his pique.

"Then, let us open a new subject. Would you be willing to tell me how it was you became a spy? You will hardly hear a word of censure fall from my lips on that score."

"I find that hard to believe. You seem prone to having hard opinions on every subject," he responded.

"I believe you may be right," she returned. "However, since I have never met a spy before, I cannot have formed a great many opinions generally. I find the subject so terribly romantic that I am more likely to admire you than not."

He could only laugh. "An oddity, indeed," he murmured. "Very well, what is it you wish to know?"

The lady before him patted her lips with her fingertips as though contemplating his question. Finally, she said, "Spying is not in the usual order of things, particularly for peers of the realm. Was your existence so dull that you felt compelled to offer your services to the Crown, or was it a matter of wishing to help in a time of war?"

He was grateful for the diversion from a subject that forced him to recall the numerous failed flirtations in which he had engaged over the years. Some of the knots in his shoulders began to relax.

He turned his thoughts toward the business at hand and

why he had initially engaged in spying. An answer to her question rose swiftly to mind. He realized he had not understood himself fully until just this moment. "One of the consequences of my having inherited a vast property and an ancient title has been that from the time I could remember, my life was settled on a path not of my own choosing. I do not repine, you understand, for that would be expressing an ingratitude which I in no manner feel. Indeed, I consider my rank and my wealth to be extraordinary gifts which I have accepted in what I hope is a humble spirit.

"However, I should have liked nothing better than to have purchased a pair of colors in a fine cavalry unit and served my country in the face of cannon fire." His heart suddenly sank to his stomach. Memories asserted themselves that filled him with a terrible sadness.

"What is it, Staverton?" she asked quietly. "Why have you suddenly grown so somber? I cannot have distressed you again since I have not yet spoken."

He glanced at her, searching her eyes and wondering if she was taunting him or intended to amuse herself at his expense. What returned to him was her complete sincerity. He was shocked, for he realized that whatever else she might be, she was not duplicitous, and he knew with a profound certainty he could trust her. The experience was so novel that he merely stared at her for a long, long moment. He could not remember the last time he had believed a woman worthy of his trust. She met his gaze unwaveringly.

"I will tell you, Anne Delamere," he said at last. "Even though I have never spoken of these things before, in this conversation they yet come to mind. You see, I had two brothers, both gallant and courageous, men of honor and principle. Both joined the army; one rose to the rank of captain in the Light Dragoons, the other had been made brevet colonel in the battle of Talavera in 1809, a distinguished officer of the Horse Guards. Each perished in the field not long ago. All the while they served in Spain, I had to remain here to tend to business."

"I see," Anne murmured.

He sat back, planting his feet solidly as the coach lurched. "Why have I told you these things?" he asked, laughing slightly and feeling completely bewildered. "My God."

"You told me because you trust me," she stated. "And I feel greatly honored by your confidences."

He laughed outright. "Miss Delamere, why should I trust a lady who kidnapped me?"

"Why, indeed?" she inquired brightly.

Once more he laughed, his spirits lightening appreciably.

"So," she stated with some finality, "you became a spy, here, in England, because it was something you could do for your country."

"Yes, that is it precisely. Whatever the risks may have been over the years, and they have been considerable at times just as they are on this journey to Bath, I never once felt I gave so much as any member of His Majesty's army."

"I admire you, Staverton. Indeed, everything you have just told me speaks of a noble character."

"Do you admire me enough to let me proceed alone on my mission?" He was curious as to what she would say. He could not guess at her thoughts.

"Of course not," she responded immediately. "You are clearly an exemplary man in the world of men, but I believe you have a great deal to answer for in the drawing room. You chose to live as though the two were separate somehow and they are not. The same nobility of character you have exhibited as the earl of Staverton and as a servant of the Crown should have been extended to the ladies of your acquaintance. Why they were not, I cannot imagine. No, I must accompany you on your journey to insure that at the end of it, you will marry my cousin." She again turned around. "Do but look, we are at Woolhampton already. I intend to eat a great deal, so be prepared. We shall probably rest here an hour, unless, of course, we discover that *my brother* is in the parlor."

When the coach drew into the inn yard, Staverton grew thoughtful. "Would you be willing to do the same as at Theale?"

"Of course," she responded. "Indeed, I had expected to do so."

"You are certainly a strange creature," he said, smiling ruefully. "Both obliging yet set on committing a crime worthy of hanging."

At that, she smiled, quite genuinely. He was taken aback, for in this moment, perched as she was on the edge of her seat, waiting for the coach to draw to a stop, and her green eyes once more glowing with excitement, she had never appeared more beautiful. He should have been wholly disenchanted with her since, even though he had confided in her and she had praised his character, she was still intent on his wedding her cousin. Yet, somehow, the tone of the exchange had caused all his former enmity toward her to dissipate. He realized he was no longer angry and, to a degree, he had begun to admire her spirit almost as much as her beauty.

The coach drew to a final stop, and as the hostler hurried to speak with the coachman, Anne descended the steps quickly. Before crossing the cobbles, she turned toward him and whispered, "I shan't be but a moment, and if possible I shall secure a parlor."

He nodded in agreement and watched her walk briskly across the inn yard. When she disappeared inside, he leaned back against the squabs. He had an uneasy feeling as though he had begun sliding down a muddy slope toward a swiftly running river. It would not be long before he plunged into the cold water, head over ears, and then what would he do?

He chuckled. Swim. By God, he would swim.

FIVE

Anne entered the inn on a cloud of exhilaration. For the second time that morning she was engaged in an act of espionage, the business for which she was beginning to think she had been born. She scrutinized the many occupants of the public dining room as surreptitiously as possible, and, not finding Bertaud within, spent the next several minutes engaged in conversation with the innkeeper. Apparently, the French spy had chosen not to stop at Woolhampton.

Securing a private parlor and a large breakfast for herself and Staverton, she realized she was a trifle disappointed. Ever since she had embarked on her journey with the earl, she had been wanting to see the man again who had tried to run her down in the lane beyond Sulhurst.

On a decidedly slower tread than when she had entered the inn, she made her way to the coach. Upon seeing that the earl remained hidden in the shadows, her thoughts suddenly grew full of him and of all that he had told her in the previous half mile of their journey. She felt she had been given a remarkable glimpse into a part of his life which he had made clear was an intensely private matter for him—the service and deaths of his brothers in the army.

She knew she had been honored by how readily he had confided in her, particularly since only a few minutes earlier he had been on his high ropes about her opinions of him.

She could not imagine, however, why he had chosen to reveal such personal events as he had unless he was attempting to ingratiate himself with her. She dismissed this motive instantly. She knew he was not such a creature as that. No, he had been entirely spontaneous and genuine, which served to nudge her heart a little. She might even be able, one day, to forgive him his many unkindnesses. She only wished he were not so devilishly handsome, and for that reason hoped he did not continue to confide in her, for she knew she was vulnerable. She had been vulnerable since the moment he had placed his lips on hers—was it only yesterday?

She smiled as she approached the coach door. She felt as though months had passed since she had first met Staverton instead of a scant few hours.

"You may be at ease," she said, as she opened the door and looked up at him. "Bertaud is not within."

"I confess I am relieved," he said, smiling.

She placed a hand on his sleeve. "You must not worry for my safety."

His smile broadened. "I must be honest with you, Anne, I was not thinking of that, but rather of my breakfast. Had Bertaud been within, we would have had to leave Wool-hampton with our bread baskets quite empty."

"Our *bread baskets?*" she queried, laughing. The use of an entirely slang expression surprised her, but, then, many things about Staverton had surprised her over the course of the morning.

She led him to the parlor, which she had not yet seen, and upon crossing the threshold, looked about her with delight and pleasure. "How lovely!" she cried. The chamber was elegantly fitted with fine bow windows, an excellent carpet and a brass pitcher, full of daisies, settled charmingly on the hearth.

"Unexpected," Staverton agreed. "I have never stopped at Woolhampton before because I thought the village too small to offer the comforts a larger town may provide. I shall not make such a mistake again."

Moving to the windows, she pulled off her gloves. "I do not think we shall see rain today," she observed.

"I should think not," he said, removing his hat and setting it on a table by the door. "There is not a cloud to be seen. August is an exceptional month, the temperature nearly idyllic most every day."

"Indeed, it is." She walked the length of the parlor several times, stretching her back and her arms. Her coach was well-sprung, but traveling was difficult under the best of circumstances.

A serving girl, quite young, appeared in the doorway with a tray laden with the breakfast she had ordered: freshly cooked eggs, pigeon pie, soused herrings, toast, berry and apricot jam, bacon, and a pot of coffee.

Staverton set to his meal with enthusiasm, eating heartily, quite at odds with Anne's tendency to carve each bite slowly and to savor her meal.

"When I first entered the inn," she said, "I overheard several of the men in the taproom speaking of a prizefight in Hungerford yesterday. Do but think, had you left Brighton a little sooner, you might have been able to see the match yourself."

"I would have enjoyed it," he admitted. "Very much so, only I find it odd in you to have mentioned it."

Anne chuckled. "Do the ladies of your acquaintance not speak of such things?" she asked.

"No," he answered promptly. "Of balls, of beaus, of fashion, but never of boxing matches. However, I keep forgetting that you are not in the usual style and so I should not have been surprised. Only, why did you bring the subject forward? You needn't entertain me if that is what you are thinking."

She waved a hand and sipped her coffee. "I was thinking nothing of the sort. By reputation, you are a notable Corinthian and boxing has always intrigued me. Do you take lessons with Jackson in London? Papa has visited his saloon on occasion."

"Yes," he responded, "I do." He continued to attack his meal, and after a moment, looked up from his plate. "I thought you said you were hungry?" A frown furrowed his brow.

"I am notoriously slow. Pay no heed to me, however. Papa usually leaves the table, all out of patience, long before I am finished."

Staverton straightened a little and poured himself another cup of coffee. "We have no reason to hurry," he said, perhaps more to himself than to her. "So, tell me a little of your father."

She watched in some astonishment as he began to match his pace to hers. This was an unlooked for politeness and she found herself thinking that there were a great many things about Staverton of which she heartily approved. "Papa is a man of simple tastes. He loves his books, his collection of firearms, shooting, a good boxing match"—she paused.

He nodded and smiled. "Indeed, what man does not?"

She chuckled softly. "He takes great pleasure in the care of his estate, and in me, of course."

"Of course."

"He is also an antiquarian of sorts, not excessively so, for he prefers his library to everything else, but over the years I have joined him on many local expeditions, to some spot or other in the kingdom about which he has developed a curiosity. He pokes about in the soil with a favorite stick and occasionally uncovers a Roman coin, that sort of thing. At Hadrian's wall, he found Latin inscriptions, which, upon interpreting them, decided they were the work of bored Roman soldiers with far too much time on their hands—*Flavius was stationed here, Antonius is a cretin*—you understand." He laughed heartily. She chuckled as well before continuing. "He has a complete indifference to society except for two or three excellent friends, and in that aspect he and I are quite similar except that I do enjoy a good fete now and then."

"Now and then?" he inquired, disbelieving.

"Yes, I know," she said, wrinkling her nose. "I have been informed that this is the prime reason I am yet a spinster. Were I to attend more assemblies, for instance, I have been promised I should tumble violently in love before the cat could lick her ear."

He dismissed this with a shake of his finger. "Do not believe anyone who would so advise you," he said, spearing another herring. "I am convinced after all these years that love is wholly capricious. You would be as likely to be shot by Cupid's arrow on this journey as in a ballroom."

She settled her cup on the saucer. "I agree with you entirely on that score," she said. "Cassie, for instance, was nearly betrothed before she went to Brighton and then tumbled in love with you, as though Mr. Chamberlayne had never existed."

"Nearly betrothed, you say? I had no notion."

"Yes," she responded. "To my dearest friend, Harry Chamberlayne. I was never more surprised than when I learned of her change of affections, but I wonder, would this have made the smallest difference to you?"

She saw a cynical expression enter his eye in that moment. To his credit, however, he said nothing.

She had no reason to doubt Cassie's love for Staverton, yet she found herself troubled that her cousin had never perceived what she could clearly see was the earl's rather hardened view of women.

Sometime later, when they left the inn, she thanked him for his kindness in eating more slowly for her benefit. She was perhaps a little more profuse in her expressions than she ought to have been, for he was immediately suspicious.

"You think me a brute, do you not?" he asked, a rueful smile on his lips as he handed her up into the coach. "A man entirely without concern or consideration for the ladies of his acquaintance?"

Her lips parted as she glanced back at him. "Not a brute, precisely," she responded. "I have merely gained the strong impression through my cousin's experience with you and that of a dozen other ladies, that your conduct toward them is as you have suggested, without either consideration or concern. So, you may imagine my surprise when you showed me such a kindness at breakfast."

"Good God," he muttered, obviously thunderstruck as he again took up his seat opposite her. "You cannot mean what you are saying. I am always courteous in society. I make a point of it." His disbelief was clear.

"Staverton, the little I know of you tends me to think that you are a man of honor. I am therefore become persuaded that you simply do not understand the fairer sex. Would you concede this might be possible?"

He harrumphed a sigh. "Perhaps, and from what little I know of you, as well, I sense that you would not have acted toward me as you have unless your belief was profound."

"Precisely," she stated with a smile. "I believe we are beginning to comprehend one another."

Anne knew that he was rather shocked by her rendering of his character, but she was grateful she had had the opportunity to express her view of him. She wanted him to have a clear understanding of just why she had kidnapped him.

A moment later, with a new team harnessed to the coach, the equipage set off at a gentle pace for Thatcham. Staverton fell silent as he glanced out the window. Anne did the same, letting her gaze drift over the countryside, which proved to be an exquisite stretch of lush meadowland, beautiful skies and fully leaved trees. The appearance now and then of flocks of sheep put her forcibly in mind of Constable's rural landscapes.

Because the road was straight, the horses gathered speed and it seemed to Anne that her coach was flying through the

Berkshire landscape at a fantastic pace. The sensation flooded her with joie de vivre. She smiled and extended her hands to either side of her seat by way of balancing herself. If the coach should hit a rut . . .

No sooner had the thought slipped into her mind than she was suddenly flung forward, landing squarely on Staverton's lap. She burst into a peal of laughter as she pushed away from him. "I am so sorry!" she cried.

The coachman's voice intruded. "Beg pardon, miss!" He immediately began to rein the horses to a slower pace.

"The roads," she said, "though much improved, are always unpredictable." She could feel a blush creeping up her cheeks.

"You must never apologize for leaping onto a man's lap. Believe me, the experience was not in the least objectionable."

"Spoken like a man," she responded, smiling. "At any rate, I will try not to do so again."

"Now you mean to disappoint me."

She could only laugh.

The slower pace, though less exhilarating, kept the bumps to a minimum. Anne once more directed her gaze to the beautiful countryside, verdant beneath a warm summer sun. Her thoughts turned to what Staverton had told her earlier about his wish he could have entered the army as his brothers did.

She glanced at him and found he was watching her. She wasn't certain the subject was appropriate but she decided to risk saying what was on her mind. "You were so kind as to tell me of your brothers and their noble service in the army that I in turn would like to tell you something of myself which no one knows, not even my father. I suppose this will sound absurd, but I had always wished, with every fiber of my heart, that I could have served in the army as well. I have no siblings and my life has been wonderfully pleasant, every desire and need provided for abundantly, and yet there has always been within me this sense of lack, of wishing that my own existence could have a more significant use. In my happier daydreams, I have been a valiant officer of a cavalry regiment—of course—experiencing the continual pleasure of knowing that I was making a significant contribution to Wellington's efforts in Spain." She felt a little silly now that she had spoken her dreams aloud. "I suppose this must sound ridiculous to you, even trifling compared to the true service your brothers performed."

He shook his head and she could see that he had listened to her with the utmost seriousness. "Not ridiculous, for as you know, I share your sentiments. I have just never heard a lady express such a desire before. A cavalry unit, eh?" His smile was crooked.

She nodded, smiling as well. "Indeed, for I love to ride and I am skilled in sword fighting."

"Equally as well as with pistols?"

She wrinkled her nose. "Nearly. I had a fencing master for five years."

"Five years!" he cried. "I cannot believe it. I am convinced you are shamming it!"

She was not at all offended. "No, I would never do so, not in the context of this sort of discussion. Do you yet understand why I am delighted to be accompanying you on your mission?"

"I am beginning to," he responded.

When Staverton returned to watching the passing view from his window, she felt free for just a moment to study him. His arms were crossed over his powerful chest and his predatory eyes scrutinized one object after another as the coach bowled along the macadamized highway. He seemed content, or at least as content as a man who was chasing a spy could be. Indeed, his muscled legs seemed tense, as though he were ready to spring into action at any moment, like a prized thoroughbred at the start of a critical race.

She could not quite comprehend him, though she could certainly understand how Cassie had tumbled in love with him. He was handsome enough to tempt Aphrodite herself. Even her own heart tended to leap at the mere sight of him. These sentiments she ignored. After all, once she had learned his identity, and that pronounced by Staverton in the most arrogant manner, she realized she could never have a serious interest in a man she had dubbed the Infidel.

And yet, there was much she admired about him, just as she had said. She found she wanted to know more of him.

"Staverton, I do not mean to give you pain when I bring forward this subject, but would you be willing to tell me how it came about you decided Georgina Patney was not worthy to become your wife?"

As he turned back to her, she could see that he was both surprised and displeased. "That is a name I have not heard for several years. Miss Patney is wed now and lives in Lincolnshire. Do I have the right of it?"

Anne nodded. "Yes. She married my cousin, a baronet, Sir Charles Wespall. She is now Lady Wespall. I know her well."

"I see. So by this do I apprehend that you have been informed of my *infamous* conduct toward her, what must it be . . . ah, yes, some five years past?"

"I have," she stated, her gaze never wavering from his. She could sense by the clipped manner of his speech that he was unhappy about discussing her cousin's wife.

"So, you wish to know how I account for myself," he stated.

"I do, for I cannot imagine how you have justified wounding Miss Patney even more severely than my cousin, Cassie."

He held her gaze boldly, and in that moment she felt all his hatred for the subject, perhaps even for the lady involved. A woman of less stern stuff than herself might have quailed beneath the hardness of his gaze, but she was not so henhearted. Indeed, she did not fear Staverton in the slightest.

When he remained silent, she added, "I spoke at length

with Miss Patney three months after the incident. She was still weeping, as though it had been but a fortnight. It seemed to me her heart had been broken. What I do not comprehend, is that the gentleman you seem to be in other respects, so noble, so courageous, even considerate, does not seem to match with the scapegrace who would injure a lady so completely as you did Miss Patney. I know you are reluctant to speak of this, but I beg you will."

He was silent for a long moment, his jaw working strongly. She could not discern whether her boldness in making the inquiry was the cause of his anger, or the memories her questions had evoked. She would not have been surprised if he had refused to discuss the matter entirely. Indeed, she knew she had been utterly provoking in having brought it forward in the first place. However, at the very moment she gave up expecting an answer, he spoke.

"I had meant to offer for her," he stated suddenly.

"What?" Had she heard him correctly? This statement was so at odds with what actually happened that she found herself shocked. "How is this possible? Why did you not?"

"I had even bought her a very special locket," he began in a voice that sounded lost and reminiscent. "A beautiful gold piece trimmed with small, matched pearls, to present to her shortly before I meant to ask for her hand in marriage. I gave it away to a woman in the East End, whom I've since learned escaped her poverty by opening a flower shop not far from Hyde Park. I think it better spent than should the locket have ever hung about Miss Patney's neck for even a moment."

At this point, Anne felt utterly confused. "Then something must have occurred to have changed your mind about Georgina," she said. "Though I cannot imagine what. I have known her some years and she is a very fine lady. Her heart is warm and giving. She cares for the poor in her village with the fervor of a saint, she is a most excellent and loving mother to her children, and a good wife to my cousin. I must ask again, what made you determine she was unworthy of you?"

"Why must I tell you any of this?" he asked, angrily.

"Because it is important to me, for Cassie's sake."

"Your questions are wholly impertinent," he growled.

She smiled faintly. "I know they are, but will you respond to them anyway? Please."

He drew in a long breath. "No one has ever asked me before," he said. "And though I resent your pressing me for an answer, I will give you one, but you will not like it."

"Whatever happened, I can bear it," she said.

He met her gaze openly. "Yes, I believe you can," he said. After a moment, he began, "When I was courting Miss Patney, fully intending to make her my wife—did she ever tell you as much?"

"No. The sense I had of your history together was that you had never mentioned your interest in wedding her. Are you certain she was aware of it?"

"Quite. I had given her numerous broad hints, what our life would be like together on my estates in Bedfordshire, that sort of thing. She cannot have been unaware of my desires, therefore I must conclude that she had her own reasons for not wanting to say as much."

Her heart began beating heavily in her breast. She had a sense that something terrible was about to descend on her, some truth that was going to overset the orderliness of her life. She was convinced now that Georgina had not told her all that had transpired between herself and the earl. Whatever Staverton meant to say to her, she had no reason not to believe him. He was many things, but she knew instinctively that he was not a liar.

"The night before I was to offer for her, we were both in attendance at Lady Burghclere's ball in Grosvenor Square. Ordinarily, I would have taken Georgina and her mother to the ball myself, but I arrived late, having escorted my infirmed mother to the fete instead. My mother was an excellent friend to Lady Burghclere, and though she did not go out much because of a serious rheumatic complaint from which she still suffers, she wanted to make this gesture to her friend. Arriving late, however, proved to be a most providential occurrence and one for which I am presently grateful."

Anne somehow guessed at what must have happened next. The very notion of it, however, gave her so much pain that she could hardly think. "You learned she did not love you," she said, her heart sinking.

His expression of great sadness as he looked inward increased her own sense of pain over the subject. He continued, "She boasted of her conquest to a friend. She was behind a gold silk drapery. She cannot have known anyone could hear her for she was never indiscreet, only in this moment when I and my beloved parent were listening. 'I do not love him,' she said. Those were her words. 'I do not love him. How is that possible? I do not love him, yet I long to be his wife, more than anything in the world.' Her friend perhaps spoke the truth of the situation more accurately. 'Who needs love when you will be a countess and have a dozen servants to wait upon you day and night.' How quickly do you suppose I forgot what was said between Georgina and her friend?"

"I daresay you could never forget any of it," she responded.

His expression grew strained. "I confronted her the next day and she flew into a rage. Somehow, she blamed me for having heard her whisper a confidence to a friend. I told her she might tell whatever story she wished as to why I did not come up to scratch, but that I had always hoped, at the very least, that the lady I should one day marry, would love me. Therefore, Anne Delamere, I must ask you this, was love too much for me to ask of her?"

"No, of course not," she responded, wiping her eyes. She was surprised to find them wet.

"You believe me, then?"

"Why should I not?"

"Because Miss Patney must have related a very different story to you."

"Not so different. What she said to me was that she had felt badly used that you had singled her out, then for a reason that seemed incomprehensible to her said you did not mean to offer for her after all."

"I see. She did not tell an outright lie, I suppose, and yet I was treated abominably the remainder of the season by dozens of young ladies and their mothers."

"Then you were badly used and I am sorry for it."

She dried her eyes and let her gaze rest on the flow of shrubs, hills and trees that continually moved past the window of the coach. The horn sounded, announcing the approach to Thatcham. She was grateful for the diversion because the air in the coach had grown sad and troubled. She did not know what more she could say to Staverton. She tried to see him as a younger man, five years past, more idealistic, deeply in love, wearing his heart on his sleeve. Somehow, she could not conjure up the image. The man before her was hardened, perhaps incapable of loving another woman, ever. At the same time, it did not excuse his conduct toward a number of other ladies since his unfortunate experience with Miss Patney, including his mistreatment of dear Cassie.

On the other hand, she could not entirely dismiss the difficulties of his situation—handsome, wealthy, a peer. If the woman he had loved and had hoped to marry would betray him, then what lady would not?

She gave herself a mental shake. She was sorry for Staverton, but she could not excuse him, not entirely.

Wishing to end the tension, however, she gave the subject a brisk turn. "Papa believes Thatcham to be nearly six, possibly eight thousand years old."

"Indeed," he murmured, glancing out the window as the coach slowed and a row of thatched cottages came into view. "I must say, that first cottage, as tumbledown as it is, might be nearly that old."

At that moment, a piece of thatching fell to the sidewalk

below. Anne burst out laughing as did Staverton, and the horrid tension between them disappeared entirely.

A few minutes more, and the coach drew into the yard of Cooper's Cottage, which served the mail coaches. Anne entered the cottage parlor, scanned the assembled customers, then quickly turned toward the serving maid and requested a cup of tea to be brought to her coach. Her heart was suddenly in her throat, for she had recognized instantly the man who had tried to run her down on the day before.

Hurrying to the coach, she opened the door and whispered urgently, "He is here. Bertaud is here!"

"Are you certain?"

"As certain as thunder after lightning." She climbed into the coach and took up her seat opposite him. "He was in the public dining room with three other fellows, one of whom was quite large, a circumstance which drew my eye to their corner in the first place. They were laughing and only stopped when Bertaud chanced to glance in my direction. I fear, for some reason, my presence soon intrigued them all."

"You are far too pretty to be a spy," he stated, a half-smile on his lips.

"Nonsense," she retorted quickly. "I believe Bertaud may have recognized me."

"Well, there is no point arguing on that head. So tell me, three acquaintances, you say?"

"Yes. Would they be at all known to you?"

Staverton shook his head. "No, not in the least. Bertaud is a solitary creature. I am beginning to think we should away, immediately."

"I requested a cup of tea. I think I should I wait for it. To not do so would arouse suspicion."

"The devil take it," he murmured. "You are right, of course."

"Draw the shades," she whispered. "On your side. Even if Bertaud should see me, what likelihood would there be that he would suppose you and I were actually traveling together?"

With the shades drawn, Anne received the tea and tipped the maid who waited on her. To her great dismay, at the very same moment, the spy emerged from the inn. She assumed as disinterested an expression as possible and sipped her tea slowly. She effected a sigh, wondering why Bertaud did not move from the doorway. She could only suppose he had recognized her. She therefore addressed the maid who was waiting on her. "Is there much trout fishing nearby?" she asked.

"Aye, ma'am. As much as you could wish for with the Kennet a stone's throw away."

"I am not much of an angler myself, but my father is greatly addicted to the sport." She drank more quickly since the spy still had not moved from the doorway.

"All gentlemen are by report," she said.

"This tea was most excellent. Thank you." She returned the empty cup to the maid, who dipped a slight cursty, then began retracing her steps. Still the spy remained on the threshold. Before the serving maid could enter the inn, however, he caught her by the arm and whispered something in her ear. Anne was too far away to hear what he had said but, oh, how she would have loved to have known what information he was seeking. She greatly feared he was asking if the maid had seen the other occupant of the coach.

Anne did not hesitate further, but gave the coachman the office to start and leaned back against the squabs with a sigh."What is it?" Staverton asked quietly. "Your eyes have the appearance of a startled doe."

Anne remained mute until Cooper's Cottage and the spy disappeared from view. Once on the road to Bath, she finally released another great sigh and said, "He was watching me the entire time from the doorway."

"Good God. Do you think he suspected—?"

"I do not know. Did the maid see you at all, for he asked her a question before permitting her to reenter the inn. I am convinced he was inquiring as to whether or not she had seen a man within my coach. Of course, I could not hear what he asked."

"No, I do not believe she saw me," he replied. Staverton was silent apace, then continued. "We are not far from Speenhamland. Would one of your servants be willing to return by horse and speak with the maid to discover what it was he asked her?"

"Of course. Shaw would leap at the opportunity. Of all my servants, he prefers to discharge the errands farthest from Sweetwater Lodge. I have always suspected he was a bit of an adventurer at heart."

"We must know the nature of Bertaud's inquiry. He is a very deliberate man and he would not have watched you as he did without his suspicions having been aroused."

How insignificant Georgina Patney suddenly seemed in this moment, in the face of the scrutiny of a French spy. How slowly the coach moved toward Speenhamland. How much Anne wished her servant was already on his way back to Thatcham, yet nothing could be done until a horse could be hired for Shaw.

"We will need to hire my servant a horse, and he ought not to be wearing my father's livery, would you agree?"

"Yes, absolutely."

She gripped her hands together. "I despise that we must wait."

Staverton chuckled. "My dear, waiting is the larger part of what a spy must do. If you are to be in the least content during the remainder of this journey, then I suggest you accustom yourself even now to this most dreadful aspect of the art of espionage. Patience is not just virtue but one's life and breath, make no mistake."

Anne sighed heavily, which again caused her traveling mate to laugh. She took his advice seriously, however, and settled her composure.

Once arrived at Speenhamland, Anne decided that her servants must be informed to some degree of their current situation. She spoke privately and carefully with all three of the men, and with Staverton's permission, related the essentials of their purpose in journeying to Bath.

All of the men were a trifle stunned but agreed readily to be of service in any manner his lordship required. When questioned as to whether they had chanced to notice the man in the doorway of the inn at Thatcham, both footmen said they had and that they would easily recognize him again since his face was so lean and sharp. Shaw, just as Anne supposed he would, volunteered to perform the task of riding swiftly back to Thatcham and speaking with the serving maid about Bertaud. A horse was hired and a black box coat unearthed from his portmanteau. Within ten minutes he was heading in the direction of the previous village.

Quince was given the task of watching the highway to see if, or hopefully, when, Bertaud passed by Speenhamland. Until then, the earl suggested he and Anne remain within the coach.

A few minutes later, Quince returned to the coach with the information that Bertaud had scarcely slowed his curricle as he drove the distance up the High Street and disappeared from Speenhamland entirely. She pressed her hand to her chest, relief once more flooding her.

"We are safe for a time," she murmured to Staverton, as Quince let down the steps.

"Yes," he responded quietly.

"We will remain here," she informed Jack Coachman, "until Shaw returns."

"Very good, miss," he said.

Staverton, meanwhile, secured a parlor in which they could await the servant's return. Anne was soon sipping a cold glass of lemonade as the earl took pulls from what he soon proclaimed was an excellent tankard of ale.

"I have every fear," Anne said, settling her glass on the

table, "that the door will open and Bertaud will be on the threshold, pistol in hand."

"Your man Quince seems fully capable of making certain that does not happen," he assured her.

"You are right, of course."

An hour passed, and then another.

Finally, Shaw entered the parlor, his brow dripping with sweat. The day was hot and the ride in the sun had been rigorous.

Anne stood up immediately, her heart beating as quickly as a bird's. "What was it he asked the serving girl?" she queried.

"Just as ye thought, miss, whether or not there were another traveler in the coach."

"Oh, dear," Anne murmured.

"What did the maid tell him?" Staverton asked.

Shaw wiped his brow with his kerchief. "That she saw a pair o' glossy boots, but that were all."

Anne glanced at Staverton, who appeared decidedly grim. Her gaze dropped instinctively to his nicely blackened and polished boots. Was it possible the spy could know of Staverton's presence in her coach merely by the description of his boots? She thought this wholly unlikely.

As she dismissed Shaw, she begged him to refresh himself with a tankard if he so desired, for they would not be leaving Speenhamland for a few minutes more.

"Thank ye, miss," he responded, his own expression worried as he quit the parlor.

Staverton moved to the window, his hands clasped tightly behind his back.

"Do you think he recognized me?" Anne asked.

"Undoubtedly."

"Though I believe he would have no basis for such a notion, is it possible he thinks you might have been in the coach?"

"Yes, of course."

"But why? I do not understand."

He turned back to look at her. "What are the odds he might see on the Bath road the same lady he tried to run down only the day before? In this profession, one comes to suspect coincidences rather highly."

Anne felt ill. She had supposed that even if she found Bertaud in one of the inns, as she had at Thatcham, that he would have had no particular interest in her. She realized that when Staverton had spoken of his purpose in following Bertaud, she had truly believed everything would progress without incident. How naive her thinking had been. She promised herself she would not be so shatterbrained again.

"What do we do now?" she asked, sitting down at the table once more. She had lost all interest in her lemonade.

He was quiet for a moment, then moved away from the window as a coach drew into the inn yard. "I want to press on to Newbury," he said. "The town is much larger than Speenhamland and we can get lost there better than here, although I daresay your coach will be easily discovered wherever we might stay."

"Should we change equipages?" she asked.

At that, he looked down at her and laughed. "I suppose we could, if you had a fortune in your pocket."

"Not at the moment," she stated seriously. "Only the housekeeping money. But I could get more if you feel it necessary. There is a bank at Newbury which will serve."

Staverton chuckled. "I forgot that you were an heiress intent on adventures, but I don't think it necessary. We need to shift our approach a little. Perhaps we could send your footmen before us as we continue on. They could form a relay in waiting for Bertaud to appear along the road, Quince pressing forward and returning to report to Shaw, who will return to us at designated locations. Primarily, we need to know where our spy means to stay the night."

"What an excellent notion!" she cried. "I only wish that I had thought of it sooner before blundering into the dining room as I did. Now I know how you felt at Reading, rather like a gudgeon."

"Well, perhaps not that bad!" he protested.

"A *complete* gudgeon," she reiterated sternly. "I remembered him, so why wouldn't he have known me upon seeing me again? He is a spy, for goodness' sake. I do feel as though I have only half a brain in this moment."

He laughed again, then resumed drinking his ale.

When Staverton drained his tankard, Anne gathered her servants together and the earl's plan was quickly explained to the men. The two footmen would journey ahead the short distance to Newbury and discover if Bertaud was at any of the inns in the large market town. "Afterward, we shall meet at the river where the barges load their corn," Anne said.

Quince also exchanged his blue livery for a plain coat of black stuff and it was not long before both servants had reined their horses in the direction of Newbury.

A few minutes later, the large elegant vehicle rolled out of the inn yard.

Having watched her servants depart, Anne grew very somber. The brief encounter with Bertaud in which she had been recognized had forced her to realize how serious the situation was.

Staverton leaned forward and took her hand. "I can see that you are overset."

Anne looked down at the hand covering her own. Another unlooked-for kindness. "Only a very little," she confessed.

"I have every confidence in you and in your servants," he said, his smile soft.

She met his gray eyes, and felt bowled over by the sympathy contained within them. "You continually surprise me, you know."

"Excellent," he returned.

Anne chuckled in response as once more she glanced at the hand covering hers. She felt a strange rush of heat in her cheeks, which had nothing to do with embarrassment.

Certain memories, which she would do well to forget, swelled through her mind. She was back in the lane in Staverton's arms and he was kissing her.

She became frightened suddenly, for it seemed to her that even Staverton's mildest touch or look caused her to feel things she should not. She drew her hand away from his and was gratified that he sat back in his seat without a word.

Glancing out the window, she observed, "It will not be long before Newbury swallows up Speenhamland entirely."

"I believe you are right," he responded in kind.

Anne was happy to continue, anything rather than to feel flushed with excitement at the mere touch of Staverton's hand. "This entire area is also quite ancient. Papa travels here once a year to poke the soil about these hills. He always finds Roman artifacts, usually coins, for nearby Speen was once the Roman town of Spinae. It is believed the Romans camped all through this area, and certainly my father's finds would support such an assertion."

"Did you never accompany him?" he asked.

"To Speen?"

He nodded.

"Yes, quite a bit when I was a child. I have my own collections stored in the old schoolroom though I must say I have not looked through them in many years. My interests have changed, as well you may imagine."

"So, hunting for Roman pottery shards is not your notion of adventure?"

She laughed outright. "Not anymore."

"What about being stared at by French spies?"

Anne met his gaze fully. She saw in his expression that he was intrigued by what she might say. She considered just how she had felt at the inn at Thatcham. "When Bertaud turned to look at me and our eyes met, even though I became alarmed, I vow I never felt more alive in my entire existence, which convinces me yet again that I ought to have been born a man, for certainly I would have been a cavalry officer."

"Born a man, eh? I for one am greatly contented you were not."

Anne blinked, wondering what he meant by saying such a thing to her and whether or not he was attempting to flirt with her. "Whatever do you mean?" she asked.

"Only that had you been a man, you would never have kidnapped me and I find I am enjoying myself a great deal more in pursuing Monsieur Bertaud with you than were I traveling alone."

"Are you flirting with me, Staverton?"

"Good God, no!" he returned. "I am persuaded you would eat me alive were I to attempt anything so foolish."

Anne chuckled. "I suppose I would," she responded with a lift of her chin. "So be warned."

He pretended to shudder, which made her laugh anew. Afterward, she shifted in her seat and let her gaze drift to the window. Having spent the morning in Staverton's company, she realized his conduct toward her was just what she liked and that she was enjoying herself prodigiously.

How fortunate, then, that the journey would be of a relatively short duration, for the vulnerability she had felt earlier seemed even more pronounced as the coach rumbled toward Newbury.

SIX

Not long after leaving Speenhamland, the ancient, pillared clockhouse on the Bath road came into view, marking the coach's arrival at Newbury. Anne drew in a deep breath, for she felt nervous about entering the town since it was much more populous than the previous three villages together. Though not so large as Reading, the traffic of several coaching inns, as well as the barge activity on the River Kennet, created a noise and bustle that could easily conceal a French spy.

Once the clockhouse had been reached, the coach turned onto Northbrook Street leading into Newbury. The wheels soon clattered over the quaint bridge that crossed the river. A few minutes more and the vehicle turned into the marketplace at the top of Cheap Street.

Anne took in another deep breath and the nervousness she had been feeling transformed into something sweet and exhilarating. She had spoken truly when she had told Staverton earlier that she had never felt so alive.

"I must say," she said, her chest swelling, "I cannot remember being so happy, despite an occasional fit of the nerves. Not only am I in the midst of an adventure, but I might possibly be doing some good as well."

Staverton shook his head as though bemused.

"What is it?" she asked.

"Are you certain you would not prefer an elegant soiree to the pursuit of Bertaud?"

"Good heavens, no!" she cried. "Have I not already told you as much? Do you not believe me? I have no interest in drawing rooms, unless, of course, there should chance to be a spy present."

He laughed outright.

The coach lumbered toward the river and soon drew to a stop in as secluded a place as such a coach and four lively horses might find. In the absence of the footmen, Staverton jumped from the vehicle, let the steps down and helped her to descend.

"Come," she said, linking arms with him. "We shall walk down to the river while we await my servants. Have you seen the barges when they are in sail?"

He shook his head. "I cannot say that I have."

"Well, then, you must. This time of year the barges are being loaded with corn for the London markets. Nothing is prettier nor livelier. Two summers past I spent several days painting them in watercolors."

Once on the banks of the River Kennet, Anne took Staverton on a tour of the riverside wharfs as well as the nearby enormous barn, all of which a bustle of activity. The sails of the riverboats flapped loudly in the breeze as though applauding the loud squawking of the Berkshire gaffers who snapped their instructions to the men carrying the heavy sacks of corn to the barges.

"Cloth is also a mainstay of Newbury's economy," she said, drawing him down the riverside path. "Last year, Papa and I happened to be sojourning in Newbury, when the owner of the Greenham Mills and a partner of his boasted they could make a coat between sunrise and sunset in one day, beginning with the wool shorn from a sheep's back. Can you imagine?"

Staverton shook his head. "I never heard of such a thing."

"Papa and I had meant to return to Sulhurst that day, but

the contest was too appealing for either of us to miss since a certain Mr. Coxeter, who had made the boast, wagered a thousand guineas!"

"Good God! A thousand! Whatever happened?"

"At five o'clock in the morning, one of the men involved in the wager brought two Southdown sheep to the mill. Everything proceeded in order, from sheering the sheep to spinning the wool and weaving the cloth. Even the cloth was scoured, pulled, sheared, dyed and dressed with I am certain even more procedures than I can presently recall. By four o'clock, ten tailors worked on making the coat from the cloth and completed the task in little over two hours. Papa and I were there to witness the settling of the wager and when Mr. Coxeter's partner, Sir John Throckmorton, appeared wearing the coat, there must have been five thousand people present to cheer him. We did not remain for the feast, but I was told that the two hapless sheep which had given up their wool also gave up their lives to feed the crowd, and that one hundred and twenty gallons of beer was served to the revelers."

"I am only sorry I missed such a spectacle. A coat made from the wool shorn from sheep on the very same day. Incredible!"

"I believe the Throckmorton family, who reside at Buckland House, have the garment yet on display."

"Were we not embroigled with Bertaud's antics I would beg an introduction merely to see the coat." After a moment, he continued, "So, these are the things that interest you, then? Barges in full sail and unexpected country events like a wager over coat-making?"

"Yes, I suppose so," she responded, never having considered the notion before.

He appeared to fall into a reverie and she could not imagine what his thoughts might be. Finally, she queried, "I suppose these sorts of things must seem sadly flat to you when your world is so large as it is."

"On the contrary," he responded. "I should have enjoyed the coat-making enormously. What I find inutterably boring are the endless string of soirees, musicales, balls and 'at homes' one feels obliged to attend during the course of the London season. By June, when I have been in the metropolis for months, I vow I feel as though my head has been stuffed full of feathers."

Anne chuckled. "We seem to be of a mind in that regard. I do enjoy an occasional assembly, but beyond that I know I would chafe at having to do the pretty day after day. And since much of the beau monde requires an attendance upon these events, I suppose that is one reason I came to accept my spinsterhood."

"You would rather be in Newbury attending a coat-making."

"Precisely," she agreed with a crisp nod of her head. "Or accompany a man, such as yourself, in his pursuit of a spy."

Staverton smiled in response and when a small stream appeared in their path, Anne did not hesitate in accepting his arm about her waist as he lifted her across the shallow rivulet.

The afternoon was pleasant in the shade of the trees and shrubbery which grew thickly by the riverside. Conversation flew in every direction for a time, encompassing Staverton's estates in nearby Bedfordshire, Anne's love of Berkshire, the movement of Wellington's armies on the Iberian Peninsula, the fortunes being made in India, and the unhappy state of the poor in London's East End.

Anne was so caught up in her discourse with Staverton that she did not at first recognize her servants when they came around the bend on the narrow path.

"Shaw! Quince!" she cried. "I am so used to seeing you in your livery. You startled me. Do you have word, then?"

Shaw nodded. "Quince and I believe he must have passed by Newbury, for none of the inns saw his maroon and black curricle and the publicans said they had seen naught of 'im."

Turning to Staverton, Anne breathed a great sigh of relief. "We may be at ease for a time," she said.

Implementing Staverton's plan, she instructed Shaw and Quince on how they were to proceed along the Bath road, that they would travel together until they discovered where it was Bertaud meant to stay the night. Shaw would then return to Hungerford where he would find Anne and Staverton awaiting word from him. Only then would a decision be made whether to continue the journey or to remain at Hungerford for the night.

The footmen were given sufficient coin for the toll booths, as well as for meals and lodging, and sent on their way.

"As for me," Staverton said, turning toward Anne once her servants had disappeared, "I am ready for my nuncheon." He drew a small silver timepiece from the pocket of his waistcoat. "The hour is nearly two."

"Where do you prefer to dine?" she asked. "The Bear, The Hatchet, The White Hart?"

"I have no particular preference."

In the end, the coachman chose for them, saying that he knew the hostler of The White Hart quite well and understood their cook to excel in her arts.

Staverton ordered a nuncheon of roast sirloin of beef, pea soup, a dish of pickles, salad, potatoes, cauliflower, apple pie and a claret that proved to be excellent, all of which suited Anne quite well. Again, the earl politely matched his pace to her slower one, and a full hour was spent in truly pleasant conversation during the meal.

By the time Anne was walking back to the coach, her arm once more wrapped about Staverton's, she was in a fair way to thinking that however much she had believed herself content prior to this journey, she had been mistaken. She could best describe her sentiments as utterly joyful in this moment.

As she glanced up at the man beside her, she wondered

just how much of her present contentment was due to his presence or to the nature of the journey upon which she had been so fortunate as to have become engaged.

A sudden panic assailed her. What if Staverton was the reason she was so happy?

She shook her head, unwilling to allow such a horrifying thought to take hold of her. Of course he was not the reason, even if they had conversed so easily all afternoon, exchanging anecdotes one after the other. No, her contentment originated in the nature of the adventure she was on. Nothing more.

Within a few minutes, the large coach was bowling up Northbrook Street, back to the clocktower and onto the Bath road. This time, however, Anne begged Staverton to sit beside her. "For it is a great deal more comfortable than sitting forward, particularly when the coach lurches as it does now and then."

He thanked her for this kindness, and for the first time on the journey, the man she had dubbed the Infidel was sitting next to her. Anne experienced a strange fluttering in her breast. Because he was tall and broad-shouldered, and his thighs of athletic proportions, he filled his side of the coach to the point that Anne felt almost cocooned. He had a warm, pleasant scent like a rich, earthy humus beneath an oak tree.

As the sun began its slow descent in the western horizon, Anne said, "It was not so long ago that a coach could not venture forth along this road at night without being asked to stand and deliver."

"The quality of the roadbeds are so superior these days and the coaches faster, that I should like to see any highwayman attempt to stop your equipage when your coachman has his team whipped to eight miles an hour."

Anne chuckled and let her gaze drift to the deepening blue of the sky. She was greatly contented and thought that this was how she would live from now on, traveling to distant cities and distant lands, seeking out adventures, living every moment to the fullest.

On the heel of this resolution, the glass window beside her shattered, something hard slanted off the side of her head, she murmured a brief, "Oh," then fell to a place of blackness.

Staverton stared down at the limp figure collapsed onto his lap. Time slowed. He heard the shouts of the coachman as though from a great distance. The coach began moving faster and faster. "Anne," he whispered, bending over her and plucking shards of glass from her gown. A telling tendril of smoke rose from her green silk bonnet. "Oh, dear God, Anne!"

He struggled to find the ribbons of her bonnet, to pull them apart, to slide the bonnet from her head. He saw the blood in her hair which had trickled down her neck. Her face was horribly pale in the dim interior of the coach. Was it possible she would die just in this manner, this very afternoon, crumpled on his lap?

What manner of fool had he been to involve her in this pursuit! If his own foolishness had slain her, he would never forgive himself!

He called to the coachman. "Do you see the assailant, Jack? Is he following us?"

"Nay. He fired his pistol from the hedges. I thought he might pursue on horseback but there is no sign of him. Is Miss Anne hurt?"

He glanced down at the still figure on his lap. He knew how devoted Anne's servants were to her. How could he possibly tell the coachman his mistress was dead?

Before he could respond to Jack's query, Anne moved in his arms and moaned faintly.

The relief he felt was so profound that his eyes began to burn with unreleased tears.

"Miss Anne has been injured," he called to Jack.

"Badly?" the shout returned to him.

"I do not know. Make haste to Hungerford. We may want a surgeon."

"Aye, m'lord." The crack of his whip above the horses' ears once more sounded like the explosion of a pistol.

Staverton winced.

"Anne," he whispered, petting her face, her neck, her shoulders. "Tell me you are all right."

To his enormous surprise, her eyes fluttered open and she sat up abruptly.

Anne felt very strange, a trifle dizzy, and a portion of her head pounded severely, but why? "What happened?" she asked. "I feel very faint and queasy. Where is my bonnet?"

"On the floor," he said. "It is ruined, I fear."

"Why? What is all this glass? The window. Where is the window?"

"We were attacked and you were struck by a pistol ball."

Anne reached up and touched her head. "I see." She felt the wound gingerly. "Oh, thank goodness. It is but a mere scratch. Do hand me my reticule."

He gave it to her from which she withdrew a kerchief and placed it a couple of inches above her right ear. After a minute or two, she removed the kerchief, which had begun to feel wet to her fingertips. There was a great deal more blood than she expected. "Would you be so good as to lend me your kerchief, Staverton? It would appear mine is not sufficiently large for the task."

"Of course." He hastily withdrew his from the pocket of his coat and gave it to her. When she pressed this against her head, he glanced down at her kerchief. "You are bleeding badly," he stated. "It cannot be a mere scratch."

"Papa said the scalp always bleeds freely. I promise you I am hardly cut at all. It feels more like a grazing."

"Anne, please tell me you are all right. You cannot know how worried I am. How do you feel?"

Anne turned to him and smiled. "As though I am the most fortunate lady in all of England!" she cried.

He scowled at her. "You are become hysterical. I knew your injury was far more severe than you have said."

"No! No!" she exclaimed. "You are mistaken." She showed him his kerchief. "There, you see, not nearly so much blood as before."

He shook his head, appearing absolutely bewildered. "Why do you say you are fortunate?" he asked.

She folded the kerchief and once more pressed it to her head. "Because I could not have asked for a more thrilling experience than to have been shot on my first adventure! You must admit how extraordinary this is."

"You are developing a brain fever even as we speak!"

Anne reached out and took hold of his arm. "No, I am not," she stated firmly. "For the first time in my life I feel as though I am truly living as I was meant to live! You must believe me. And I am perfectly well. Feel my heartbeat."

She took his hand and pressed it against her throat. "Do you see how steadily it pulses? Were I hysterical, would you expect my heart to be so regular, so determined?"

"Anne, what you do not seem to understand is that you might have been killed. Indeed, I thought you had been!"

"Nonsense," she stated optimistically. "Besides, when it is time for me to pay my debt to nature, then so I shall. Until then, well, I could not be happier. And see, the bleeding has already stopped."

She again held the kerchief out for him to see. There was very little blood on the folded portion of the white kerchief.

The coach jolted several times. "Jack!" Staverton called out. "Miss Anne is perfectly well! You may slow the coach now."

"Thank God!" Jack cried, reining in the horses.

Staverton felt quite peculiar as he looked at the beautiful, brave creature next to him. Now that he was convinced she was not badly injured, he was finding he could not tear his gaze from hers and that his chest had become filled with a powerful desire to do something he knew he should not.

He felt utterly enthralled and excited by Anne Delamere, who had shown such tremendous sangfroid in the face of the recent attack. Would Georgina Patney or Cassaundra Bradley have done anything else but fall into a swoon? Of course not. Any lady would have fainted, any lady except the one beside him.

He whispered her name. "Anne."

Her expression grew solemn. Her lips parted. "Yes?" she murmured in hushed response.

He saw the soft invitation in her eyes. He dragged her onto his lap, cradling her with one arm so that with the other he could pet her face, stroke her cheeks, her chin, and find her lips with his own. The kiss he gave her began gently, a delicate search as though he feared wounding her further.

A sweet moan sounded in her throat. Staverton drew back and looked at her. He saw the glitter in her eye. "Anne, whatever am I to do with you?"

"Kiss me again," she whispered, slipping her arm about his neck.

He pulled her tightly against him, holding her fiercely. The second kiss became wild and uncontrollable, as though the heat of the recent attack had entered his veins, burning at such a pitch that he could only dampen the flame by kissing her again and again, plumbing the depths of her mouth with the softness of his tongue. He held her so tightly that he was not certain where he ended and she began. Her fingers slid into his hair and he kissed her fiercely in response.

The impassioned embrace lasted for a few minutes more until the coachman sounded the horn announcing the next toll gate through which the vehicle soon passed. Only then did Anne withdraw from him, rising up beside him and staring at him strangely. One of her hands remained resting on his chest. He covered it with his own. For a long, long moment, he kept her gaze fixed to his.

"How you kissed me just now," she murmured.

She tried to think back, to recall precisely how it had been that she had become wrapped up in his arms without hesitating even a trifle. She remembered looking at him and seeing the strange, almost wild look in his eyes. She had read his thoughts as though they had been her own. She had, in that moment, wanted only one thing, to be held by him in a powerful embrace and to be kissed by him as thoroughly as she had been yesterday. And so she had.

She did not understand what was happening to her or why she had permitted Staverton to kiss her so passionately, or why she had kissed him back with an equal degree of passion. She felt her cheeks burning. What must he think of her in this moment?

"You should not have kissed me," she whispered. "And . . . and I do beg your pardon for having returned your kisses so . . . so forcefully."

He chuckled softly. "Dear Anne, you delight me so very much."

"And to think I was always used to call you the Infidel," she said wonderingly.

Staverton appeared stunned. "I beg your pardon?"

"The Infidel," she reiterated. "Surely you have heard the appellation before?"

His gaze slid away and a familiar hardened expression overtook his features. She knew she had erred in speaking the unhandsome nickname at such a moment, yet she had not expected him to react in such a manner. "I have offended you, and for that I am sorry," she offered.

"Did you think I would find it amusing, to hear that truly wretched name spoken just now?"

"No, not at all," she responded. "However, I hardly thought you would take a pet because of it." The coach hit a small bump and she balanced herself.

"Take a pet?" He appeared astonished. "For years, I have heard myself referred to by that terrible epithet and wondered what manner of person would have created such an odious sobriquet."

Anne folded her hands on her lap quite tightly, the kerchief tucked between her palms. Such had been their former rapport that she felt compelled to tell him the truth even though she could see how deeply he was distressed. "There is something I feel you should know, then," she said quietly.

He turned toward her slightly and waited.

"I believe I was the one who instigated the use of 'the Infidel' as your, er, sobriquet."

His lips parted in obvious disbelief. *"You* created this charming nickname?" he asked, a frown furrowing his brow. "But why? You never even met me until yesterday."

"Because of Georgina," she responded. "I was outraged by what I supposed your conduct had been toward her and I had no reason at the time to doubt she had spoken the entire truth to me."

He shook his head as though bewildered. "Do you tell me that I have you to thank for a name I hear whispered whenever I but pass through a room?"

Anne drew in a deep breath. "I suppose you do."

"And I kissed you," he murmured. "Twice."

Anne suppressed a chuckle. "Rather ironic, I think."

He cast a sharp glance at her. "To say the least," he said.

She could see that he was offended, as perhaps he ought to be, particularly given the fact that Georgina had withheld from her a critical part of what actually happened between herself and Lord Staverton so many years ago.

"Staverton, I will in this moment apologize to you for your nickname. I must confess, in the past few hours, since having kidnapped you this morning, I have grown to see you as a friend, a friend I hope to have for a long time. However, if I have shown prejudice toward you, it is not only because of Miss Patney. There have been so many others with whom I have been acquainted, all speaking of unhappy experiences with you, that the epithet, instead of diminishing in strength, seemed to grow with each passing year."

"So, then, you are not truly to blame?" he countered, angrily.

She considered this. "You are right," she responded. "I am to blame, for every time I learned of your mistreatment of yet another lady, I became outraged and tended to refer to you more and more as the Infidel. However, in this moment, I am sorry and I do apologize."

She winced slightly and drew in a deep breath. She realized her head had begun to ache and she felt a twinge of nausea turn her stomach. The sway of the coach did little to soften the experience.

"Perhaps we can discuss the matter another time. For the present, however, I had rather hear nothing more on the subject."

"That would probably be best," she said quietly.

Staverton turned away from her. He was overset by having learned the lady he had just kissed, and that so passionately, had been the very one to have first called him the Infidel.

Good God, *the Infidel!*

He had borne the stigma for five years now, and whenever a lady was in the least piqued by his disinterest, he could be assured that he would very soon hear himself referred to, yet again, as the Infidel.

And Anne had been the cause of it.

He felt oddly downcast. In the course of the day, he had come to think of her as very different from all the ladies he had known. However, in learning she had been the actual author of the odious nickname, his opinion of her had begun to sink. It seemed possible she was no different from the majority of the females he had known through the years, except that she had maligned his character on behalf of someone else rather than as a result of her own experience with him. He was not certain this was much better.

He turned toward her. "We are nearly at Hungerford. I have friends who . . . Anne, what is it?"

"My head has begun to ache and I feel a trifle dizzy."

He glanced out the window. "We are not far from Farleigh's house," he murmured. "Anne, with your permission, I should like to take you to Hawkeridge Court. I have friends there who can tend to you. It is unlikely Bertaud would follow us; you would be safe, and I could summon a surgeon to examine your wound. Will you allow me to direct your coachman?"

"What of Shaw?" she asked.

"When you are settled, I will make my way to Hungerford and arrange matters as best I can, only I think you should see a doctor."

"Very well," Anne agreed.

Staverton called to the coachman and within ten minutes, the large equipage turned up the lane leading to the house of his good friends, Robert and Lady Katherine Farleigh. Robert had been his bosom beau since Eton days and Lady Katherine an excellent friend since her first London season eleven years past. They resided at Hawkeridge Court, an ancient Elizabethan manor which had been in Farleigh's family for nine generations. They had a young son who was his namesake—Hugo, and *not* the Infidel—and from recent correspondence he had learned that Lady Katherine was increasing again.

Glancing at Anne, he saw that she was rubbing her forehead and wincing.

"You are not well," he said quietly.

"It is nothing to signify," she returned. "A good night's sleep and I shall be as right as rain, I am certain of it."

"Katherine will tend to you. A more generous and competent nurse you will not find."

Anne nodded, but said nothing more.

When the coach drew to a stop before the fine old mansion, Staverton let down the steps and helped Anne to the gravel drive. When she wobbled on her feet, he did not hesitate but gathered her up in his arms.

"I can walk," she managed, though rather feebly.

"It is my fault you are in this condition," he said. "I should not have kissed you."

Anne chuckled softly. "Do you mean to boast to your friends about the effects of your embraces upon me?"

"Of course," he murmured.

She leaned her head against his shoulder. "I am sorry about the Infidel."

"Hush," he murmured quietly in response.

When the door opened, a familiar face greeted Staverton. "Hello, Langford," the earl said, addressing his friend's ancient butler. "Is Mr. Farleigh at home?"

"Yes, m'lord," he said, glancing impassively at the figure in his arms. "Mr. Farleigh and Lady Katherine are in the yellow salon."

"Will you please send for a surgeon? We suffered an accident on the road."

The well-trained retainer merely lifted a brow at this request. However, his quickly, if quietly, snapped commands sent a body of footmen flying in several directions at once— to fetch the surgeon, to inform Lady Katherine of her guests, to prepare a sustaining brandy for the young lady and his lordship, and to make rooms ready for them both.

An hour later, Anne found herself in the ministrations of a wonderful woman nearer to Staverton's age than her own. She was Lady Katherine Farleigh, the daughter of a duke who had tumbled in love with and married a mere Mr. Robert Farleigh, one of Staverton's dearest friends. While waiting for the surgeon to arrive, Lady Katherine took charge of Anne, sending her servants to fetch her portmanteaus and situating her in a comfortable bedchamber in which she had a small fire built against the night air. "For you have suffered a shock and I will not be surprised if you begin to have the chills."

"You are too kind," Anne said. She allowed herself to be dressed in her softest nightgown and led to a large chair where Lady Katherine cleansed the wound herself.

"It does not appear to be very deep," she said. "You were fortunate. I did not know highwaymen still plied their trade along this road, the punishment being so severe. Was the bandit masked?"

Anne was suddenly very tired and could not give her an answer. Lady Katherine, seeing her fatigue, began telling her of Hawkeridge Court and how she had met both Staverton and Farleigh many years ago at a masquerade at Vauxhall.

Lady Katherine's quiet prattle was like a soothing tonic to the thumping inside Anne's head. Much of the pain had diminished by the time she was tucked in a comfortable bed, in a room lit with but one candle and the glow of the fireplace. She closed her eyes and the room disappeared. It only came into focus a little later when a man stood over her, speaking softly to her.

"Miss Delamere, can you hear me?"

"Yes," she whispered, her eyes opening to bare slits.

"Have you a headache?"

"Yes," she returned. "But only a little."

"You must drink this and I promise you will feel a great deal better in the morning."

She felt herself lifted so that she could imbibe what she soon discovered was a glass of laudanum and water. When she had drained the last of it, she murmured her gratitude, turned on her side and fell promptly asleep.

SEVEN

On the following morning, Anne awakened slowly as her dreams merged with the remarkably loud sound of squabbling birds just beyond her window. Opening her eyes, she found she was lying on her side with her hands tucked beneath her cheek. She was being observed by a plump yellow cat sitting on a nearby chair.

"Hello," she murmured, squinting her eyes against the sunshine filtering through the curtains.

The cat twitched his ears, but gave no evidence of being interested in her otherwise.

"Were you sent here to guard me?" she asked, smiling.

The cat responded by softening his orange eyes and once more twitching his ears.

"I begin to believe you might be a spy."

The cat yawned.

"And I can see that you are trained in all manner of subterfuge."

When the cat offered a strangely hoarse meow, she rolled onto her back, chuckling, then extended herself into a satisfying stretch.

She looked up at the pretty rosette in the center of the pink moire silk that formed a canopy over the comfortable bed. She felt warm and safe beneath the soft blankets, and her head no longer ached, the happy effects of laudanum.

For a moment, she desired nothing more than to remain where she was for perhaps an eternity.

She wondered lazily whether or not the house was yet astir, and if Staverton's friends partook of a hearty breakfast, for she realized suddenly she was famished. How much she would enjoy a steaming cup of hot chocolate, bread dripping with butter, and a scrambled egg or two. Her stomach rumbled in a completely unladylike fashion.

Her thoughts drifted about contentedly in this manner until they landed upon Staverton and all they had endured together thus far on their journey to Bath. The entire day had felt like a very hilly lane taken at breakneck speed, up and down, up and down, in a racing gig. She had begun the morning with a kidnapping. Throughout the middle hours she had chased a spy, gotten shot for her efforts, then found herself kissed more passionately than she would have ever believed possible. In the end she had climbed into bed with a headache, a dose of laudanum and the sure knowledge she had deeply offended his lordship by revealing that she was the author of his most hated nickname.

She sighed deeply, feeling very confused. Her opinions of the earl, while by no means having completely turned around, were certainly undergoing a change, which had begun with the truths surrounding his courtship of Georgina Patney.

Previously, she had supposed his actions had had no particular basis other than that for some reason he took pleasure in tormenting females in general. She was now convinced he acted from a sense of betrayal, perhaps first begun when he overheard Miss Patney telling a friend that she did not love him but still intended to become his wife. In consequence, she thought it a fair assumption that he simply did not understand the devastating nature of his attitude toward the ladies with whom he flirted. The only fault she could presently find in the entire history was not with Staverton so much as with Miss Patney, who had allowed rumors to run rife without once defending the earl's reasons for abandoning her.

The fact that Anne had settled the horrid nickname upon him now seemed to her shame, even though she had been utterly convinced at the time that he had been worthy of so wretched an epithet as the Infidel.

As for the kiss, Anne dismissed it entirely. The excitement of the moment must have created her desire to fall into Staverton's arms, which was perhaps the same reason she had allowed him to kiss her in the lane two days past when she was covered with raspberries. Any notion beyond this, that there was a possibility her affections were beginning to be engaged, she absolutely refused to allow. Once the documents had been replaced, she would return Staverton to Berkshire and to Cassie. She would somehow force him to wed her cousin and the pair would live happily ever after. Yes, regardless of a harmless kiss or two with Staverton, this ridiculous jaunt to Bath would end in a wedding in Berkshire.

With these thoughts creating a well-ordered mind, she left the warmth of her bed and padded quickly across the floor to the bellpull. The yellow cat jumped from his chair and trotted beside her, asking loudly to be let out from the chamber. Opening the door for the poor creature, she gave the bellpull a tug.

She remained by the door, her mind suddenly swamped with the possibility that Staverton might have already left Hawkesridge Court. She hadn't the least notion of the hour, but she knew the earl would not want to tarry. If he thought her too ill to travel, he would leave her behind in a trice. She remembered he had said he would go to Hungerford and wait for Shaw to come to him. She felt panicky suddenly. What if Shaw had returned with news that Bertaud had not stopped for the night but had continued on to Bath, which, after all, was not so very far distant. Staverton undoubtedly would have pressed on without her.

She gave a little whimper and rang the bellpull again,

only this time she gave three sharp tugs. She would be devastated to find she had been inadvertently left behind and all because she had been shot up a little.

Within barely a minute, a maid arrived out-of-breath. "I was that worried, miss!" she cried, entering the chamber. "Do ye need the surgeon?"

"No, no," Anne assured her. "I must know, did Lord Staverton leave yet? Is he gone?"

"No, miss," the young serving girl replied, obviously relieved by her appearance of health.

Anne released a great sigh. "Thank goodness," she said. "I feared he might have departed already."

"No, he has not. I believe he is in the morning room partaking of his breakfast, although he must intend to leave quite soon. The coach he hired in Hungerford is being harnessed even now."

"He hired a new coach?" she asked, startled.

"Yes, for he could not get the window of your coach repaired in time to continue his journey."

"Yes, of course," Anne said. She had forgotten entirely that her coach was now lacking a window. "You must dress me quickly, then, for I do not wish to keep his lordship waiting. The simplest fashion for my hair will do and the Sardinian blue carriage dress with the matching bonnet. The latter you may take to the entrance hall after you have finished packing my portmanteaus. I shall require everything to be ready by the time his lordship means to board his coach."

"Yes, miss."

Lord Staverton sat in the morning room, bent over at the waist, his hands clasped loosely between his knees, staring at nothing in particular. He had just finished his meal and was answering Farleigh's and Lady Katherine's questions as best he could. The task was not simple. He had been attempting to explain just how he came to be in Anne's company as well as the incident on the highway.

"So, you have not the faintest notion who it was that shot at your coach?" Farleigh asked.

Staverton shook his head. This particular aspect of his journey with Anne he did not feel he could discuss. "I suspect a highwayman," he prevaricated. "Who can say."

"But that makes no sense at all," Katherine said. "Why, then, did the bandit not actually stop your coach?"

"It is a mystery," he responded.

He noted from the corner of his eye that his friends exchanged a confused glance.

"As for Miss Delamere," Katherine prodded, reverting to the original topic, "you are saying she actually kidnapped you." She sat adjacent to him, coffeepot in hand.

He nodded. "Just a half cup, thank you. Yes, she bound my hands quite expertly with a length of rope, all the while holding a pistol at my back. I suppose I could have attempted to escape at that moment, but I feared the pistol would discharge accidentally and one or the other of us would have been injured."

"Whyever did she feel she must kidnap you?" Farleigh asked, dumbfounded.

"Apparently, she feels it is time I tied the connubial knot." When both his friends waited for further elucidation, he added with a sigh, "Her cousin is Miss Bradley."

"Ah," Farleigh said, finally enlightened.

"That charming young lady you pursued in Brighton?" Katherine queried. She and Farleigh had spent a week early in July at the seaside watering hole. "I had thought your heart won at last when I saw you together, indeed I did. I can only suppose you did not offer for her after all?"

Staverton was shocked. "Of course not!" he responded. "I was not in the least in love with her."

"Oh, I see."

He did not like the frown on Katherine's brow. He accounted her a most excellent friend and had been overjoyed when she accepted Farleigh's hand in marriage. "So you believed I was in love with her?" he asked, almost fearing to hear her answer.

"Yes," she responded simply.

"But, what would have made you think so?"

"There were moments, when I saw the pair of you together, that I thought you happy, truly happy."

He considered this. "I suppose there might have been. She was an agreeable companion, but, I never loved her."

"Then why on earth did you single her out as you did?" she asked warmly. "She must have been heartbroken when she returned home. Had you made such a fuss over me, as you did Miss Bradley, I promise you I would have been ordering my bride's clothes before ever I left Brighton."

Staverton was shocked, for she was echoing very nearly what Anne had been telling him yesterday. "If I singled her out," he said quietly, "it was to teach her a lesson, for she had set her cap at me and yet I did not believe for a moment her affections were engaged."

"Oh, dear," dropped from Katherine's lips.

Staverton groaned inwardly. "None of this is to the point, really." He took a sip of his coffee before continuing. "Whatever my relationship to Miss Bradley, I only brought it forward to explain how it was Anne, that is Miss Delamere, came to be in my company."

"I can understand much of this, but why, then, are you traveling to Bath?" Farleigh asked logically.

"I have business there which must be concluded before I can return to Berkshire with Miss Delamere."

"This all sounds mighty havey-cavey, Hugo. Why must Miss Delamere attend you?"

"She will not have to now, of course. I am certain she will want to return to Berkshire because of her injuries."

Farleigh narrowed his gaze. "Then there is no connection

between the kidnapping and the shot fired which wounded Miss Delamere."

"None at all," he responded truthfully.

Farleigh snorted. "There is something you are not telling us."

"That much is true," he responded. "However, I beg you will ask me nothing further on that subject."

"There is one thing I wish to know," Katherine said, pouring more coffee for herself. "What of Miss Delamere? Has she thrown herself at your head as well?"

"Good God, no," he responded. "She is forever reminding me of my faults and it perhaps will not surprise you to learn that only last evening, after she had been shot, she informed me that she was the very one who had created the appellation the Infidel."

"Indeed? This is most singular, almost portentous, surely," Katherine cried, smiling. "Although, I daresay you came the crab and frightened the poor child out of her wits."

At that, Staverton could only laugh. "She could never be frightened in such a manner. She is the bravest lady I have ever met. Oh, now do not look at one another in that manner, as though you mean to have secrets about the state of my heart."

At that moment, their son, just turned five, entered the breakfast parlor. When he caught sight of Staverton, he broke into a run. "Uncle Hugo!" he cried, launching himself into the earl's arms. Staverton rose to his feet just in time to receive him and whirled him in a circle. "Nurse said you were here and I had to find out if it was true."

"Quite true, and how happy I am that you came downstairs to greet me; only look how you have grown! I vow you will be as tall as your father in a year or two."

Little Hugo, chuckled. "No-o-o," he countered, grinning. "Not for many years, that is what Mama says."

Katherine said, "I must say I do not care what ill wind

brought you here, only that you are here. Can you stay with us for a day or two?"

He shook his head. "I'm 'fraid not. In fact, I shan't be staying more than an hour."

"You mean your business in Bath will not wait even a day?" Farleigh asked suspiciously.

"No, it cannot," he responded firmly. He carried Hugo to his mother and settled him on her lap. Taking up his seat once more, he cradled his cup of coffee in his hands.

"Then you must at least tell us why you spent most of the evening at Hungerford last night," Farleigh pressed.

"Leave him be," Katherine said, addressing her husband. "Staverton has always been a trifle mysterious, disappearing for weeks at a time, without a word to anyone of his whereabouts."

"Havey-cavey," Farleigh reiterated. "Does Miss Delamere know what your business is in Bath?"

"Yes," he responded. "Speaking of which, I was wondering if you would permit her to remain here until she feels ready to return to Sulhurst?"

"Of course," Katherine said. "I only wonder how she fares this morning."

As though her concern had summoned Anne down the stairs, she was suddenly in the doorway.

"Good morning," she called out. "Do I smell bacon? What a heavenly aroma, for I find I am starved."

Staverton rose from his seat as did Farleigh. "Good morning to you, Miss Delamere," Lady Katherine called to her.

"A very fine morning, indeed," Anne responded cheerfully as she moved into the room.

Katherine whispered to the earl, "She appears ready to travel, Hugo."

"So she does," he murmured, a little stunned. Ready to travel and more beautiful than even yesterday, he thought. His night's sleep seemed to have robbed him of his memory. With light from the windows of the morning room glinting off her blond locks, he felt as though he were seeing her for the first time.

She was gowned elegantly, just as she had been the day before, sporting a lovely blue carriage dress of a sturdy twilled silk, made high to the neck with narrow ruffles. The sleeves were long and puffed at the shoulder, the front of the gown was scalloped along a row of pearl buttons which descended to the hemline, with gold braid adorning the high waist of the empire gown. About her neck was a simple gold locket.

She would certainly make even Aphrodite envious.

"How are you feeling this morning?" Katherine asked.

"Extraordinarily well, thank you," she responded, approaching her hostess. "And I have you to thank for it. The bed was so comfortable and your physician knew precisely the dosage of laudanum I needed. I feel as though I slept a hundred years last night." She greeted both Farleigh and Staverton in turn, then addressed little Hugo, still seated on his mother's lap. "And who might this be?"

"Young Hugo, my namesake," Staverton offered, smiling.

"That's right," Katherine said. "But when he has been very bad we call him the little Infidel."

"You do not!" Staverton cried in disbelief.

Glancing at Anne, he saw a rather startled expression in her eyes. "I see you have heard of my mischief," she said, a blush on her cheeks.

"Nothing pleased us more," Farleigh responded, smiling wickedly upon Anne, "than to learn we had met the author of Staverton's epithet. Admit it, Hugo, your reputation in certain circles is so vile that nearly half the matchmaking mamas warn their daughters away from you at the beginning of every season."

"It is too bad of you, Robert," he cried. "Just when I had Miss Delamere convinced she had served me quite ill by settling that horrid sobriquet upon me, you must somehow justify it!"

Robert merely laughed, leaning back in his chair.

Katherine wagged her finger playfully at her husband, then turned and made a more formal introduction of her son to Anne.

"So you bear Lord Staverton's name?" Anne asked.

"Yes, I do," he stated. With his mother's encouragement, he slid off her lap and offered her a bow, to which she responded with a bow of her own.

"I am pleased to make your acquaintance," she said. "And what a handsome fellow you are. You must be seven I should think, by how tall you are, possibly eight? Do I have the right of it?"

Staverton watched little Hugo's chest swell with pride.

"I am just turned five," he cried. "Did you hear that, Papa? She thinks I'm eight."

"Yes, indeed," Farleigh responded, beaming upon his young son.

"Well, if you are, indeed, Lord Staverton's namesake," Anne continued, "then I must say, you are already bearing his name well, for you appear to be a strong lad. But I must warn you, besides being strong, you must also be very courageous, for this, I believe, is his lordship's finest quality."

"I am brave, too," Hugo stated enthusiastically. "I do not even cry when my pony tosses me to the ground."

"I am in no doubt of it," Anne responded with deep sincerity.

"Are you going to marry Lord Staverton?" the boy asked artlessly. "If you do, then you could visit me."

His mother intervened. "Darling, it is not considered polite to discuss such things."

"Why?" he asked, glancing back at her.

She leaned forward and hugged him. "Because, only Lord Staverton has the right to ask Miss Delamere to marry him."

Anne saw the disappointment in his face and quickly asked, "May I visit you even if I am not to marry his lordship?"

At that, the lad beamed and nodded. "Will you sit beside me at breakfast?" he asked.

"I should be honored."

He took Anne's hand and led her to the sideboard, where he instructed her on how to fill her plate.

Staverton only became aware that he was still standing and also staring at her when Farleigh cleared his throat several times. "Your coffee is getting cold, Hugo."

Staverton glanced down at his cup. "So it is," he said, taking up his chair once more. Still, with only the strongest discipline could he keep his gaze from straying in her direction.

When little Hugo led her back to the table, he proffered a new question. "Would you be my wife, then?" he asked, "Since you are not to marry Lord Staverton? I think you are very pretty, and you smell good, too."

Staverton wondered what Anne might say to this odd, little-boy's request. Even his friends seemed enrapt as to what her answer might be.

"I must say I am honored by your offer of marriage, Hugo. However, I cannot give you an answer since you are not of an age to marry anyone."

"When I am older?" he asked, hopefully.

"Perhaps," she said.

Hugo smiled happily.

Farleigh bid his son eat his breakfast, which he did quite eagerly, so that he might converse a little with Anne himself. He asked about her home and inquired about her father when the subject arose.

"Delamere," Farleigh mused. "The name is familiar. Have we met in London?"

"I do not think so, for I rarely visit the metropolis."

"Not even for the season?" he asked.

"No," Anne returned, smiling faintly.

"This is a great curiosity," he cried. "How is this possible? I thought every young lady yearned to be presented at court."

"I know it will seem odd in me," she said, "but I never much fancied the notion of the annual season. An occasional ball is all well and good, but many of my friends regaled me with the rigors of one's social obligations during a London springtime, and I vowed I would never cross the Thames for such a reason. I cannot imagine how anyone attends as many as four events in one night! Although, I must say I would have enjoyed riding out every afternoon at Hyde Park, but this still would have been hardly sufficient reward for the rest of it."

Katherine laughed. "I must confess, I was never very fond of the season myself, nor is Farleigh, particularly. We have been to London but a handful of times in the six years we have been married. The society about Hungerford and Newbury suits us perfectly, and when we are in need of a change, we visit my family in Staffordshire. I have three sisters settled there."

"And is it true that you first met Mr. Farleigh and Lord Staverton at a Vauxhall masquerade?" Anne asked.

Katherine's expression softened appreciably as she turned to her husband. "Indeed, it is quite true," she responded.

"I call that an adventure," Anne said, between bites of scrambled eggs and bacon. "Should I ever tumble in love, I hope it will be from having met my husband at a masquerade."

"What about at a kidnapping?" Farleigh asked playfully.

Anne drew in a shocked breath. She turned to stare at Staverton. "You told them?"

He shrugged and smiled. "I did not know how else to explain the circumstance of my traveling with a lady, who, until two days ago, was completely unknown to me."

"But we are *cousins*," she said, smiling. "Or have you forgotten?"

Farleigh entered the conversation. "That wouldn't fadge, Miss Delamere, not by half. I know nearly all of Staverton's family and I would certainly have known of a cousin as beautiful as you."

"Indeed?" Katherine queried, turning to stare down her husband. Her expression was quite arch.

"You must admit she is lovely, my pet," he soothed, leaning toward her and covering her hand with his own. "Of course, she does not hold a candle to you."

"How provoking you are," she returned. Her eye was caught by something on her son's plate. "Hugo, whatever are you making with your bacon?"

"A coach and four," he answered proudly.

A general laughter ensued.

Staverton glanced at the clock on the mantel and saw that the hour was advanced. He decided the moment had come to inform Anne that she would not be traveling with him to Bath after all. That she was dressed for the road was not lost to him, but from the moment she had been shot, undoubtedly by Bertaud, he had been determined that she would return to Sulhurst, where he knew she would be safe.

"The Farleighs would like to extend their hospitality to you," he began, "until you are perfectly recovered and ready to return to Sweetwater Lodge."

Until this moment, Anne had been enjoying herself exceedingly, but Staverton's announcement, so coolly proffered and without the smallest evidence he meant for her to decide her own mind, caused her to pause in cutting a slice of Yorkshire ham. She turned toward him in a meaningful manner. "Are you saying you intend to go on without me?" she asked quietly.

He met her gaze unflinchingly. "Yes," he responded firmly.

Anne settled her knife and fork on her plate and continued to eye Staverton, hoping he would read the full intention behind her words. "My lord," she said formally, "I beg a word with you—*in private.*"

She watched the earl's features harden. "Farleigh and

Lady Katherine are most happy to have you stay with them. You will return to your father and I shall continue my journey to Bath. The matter is settled and there is simply nothing more to say on the subject."

Anne could not believe his high-handedness. "Oh, but I believe there is much more to be said," she responded coldly, through clenched teeth. "Though I would rather do so in private."

"Mama, why is Miss Delamere so angry with Uncle Hugo?"

"I do not know, my pet," Katherine responded. "However, I hope his lordship will have the goodness to discover what is distressing Miss Delamere, say, in the blue parlor?" She glared at Staverton, then inclined her head purposefully toward her son.

"Yes, of course," the earl said, rising immediately to his feet.

Anne was but a half second behind him.

The blue parlor, which overlooked the duck pond, adjoined the morning room through a small antechamber. Once within, Anne closed the doors and rounded on Staverton. "You will not discard me as though I am a—a mere sack of corn or the like! I will go with you, just as we agreed on at the Grey Castle, or have you forgotten that you are my prisoner!"

Staverton laughed outright. "All that is changed, Anne! For goodness' sake, you cannot still be holding to your original scheme? I cannot marry Cassie, I do not love her!"

"Whether you love her or not has never been the issue and well you know it. I kidnapped you because of what *you owe to my cousin,* to a woman whose hopes you raised so high by your own conduct, nothing more. However, I do not mean to argue with you on that score. As delightful as your friends are, I have no intention of remaining here. I am going to Bath with you, today!"

He saw the pronounced color on her cheeks and the way

she had settled her hands on her hips, her arms akimbo, quite stubbornly. There was a pout to her mouth which he found utterly adorable. "You are not well," he stated. "Or have you forgotten that yesterday you were shot and had to be dosed with laudanum because of the severity of your headache."

"Do I look unwell to you, my lord?" she asked hotly.

"No, you do not, but none of this is to the point."

"It is very much to the point. I am quite fit to travel and mean to do so." She turned her head for him. "Do but look! You cannot even see the wound, it was so small! And I do not have the headache this morning at all, if that was truly your concern, or do you just mean to be mulish?"

"Not mulish, Anne," he responded, shaking his head. He could not believe she had suggested he check her wound to detect its size. He realized she possessed the unique ability to surprise him at every turn. "I did not mean to appear obstinate. I had only one thought—the worst fear that though you escaped serious injury yesterday, you might be mortally wounded yet on this ill-starred journey. When you lay so quiet and unmoving in my arms after you had been shot, I felt as though my heart would break at the likelihood I had brought your life to an untimely end. That is my only thought now. I do not believe I could bear it were I to be the author of your death."

Anne was stunned. She had supposed he was merely attempting to dispose of her for entirely selfish reasons, primarily to avoid wedding her cousin. His profession of his fears for her safety came as a shock. "Is this truly how you feel?" she asked.

"Anne," he cried. "I may be many things, but I am not so unfeeling as you think me."

"Then I beg your pardon," she said, her temper gentling. "From the moment you told me you were insisting I remain here, I believed only that you were thinking of your own comfort. Since this is truly how you feel, that my safety was your primary concern, then I can only say I am much gratified."

"I am glad of it, for I am, indeed, deeply anxious. It is one thing for me to risk my own life, but it is an entirely different matter to be risking yours, especially when it is not in the least necessary."

Anne moved to the windows. The ducks were swimming gently on the pond for the moment. She concluded there was no possible way she could dispel his concerns, and for that reason addressed her intentions. "Sulhurst of the moment holds no particular interest to me. If you leave without me, I will simply follow in your wake. I will hire myself another coach, just as you have, and make my way to Bath on my own. However, I beg you will allow me to travel with you, or have you forgotten that it is my servants who are at present keeping pace with Bertaud?"

"I have not forgotten," he murmured.

She smiled faintly. "Please do not refuse me in this, Staverton. We have already come so far. Besides, we are losing time in arguing in this manner and I have begun to feel as though we should leave quite soon. It would not do to permit Bertaud to place too much distance between us."

At that, he shook his head, grimacing, yet with all the appearance of holding back a smile of his own. "I will regret this," he said more to himself than to her. "Are you aware of the severity of the risk you mean to take?"

"Of course," she cried. "Why else do you think I want to come?"

He laughed outright. "You are an oddity, Anne Delamere. Do you know how strange what you just said sounds?"

"You must understand that I am merely speaking the truth from my heart. I have not been so happy in ages as I was yesterday, even after being shot."

He was still shaking his head in disbelief. "Do you truly comprehend the dangers you—that we—are facing?"

"I do. I want to go with you until you have completed your mission."

"Very well," he said at last, throwing up his hands. "Have it as you wish."

"Excellent," she said, smiling. "Now that we have this settled, pray tell me what you discovered at Hungerford. Did Shaw find you last night?"

"Yes. Bertaud made plans to stay the night at Chilton Foliat, at the Boot Inn. I arranged for Shaw to return to Hungerford with news of Bertaud's intentions once he quit the Boot Inn. He should be waiting for me—for us—even now."

"Then we should go."

"Yes, we should."

In the morning room, Mr. Farleigh, having overheard the entire exchange because he told his son to go make a crack in the door to the blue parlor, glanced at his wife and asked quietly, "Do you know to what dangers he is referring? To what mission?"

She nodded. "For some time he has served the Crown in matters of"—she paused and glanced at her son—"of national concern."

"Good God. How is it you know of this but I do not?"

"Because *your* brother is not secretary to the prime minister."

"Oh, I see."

"Precisely."

"Well, I never would have believed it," he said.

"What? That Staverton would take up so dangerous a career?"

He smiled. "No, I can believe that readily enough, for he was always full of pluck, even as a lad."

"What, then?" his wife asked, moving to stand behind him and slipping her arms about his shoulders.

He reached up and placed a hand over hers as he had done earlier during breakfast. "That Staverton has at long last met his match, someone who will bring his ill temper to heel."

Katherine leaned down and kissed him on the cheek. "I could not agree with you more."

A half hour later, Anne was seated beside Staverton in the newly hired coach as it drew away from Hawkesridge Court. She felt entirely well-satisfied at having won the day.

"You needn't appear so smug," he said with a twitch of his lips. "Bertaud may yet find his bullet true and I shan't repine one whit since you have been stubborn in the face of sense."

"I would not expect you to mourn," she retorted, "although I do request that you ship my remains to my father with a note pinned to my bonnet stating that I perished being very brave. That will please him immensely and I shall be content."

He chuckled. "You will not be content, you will be dead."

"So I will!" she responded happily. After a moment, she asked, "Why did you permit me to come with you?"

"Well, besides the fact that I already know you well enough to believe you would follow through on your threat to chase after me, the truth is, I quite agree with young Hugo—I, too, think you are pretty, and you smell good as well."

Anne laughed heartily and, knowing herself forgiven, at least for the present, settled her gaze out the window, intent on enjoying the day.

EIGHT

As the coach crossed yet another bridge over the River Kennet, Anne gripped the carriage rope to steady herself. The vehicle Staverton had hired was not nearly so well-sprung as her own traveling coach and she seemed to feel every bump in the road as though it were a small mountain. More than once she apologized to the earl for jostling him accidentally.

Leaving the bridge, a sudden dip in the road sent her flying forward, her momentum halted fortuitously by Staverton, who caught her about the waist and pulled her back onto the seat.

"Thank you!" she cried. "I am not at all used to such a badly sprung conveyance as this."

"It is pretty awful," he responded, "although I daresay you are suffering a great deal more than myself."

"I have noticed as much. Your booted feet at the end of a pair of long legs keep you anchored rather nicely against the bottom of the opposite seat. My legs are not quite long enough to make myself secure."

"I could put my arm around you?" he suggested.

She caught his teasing glance and could only laugh.

Approaching the village of Hungerford, Anne asked, "Where did you tell Shaw we would meet him?"

"There is another bridge behind the Bear Inn, from which

I have often fished for trout, Hungerford being famous for both trout and crayfish. When I am able to pass a few days at Hawkesridge Court, Farleigh and I make at least one trip to this particular bridge. I suggested the place to Shaw because it was less conspicuous than the inn yard or even the street. I hope this is agreeable to you?"

"Of course," she said. "I have every confidence in your judgment."

Anne glanced at him, aware that though he had acquiesced to her presence on the journey, he was by no means content. His gaze was restless as he scanned the surrounding countryside from both windows of the coach, and there was a tension in the set of his shoulders and in the grim lines about his mouth that had not been present yesterday. More than once, she had felt his fingers lightly on her shoulder as some movement of shrubbery or the approach of another carriage alerted his senses. She doubted there was anything she could say to set his heart at ease where her welfare was concerned.

Withholding a sigh, Anne let her gaze drift to the windows as well. Berkshire would soon be left behind since Hungerford was situated in close proximity to the Wiltshire border. Their journey to Bath from Sulhurst was already a third accomplished.

Once at Hungerford, the coachman drew the vehicle to the bridge behind the inn, and shortly afterward, Anne's servant rode up to the coach on a black horse. "Did you and Quince see Bertaud this morning?" she queried, opening the door in order to better converse with him.

He nodded and doffed his hat respectfully to each of them in turn. "Aye, miss. The Frenchman took the old road to Chilton Foliat. He passed the night at the Boot Inn, just as I told Lord Staverton he meant to do. Quince is yet on his heels. He said he would leave messages for me at Knighton, Ramsbury, Axford, and Mildenhall."

"We will follow after you," Staverton stated.

Anne, however, had a different notion entirely. "Perhaps

we should consider taking the new road," she offered, addressing the earl. Her father had once told her the history of the two routes to Marlborough. Prior to the year 1744, the road to Bath after leaving Hungerford rambled through Chilton Foliat, past Littlecote Park, through Ramsbury, and finally reached Marlborough. However, during that year, a new turnpike was created which led the traveler to the city of Marlborough through Froxfield and the beautiful Saversnake Forest. "I have every confidence Shaw and Quince will be able to keep Bertaud in sight, and later, at Mildenhall, Shaw could easily turn in a southerly direction, pass through the forest, and meet us at the top of the hill before the descent to Marlborough. This would give us a few miles on the road without fear of discovery."

Staverton nodded. "If your men are willing to continue their pursuit, I must say the notion is an excellent one. We will certainly run little risk of crossing paths with Bertaud, at least not until we reach Marlborough." He turned to her footman. "But what do you say, Shaw? Bertaud has slain more than one good man in his time and I do not want you ignorant of the dangers involved."

" 'Tis my duty as an Englishman," the servant stated firmly. "Both Quince and I are proud to be of use in this situation. 'Tis little enough, what with so many English soldiers dying in Spain as they are, or coming home crippled."

"Good man," Staverton said seriously.

Anne was proud of Shaw and Quince, and of Jack Coachman, as well, for that matter. All of her servants were brave, patriotic men who were willing to take up Staverton's cause in the face of the obvious dangers involved in trailing a spy.

As for Staverton, she knew what he was thinking, that for the next three leagues or so, he need not be so anxious for her safety as he had been for the past several miles.

Having arranged with Shaw to meet him at the top of the hill before the descent to Marlborough, Anne settled back in her seat. Staverton closed the door and glanced into the west. "The air feels different somehow. I wonder we do not have a rainstorm before nuncheon."

"I do not see any clouds," Anne remarked.

"Nor do I; still, there is a change, a slight breeze perhaps, a smell to the air."

Anne took a sniff. "I smell nothing," she said. A moment later she wrinkled her nose. "Except the horses."

Staverton laughed and bid Jack Coachman take the southerly route to Froxfield.

Once the coach left Hungerford, Anne retrieved her pistols from their case in order to examine and clean them. She had not used them in some time, so the pans and barrels of both were in excellent condition, but her father had taught her that it was always a good idea to keep the firearms polished and oiled, regardless, so that when they were needed, they would neither fail her nor explode in her hands.

She went about the business quietly, overlaying the delicate blue silk of her gown with the carriage rug for protection and settling the pistols on the rug itself. Her thoughts, however, flitted in other directions entirely. For no particular reason that she could deduce, her mind became filled with the images of having been kissed by his lordship on the day before.

Earlier, she had refused to assign even the smallest significance to the experience, but now she was not so certain she had been wise in dismissing what had been an extraordinarily passionate embrace. For one thing, she was not in the least convinced that the only reason she had allowed the kiss was because of the excitement of the moment as she had previously thought. She paused in her rubbing of the inlaid wood patterns along the stock of her pistol. Staverton had pulled her fully onto his lap. He had comforted her tenderly by petting her face in the gentlest manner possible, as though reassuring himself that she was still alive. He had taken a deep breath and whispered to her, *Anne. Whatever am I to do with you?*

She resumed rubbing the stock in small, slow circles with

the tip of her cloth-covered finger. What had he meant by uttering these words? He had seemed so lost. Only then, as she was examining the memory, did she realize she had actually commanded him to kiss her again!

She gasped ever so faintly, but apparently Staverton overheard her, for he turned toward her. "What is it?"

She blinked several times. "I . . . I thought I detected a scratch on the surface of this square of inlay, but I can see I was mistaken."

"Indeed," he murmured.

She glanced up at him and saw that his smile was crooked.

She ignored his knowing expression. She could see that he was fully aware she had just told a whisker, but she wasn't about to confess it to him, especially since she could hardly tell him her thoughts.

In truth, she had felt cared for deeply by the gentle nature of his first kiss, which was why she had begged him to kiss her again—she had expected more of the same. That the ensuing kiss had become passionate in the extreme was what she found inexplicable. Was this what usually happened when he kissed a woman? Should she be careful not to ascribe too much meaning to the experience? But most importantly, was it possible the manner in which she tended to become wrapped up in his arms indicated her heart was being affected by the man sitting so closely beside her even now?

Was this how he hurt the ladies with whom he flirted? Did he lead them to believe by his actions that his affections were truly and deeply engaged when they were not?

She could not say. What she did know for certain, which was probably the most distressing aspect of the most recent kiss she had shared with Staverton, was that she doubted there was anything that would give her greater pleasure than being embraced, touched and kissed in such a fashion again.

She lifted her gaze to him for a brief moment and saw that he was looking out the window, his expression solemn.

His gray eyes surveyed the passing landscape sharply. There was something in his demeanor that spoke of power beyond his strong physical presence. She admired this about him, the sense of command which belonged to him, as snugly as the well-tailored coat he sported of an elegant Egyptian brown. He was dressed to perfection in a waistcoat of bishop's blue silk, fawn-colored pantaloons and glossy Hessians dangling with gold tassels. His black top hat was of a fine beaver felt, rolled fashionably at the sides.

She returned to tending the fine-grained wood of her pistols. Everything about her firearms was first-rate, not unlike Staverton—polished, honed, balanced, proportioned, powerful, even deadly. These attributes which the earl possessed, coupled with his ability to give an impression of deep concern, made him capable, as Cassie had once said, of making any lady he chose to tumble in love with him.

Was she herself, then, in some danger of losing her heart to the Infidel? She simply did not know. She believed, she *hoped,* she had more sense than that. However, one soulful look, and she had begged for a second kiss.

She thought it prudent, therefore, to open a subject that surely would illuminate Staverton's character in such a way that she might be relieved of a little of her admiration for him. Clearing her throat, she began, "I have been meaning to ask you for some time, at least since we left Hawkesridge Court, about another young lady, a cousin of mine, who for many years held a grievance against you." He turned toward her and, lifting her gaze to him, she noted the stilled expression of his features. "Would you be willing to discuss the matter with me?"

"You expect me to justify my conduct again as I did concerning my history with Georgina Patney?"

"May I speak plainly?"

There was a considerable pause before he nodded his assent.

"When you told me of your experience with Lady Wespall, with Georgina, I was astonished. I had never expected to hear a version of the incident which would cause me to alter my opinion of you, but so I did. I will confess that it would be much easier for me to continue in my prejudices against your character but I would appreciate very much if you would tell me what you perceive happened between yourself and Prudence Marsh."

At that, he seemed to relax. "Miss Marsh is your cousin?"

"Yes."

He chuckled slightly. "I begin to fear you have so many cousins scattered throughout England that I shall be obliged to spend the next decade of my life justifying my conduct to you on one matter or another."

Anne loved that he had broken the tension with a joke. "Not a decade," she assured him. "Five years at the most."

He laughed. "Well, I will tell you of my experiences with Miss Marsh. However, I will only do so on one condition."

She could not imagine what he would require of her but she agreed readily. "Anything you wish for," she said.

"That you cease pointing your weapon at me."

Anne glanced down at the pistol she had been polishing and saw that it was fairly aimed at his heart. "Oh, I do beg your pardon!" she cried. "The first rule in managing one's weapons! I am sorry." She turned the barrel of the pistol away from him and encouraged Staverton. "Pray begin when you are ready. I cannot tell you how anxious I am to hear what you would tell me of your pursuit of her some four years ago."

"Miss Marsh," he murmured. "She was an unusual female, to be sure, and quite lovely to behold. I was sorry to hear she had become something of a recluse, living out her days buried in the Cotswolds, refusing all suitors."

"I have not received a letter from her in over a twelve-month, but I did hear from her mother, my aunt, that she is grown as thin as a knitting needle."

He chuckled. "Perhaps not quite as lean as that, but I can attest to her rather frail appearance for I saw her Christmas

We'd Like to Invite You to Subscribe to Zebra's Regency Romance Book Club and Give You a Gift of 4 Free Books as Your Introduction! (Worth $19.96!)

If you're a Regency lover, imagine the joy of getting **4 FREE Zebra Regency Romances** and then the chance to have these lovely stories delivered to your home each month at the lowest price available! Well, that's our offer to you and here's how you benefit by becoming a Regency Romance subscriber:

- **4 FREE** Introductory Regency Romances are delivered to your doorstep

- **4 BRAND NEW** Regencies are then delivered each month (usually before they're available in bookstores)

- Subscribers save almost $4.00 every month

- You also receive a **FREE** monthly newsletter, which features author profiles, discounts, subscriber benefits, book previews and more

- No risks or obligations...in other words, you can cancel whenever you wish with no questions asked

Join the thousands of readers who enjoy the savings and convenience offered to Regency Romance subscribers. After your initial introductory shipment, you receive 4 brand-new Zebra Regency Romances each month to examine for 10 days. Then, if you decide to keep the books, you'll pay the preferred subscriber's price.

It's a no-lose proposition, so return the FREE BOOK CERTIFICATE today!

last in Bath. I almost did not recognize her. She approached me in the Pump Room, smiling. I vow, she truly seemed content. She even apologized to me."

Anne stopped swirling the ramrod down the barrel of her pistol and turned to stare at him. "She apologized to you? Is this, indeed, true? But whatever for? Did she seem sincere?"

"Yes, it is true, and I do take a measure of offense in your having questioned as much, and yes, I believed her quite sincere."

"What did she say at the time? Did she in any manner refer to her sojourn in the Lake District when you sat in her pocket the better part of three months?"

"Yes, as it happens, she did." He seemed pained. "She said that she had behaved foolishly in the boathouse—you do know about the boathouse?"

She nodded. "A wind had arisen, as I recall."

"A monstrous wind like nothing I had ever seen before, but no rain. It was most unusual. At any rate, we became trapped in a boathouse on the far side of the lake for several hours together. But when I met her recently in Bath, she told me she had regretted her conduct for many years and had wished it undone a thousand times."

"I do not know if this question will seem impertinent, but what did happen in the boathouse?"

"Nothing to signify," he responded. "I behaved the gentleman and only kissed her once." He paused for a moment and stared hard at Anne. "But that kiss, it was not even in the remotest sense like the kisses I have shared with you."

Anne felt a strange quivering inside her as his gaze drifted to her lips, as though he was remembering. The expression on his face caused her to remember, as well, just as she had a few moments earlier. She felt the most ridiculous impulse to beg him to kiss her yet again.

He looked away from her and gave himself a strong shake. "None of that is to the point. Where Miss Marsh was concerned, as with Lady Wespall, I had been on the verge of offering for her. I might even have done so that windy afternoon, when the lake was whipped to a frenzy, had she not pressed me in the oddest way. We had been trapped there for at least three hours when she clamped her hands together and with a rather mulish expression stated, 'you must marry me, you know, for I am forever compromised.' "

"She never said so," Anne remarked. "Please tell me you are bamboozling me on this point."

"Her very words. Did she never tell you?"

Anne shook her head. She could not credit that, for the second time, the lady in question had not told her the entire truth. As with Georgina, Prudence's conduct could hardly be accounted either self-respecting or sensible. "Pru always was a bit of a ninnyhammer. I mean, even if she desired to marry you more than anything, why on earth did she not have enough dignity to wait for you to offer for her in a proper manner? 'You must marry me,' " she effected in a theatrical manner. "I vow, I should have tossed her in the lake for saying anything so absurd!"

At that, Staverton burst out laughing. "My dear Miss Delamere, have you forgotten you have already told me that *I must marry your cousin!*"

"That is a different matter entirely. I vow Cassie never once said anything so wretched to you during her stay in Brighton."

Staverton was silent apace, as though searching his memory. "No, she did not," he responded quietly. "She was always perfectly genteel in her manners and discourse."

Anne met his gaze. "Do you see, yet, how badly you misjudged her, regardless of Prudence's reprehensible conduct or Georgina's?"

"I did not think so at the time, but even Katherine was surprised that I had not offered for Miss Bradley."

"There, you see," Anne said. She might have been completely satisfied with this admission except that she had just succeeded in strengthening her case that Staverton ought to marry her cousin. Somehow, in this she was not nearly so content as she had been previously. She wondered, for instance, what Staverton thought of the fact that Cassie had been nearly betrothed to Harry Chamberlayne at the time she had met the earl in Brighton.

For a moment, Anne wondered what she thought of Cassie herself. She had much to contemplate in all that the earl had just told her. She returned therefore to the quiet task of cleaning her pistols.

Staverton was content that the subject had finally worked itself out. He was never comfortable either thinking or speaking of Prudence Marsh. He knew he was not responsible for her decision to essentially renounce society and live as a recluse in the Cotswold Hills, yet the suspicion had always nagged at him that he had not managed the business well. What he did not tell Anne was how coldly, how badly, he had treated Miss Marsh the remainder of that afternoon, telling her he refused to be bullied into marrying anyone. She had wept, wailing at times that he was breaking her heart. Still, he had remained resolutely set against her.

When he had seen her in Bath last year, she had teased him a little. "Have you found anyone who meets your extraordinary standards?" she had asked.

He had been shocked that she would say such a thing to him. Was he so impossible to please?

He glanced at Anne, who had bent her head over her second pistol and was examining what he could only suppose was possibly another scratch on the surface of the beautifully inlaid wood. He had never met anyone like her before; certainly he had never met a lady who valued her pistols as much as any man of his acquaintance, more than some he could name.

"May I have a look?" he asked.

"Of course," she responded. She handed him her pistols with obvious pride, and as soon as he held each in hand he realized she was perfectly justified in her sentiments. "Very nicely weighted," he said. "Excellent balance, both of them. And you are a keen shot you say?"

She nodded. "I do not mean to boast, but Papa would let me be nothing less, particularly since last year he set a new record at Manton's in London."

"Delamere," Staverton mused, frowning as he tried to place the name. "Good God! I have met him. He overset my record. Is he a fellow with a balding pate, an easy manner and a very dry wit?"

"You have described him exactly."

"And you are his daughter?"

"Yes, indeed."

"Were you in London as well at the time?"

"No, as I have said before, I have little interest in the metropolis."

"That, at least, is something we agree upon."

"You are not enamored of coal smoke, disease and poverty either?" she asked facetiously.

He chuckled. "I can hear your father speaking now."

She resumed her task, and once she was satisfied with the condition of her weapons, she settled them in the case.

A stiff breeze suddenly buffeted the coach. "Do but look!" Anne cried, gesturing for Staverton to cast his gaze to the western sky. "Your clouds have arrived at last, and quickly, too."

At Froxfield, Anne remained in the coach as did Staverton as the horses were changed. The coach swayed several times as the two new teams were placed in harness. Nearly to the precise moment of the coachman giving the horses the office to start, a steady rain began to fall.

Several miles down the road, the coach entered the Saversnake Forest. The beauties of oak, elm, ash, beech and thorn brought a companionable silence between herself and Staverton. Her gaze was fixed to the moving picture of the forest as it passed by her window. The air of the lush woodland seeped into the coach, pungent with the scent of fern and wet oak leaves.

Anne once more drew the carriage rug over her legs, for the temperature diminished almost immediately. She felt deeply relaxed and removed her bonnet that she might lean her head against the squabs, just for a moment or two. Her eyes closed of their own volition, and the gentle swing and sway of the coach, as well as the steady beat of the raindrops on the roof of the coach, worked on her mind like a cup of warm rum punch. She stifled a yawn and before long her thoughts became a rambling that made no sense at all as she drifted into sleep.

Sometime later, she awakened slowly, though she did not open her eyes. She found she was leaning sideways, her head buried in soft cloth. Her arm was wrapped about something very warm and she could smell the faintest scent of a fine grade of soap.

She felt unreasonably content and perhaps would have stayed all snug and comfortable had her left hand not started tingling. It was bent at an odd angle and was beginning to hurt. She shifted slightly and felt the warmth beneath her arm move about with her.

She awoke with a start, realizing she was once more engulfed in Staverton's arms, that he had been holding her while she slept.

She leaned back only to find his amused smile beaming down upon her. She met his gaze and for the longest moment became lost in his eyes. Perhaps she was still asleep and just dreaming. She felt as though she was seeing all the way to his soul, even that she understood him and that in this moment he comprehended her.

A river of longing coursed through her entire body. The sensation was so profound that it was only with some difficulty she began to disengage from his strong gaze and the comfort of having been enveloped in his arms.

"Good heavens," she whispered. "Did I actually fall asleep?"

"Yes," was his succinct answer.

"But how could I have done so?" she asked, pulling away from him. "I remember leaning my head against the squabs, the rain was pelting the top of the carriage and the smell of oak was heavily in the air . . ."

"Actually, you were reclining awkwardly against the seat, your neck became bent and you kept whimpering. I could not help but take pity on you. I coaxed you onto my shoulder and you murmured a very sweet, 'thank you, Hugo.' Do you not remember?"

"No, not at all. I do beg your pardon, Staverton. I never meant to be so familiar with you, nor to trouble you so."

"I would hardly call cuddling a beautiful young lady while she slept a particularly difficult trial to bear."

Anne smiled and stifled a yawn. "How long did I sleep?"

"An hour."

"It has nearly stopped raining, as well."

"Almost," he murmured. "I believe we are about to leave the forest."

At that, Anne sat up straighter still. Putting her bonnet on, she cried, "Ah! The most exciting part of the entire journey is just ahead of us."

"You mean seeing what Shaw has to tell us?"

"No," she returned, laughing as she tied the ribbons beneath her chin. "Going down the steep hill."

"My dear Miss Delamere, have you no sensibility? Do you not know how many coaches have crashed on this particular descent?"

She giggled. "I have every confidence we shall not come to grief, for my coachman is one of the finest in all of Berkshire. Once Shaw arrives, he will place the skids properly and you will have no reason to doubt we will be perfectly safe."

"Well, I certainly hope so."

When the coach drew off to the side of the road at the top of the hill in order to await Shaw's arrival, Anne walked to a southern prominence, the wind buffeting her firmly and whipping her blue carriage dress about her ankles. The rain had ceased, and in checkerboard parcels of blue and gray the sky was beginning to clear. Below her, the city of

Marlborough sat on the slope of a great down with the River Kennet rambling through the valley like a silvery serpent.

Staverton joined her, standing beside her and remarking on the beauty of the landscape. Anne drew in a deep breath, her contentment rising again in her breast. She could only wonder whether it was the rain-drenched downs which made her feel as though the world had been made anew, or whether it was the man beside her. She felt peculiar, remembering how very recently he had cradled her while she slept. For some reason, she longed to take his hand in hers, to give his fingers a gentle pressure as a way of sharing this moment with him.

She felt her hand turn at the wrist. She glanced down and saw that his gloved fingers were very near. If she turned rapidly, she would brush his hand with the tips of her fingers—an accident, only!

She smiled, thinking how ridiculous this was, to be imagining just how she could go about touching Staverton's hand. The man next to her was Cassie's betrothed, and the desire she was experiencing probably had more to do with the exquisite nature of the view before her than anything else.

At that moment, her servant arrived on horseback from a nearby track through the forest. Anne, hearing his name called by her coachman, turned sharply, and just as she had planned, her fingers brushed against the back of the earl's hand. A current flowed through her so sharp and heady, that she blinked several times, all the while apologizing to Staverton for having touched him.

He laughed. "You did not injure me," he stated. "And you have no need to apologize."

She met his gaze briefly, startled by the odd sequence that had made her imaginings actually happen. She drew away from him and turned briskly toward her servant. "What have you learned, Shaw?" she called out.

The servant guided his black horse close to her. "Bertaud passed through Marlborough," he said. "He did not even pause to change horses. Quince left word at Mildenhall to the effect that he has stopped at Beckhampton for the night. He arranged for a room and the horses are unharnessed from his curricle."

Anne breathed a deep sigh of relief. She could be at ease once more, as could Staverton.

After Shaw had placed the skids properly in front of the back wheels of the coach, she thanked him for his efforts concerning Bertaud, then bade him wait at the bottom of the hill in order to return the skids to Jack once the coach made its descent.

Shaw nodded his acquiescence, remounted his horse and began a slow and careful progress down the steep hill. Anne's heart raced as she boarded the vehicle once more, and with Staverton beside her, commanded the coachman to press on.

Even with the skids, and the horses held tightly in check, the coach more or less plummeted down the hill, much to Anne's delight. Staverton braced his booted feet against the seat in front of him, and with her permission, held her tightly about the waist. She delighted in the entire descent, laughing the entire way.

Staverton laughed with her. "I would never have imagined that chasing after Bertaud could hold such enjoyment."

Anne smiled. "That is one of the kindest things you have said to me." He still held her about the waist, quite scandalously. A warmth climbed up her cheeks. "You had best release me now," she murmured. How odd that she wished he would not.

A slow smile spread over his features. "Must I, Miss Delamere?" His brow was crinkled in a theatrical manner.

She took one of his hands and forcibly removed it from about her. He groaned playfully. "Oh, very well." After which he released her entirely.

Once Shaw had removed the skids and given them to the coachman, Anne bid her servant continue on to Beckhampton where he was to meet with them on the morrow with further word of the spy's movements.

Shaw waved farewell and set his horse toward the High Street, where he soon disappeared in the increasing traffic.

Marlborough was a fair-sized town and saw not only Bath and London travelers, but those from the north and south as well.

The coach eased its way into the general flow of every manner of conveyance, from fine barouches to the public coaches, from carts and wagons of every description to high flyers and spirited gigs.

"This must be the widest road in all of England," Anne said as the coach turned up the High Street. The shops overhung the sidewalk, forming a delightful arcade, and two churches, one at either end of the broad avenue, hemmed the street in like bookends.

At that moment, the rain opened on the town again with a sudden burst of fury. Riders slumped their shoulders and spurred their mounts toward the inn yards, ladies walking along the street squealed their displeasure as they ran for shelter, and gentlemen in open curricles could be heard cursing.

"At least we are safely within our coach," Staverton remarked. "Shall we nuncheon at the Castle Inn?"

"That would be delightful."

Entering the courtyard of the inn a few minutes later, the cloudburst ceased as quickly as it had begun. Unfortunately, the inn yard had become a miniature lake.

Staverton descended from the coach first and turned to assist Anne. "I suppose there is nothing for it," she said, frowning at the water flowing happily over the toes of the earl's glossy boots.

Staverton, holding Anne's hand and arm, suddenly swept his arm about her waist and caught her up as he had the first day of his acquaintance with her.

Anne, surprised, laughed heartily and quickly slid an arm about his neck. "The advantage of pantaloons and Hessians!" she cried. "How I envy you, for had I stepped in the water, I should have dampened more than one garment and soaked my half boots through entirely."

He smiled, carrying her easily through the deep puddle as the coach moved away toward the stables. Anne glanced at the sky overhead and cried out, "A rainbow!"

Staverton whirled her about until he, too, saw the lovely arc of color. "So it is. An omen," he added. "A good one, I trust."

"Of course," she agreed readily. "On such a vital mission as ours, I would expect nothing less."

He glanced down at her. Anne met his gaze and smiled. "You were very kind to carry me, my lord."

"You are always setting down to kindness that which a man does for pleasure."

"Regardless," she said, chuckling. "I am still grateful. Also, I do believe you could put me on my feet now. We are long past the puddle."

"So we are," he agreed, glancing down at the cobbles below. "However, since I cannot be assured of precisely when I will have the opportunity of holding you again, I do not think I shall."

"Never?" she asked in the same light tone.

Staverton did not know how it had come about, but his initial, rather harmless gesture of carrying Miss Delamere across the Castle Inn's lake had turned into something quite dangerous, for in this moment he was experiencing a profound desire to kiss her again. He was charmed by Anne Delamere, who cleaned her pistols, kidnapped peers and generally took him to task whenever it pleased her. It was entirely true that he had never known such a lady before, certainly not one with such an inviting mouth and smile.

He would kiss her. He decided as much. The moment could not be more advantageous since the inn yard was presently empty; not even a stable boy was about. He leaned forward, but the door, some six feet away, suddenly opened and a large man and two companions crossed the threshold.

"Oh, I say, guv'nor," the first man said. "I do beg yer

pardon." He tipped his hat and walked past them both, tramping through the puddle as though it did not exist, his compatriots in tow.

Anne realized she was trembling, not because the men had startled her, nor because the air was chilled from the recent rain, but because Staverton had meant to kiss her. Had the moment not been disturbed, she had every confidence he would have pressed his lips to hers. What was worse, she thought, as he finally settled her on her feet before the door, was that she would have welcomed the kiss.

She felt wholly undone by the sure knowledge she could not trust herself with Staverton, that he had but to flirt with her a little, to play the gallant by carrying her across an inn yard, and she was willing to allow him to kiss her.

Entering the inn and watching Staverton secure a parlor, she felt utterly bemused. The previous two kisses she could to some degree explain as having been the result of the danger and excitement of the moment—in the lane when Bertaud had nearly run over her, and, later, when she had been shot. However, there had been no danger in crossing the cobbles just now, merely a closeness that seemed to arouse all manner of sensation between herself and Staverton. She wondered what his thoughts were.

As Staverton spoke with the landlord and arranged for a parlor for himself and Anne, he made a concerted effort not to meet her gaze, at least for a time. He could not believe he had almost kissed her again, a circumstance that was forcing him to take stock of what was happening between them. He had known her but three days and already he could barely keep from touching her. Did she know the restraint he was showing? Had she the smallest notion how much he had enjoyed holding her while she slept during part of the journey through the Saversnake Forest? Was she aware that, given the smallest opportunity, he would kiss her again?

And yet, what good could possibly come of such reckless conduct? No good whatsoever, particularly since at the very least he had the rather ticklish situation to overcome of finding a way to convince Anne that he should not marry Cassaundra Bradley.

He debated whether or not to discuss the matter with Anne, but in the end, as they entered the parlor and removed hat, bonnet and gloves, he decided it would be best to keep all their conversation on less intimate subjects. He was happy to see that Anne, herself, seemed rather strained in her composure and that when he asked her what she desired for nuncheon, she relaxed visibly.

The next few minutes were spent discussing their preferences for the meal—hardly an objectionable topic, surely!—and once more a sense of equanimity was restored between them.

During nuncheon, Anne found herself grateful that Staverton kept their discourse relegated to matters as far removed from the state of her heart as possible—the weather, the beauties of Marlborough generally, the quality of horses he had purchased for his stables in the past several years, the progress of the war on the Peninsula, the predictions by the government that Napoleon meant to invade Russia in the near future, the latest scientific papers of Humphry Davy, and the excellent claret the inn served with their Davenport chicken, roast lamb with spinach, baked fish, salad and mince pie.

With an entire afternoon and evening to dispose of, Anne suggested a game of backgammon and a variety of card games blended with walks through the ancient town when the weather permitted. Sudden brief showers seemed to be the order of the day.

For herself, Anne was exceedingly content. Staverton was an excellent opponent in the board and card games in which they engaged, and an agreeable companion as they explored the churches at the top and bottom of the High Street and the numerous shops between. He bought her several yards of an exquisite Brussels lace, three candles infused with rose oil, and burgundy sealing wax since her supply at home was nearly gone. For himself, he found a small, exquisite knife with a carved ivory handle, which Anne insisted on paying for.

"To return the compliment," she responded. "And because you have been a good sport throughout the kidnapping."

He could only laugh. "I would suspect that in all of history this has been the most unusually pleasant kidnapping anyone has ever been forced to endure."

"I take that as a compliment," she said playfully.

Later, as she prepared to dress for dinner, with the assistance of a serving maid from the inn's staff, she had some difficulty choosing precisely which of her several gowns to wear. Having believed initially that she would be headed to Gretna Green in Scotland, she had packed extensively for the trip so that she had a number of choices before her. The maid had laid out three of her gowns, exclaiming over each one—which indeed she had every right to do, since the fabrics were of the finest silks and each made up by the hand of expert seamstresses in Sulhurst.

She paced her bedchamber, unable to decide. Her quandary was simple—she found herself leaning toward wearing the prettiest of the gowns, but to what purpose? Why should she don her best dress? Was she hoping to entice Staverton into kissing her again? Goodness, what foolishness was this?

She turned away from the bed, an unexpected lowness depressing her spirits. Prudence's admission of wrongdoing had caused Anne to reevaluate, yet again, her opinion of Staverton. However, though he had redeemed himself a little, in both his polite attentions to her as well as in his recounting of his history with Prudence, still she could never permit him to be of any real interest to her, even if much of her former hostility toward him had diminished. He was still the man she had kidnapped on behalf of her cousin, and whatever blossoming of interest or affection that seemed to be occurring between them ought to be nipped in the bud right now.

For that reason, she turned back to the bed and announced

that she would wear the rather dullish peach silk, a decision which caused the maid's expression to fall. "But, miss, the lavender would set your beautiful complexion to such advantage as well as the green of your eyes. And with so much lace—!"

Anne withheld a very deep sigh, for she was in complete agreement on that score. "The peach, if you please." It would only be proper.

"If that is what ye wish, miss."

She could hardly explain to a complete stranger that what she wished of the moment had nothing to do with her final selection, and that she wished more than anything Staverton might see her gowned splendidly in a creation that only two months past had appeared in Ackermann's Repository. Sighing deeply, she braced herself to the more honorable path. She must think of Cassie and only of Cassie.

A half hour later, when she was summoned by another servant to dinner, she descended the stairs satisfied that she had done what was right and good.

Staverton happened to be looking in the direction of the doorway of the parlor and so it was he saw Anne the moment she arrived. Faith, but she was so very pretty and carried herself with a lively dignity he found infectious to his general mood. He always seemed to become oddly lighthearted when she but entered a room. Her hair had been combed and dressed in elegant curls atop her head, and she was wearing a lovely gown of peach silk that seemed to accentuate her beauty, the emerald color of her eyes, the honeyed hues of her hair, and the milky quality of her fine complexion. He wished she had not worn something quite so appealing, for he found his thoughts drifting in places they ought not.

He felt the struggle deeply within himself to keep from tumbling in love with her. This, he had never expected within the strange alliance he had formed with Anne Delamere, that his heart might be in some jeopardy. Yet, he could acknowledge this much, that he felt a tug of attraction toward her and that no matter how many times he had lectured himself on remaining aloof, he always found himself drawn into the delight of her conversation.

She entered the parlor on a cheerful note. "Good evening, my lord," she called out.

Anne was unable to read the expression on his face. He seemed distressed in some manner that she could not fathom. At the same time, her good intentions to keep her heart in check faltered as she took in his strong figure and fine looks. He was wearing black pantaloons and a black coat, much in Brummell's elegant yet simple style. His white neckcloth was tied to perfection and his shirt points rose at just the right height up his cheek. He appeared in this moment so the model of masculine excellence that she actually drew in a sharp breath. "You ought not to be so handsome you know," she stated lightly, crossing the room to him. "It is no wonder you have scarcely known how to conduct yourself in society. Cassie told me she had but conversed with you for a minute when she found herself tumbling in love with you. In this moment I can understand why."

He smiled, if ruefully. "I do not know whether to be offended or flattered. Is there any chance you might have tumbled as well?"

Anne felt a blush rise on her cheeks but she quickly composed herself. "Of course not. You are, in effect, betrothed to my cousin. I hope I am not so foolish as to fall in love with a man who is presently betrothed."

He chuckled and moved away from the fireplace. "Then I will only say that you are quite one of the most beautiful ladies I have ever known. You have an unerring eye for style, and with such a sweetness of temperament, I would find myself at certain risk of tumbling in love myself had I not, of course, already been engaged."

She met his gaze and saw the teasing light in his eye. "You are flirting with me!" she cried. "I take it most unkindly in you. I was at least speaking the truth from my heart."

"Are you saying I am not?" he asked in just such a way as made Anne pause.

"Are you then?" she asked in her straightforward manner.

"Yes, as it happens, I am. I like your plain manner of speaking, Miss Delamere, and was returning the compliment. Your gown is exquisite, by the way. I believe this particular light shade of orange is perfectly suited to your golden hair and lovely green eyes. Do you care for a little sherry?"

"Yes, thank you," she murmured, feeling a trifle stunned by so much sincere admiration.

As he moved to the table near the window, on which sat a decanter and two small glasses, she realized that he was not only being perfectly serious in his compliments but equally as forthcoming as well. She thought it quite ironic that he should like her gown when she had worn it because it was, in her opinion, the least pretty of her entire wardrobe.

Oh, dear.

He returned to her and with a soft smile offered the glass to her. She took it, smiling in return. She gazed into his extraordinary gray eyes and began feeling lost all over again, just as she had when he had first held her in his arms in the lane beyond Sulhurst. What was this hold he had on her?

A scratching on the door diverted Anne's attention from the earl, for which she was grateful since she was beginning to feel all of her vulnerability return to her.

"Come," Staverton called.

A young serving girl entered the chamber with a curtsy. "A letter is arrived for ye, m'lord." She smiled and curtsied again.

"Bring it here, child," he said.

The girl moved forward on a quick step, obviously nervous. She blushed deeply as she handed the missive to Staverton. He rewarded her handsomely, which caused her to gasp slightly. "Thank ye, m'lord." She then curtsied what seemed like a half dozen times more before quitting the parlor.

Anne chuckled and sipped her sherry.

He met her gaze. "This happens all the time. It is my rank."

She laughed outright. "You cannot be serious."

"I am," he stated, scowling.

"Then you have little comprehension of the fairer sex."

"And you are being ridiculous."

"Am I? What I believe is that you haven't the smallest notion how your physical presence affects even a mere, and quite young, serving girl."

Staverton searched her eyes for a long moment. "You are serious," he stated, as though rather astonished.

"Very much so," she responded. "I begin to understand your difficulty."

"*My* difficulty?" he queried.

"Yes," she responded.

"And what would that be?" he asked lightly.

"I am come to believe that most of the ladies who have ever felt a *tendre* for you have done so merely because of your quite astonishing appearance. In contrast, you have assumed such interest has been mercenary, that it is your rank and your wealth which have been the focus of pursuit. Men are not the only ones to be led astray by a pretty face. Women are equally as susceptible, particularly if the man appears to have been sculpted by Michelangelo from head to toe!"

He barked his laughter. "Now you are taunting me," he cried.

"On the contrary," she said evenly. "I was never more serious, Staverton, than in this moment."

He searched her eyes. "Good God, is that how you see me?"

She nodded. "If you could only hear how the ladies I know describe you, I vow you would be even more horrified than you are at present. Do you never look in the mirror?"

"When I chance to make use of my looking glass it is to determine if my neckcloth has been tied properly and whether I am still bleeding from having been shaved."

Anne laughed. "No one, then, could ever accuse you of vanity."

"I should hope not."

"Then from whence does your arrogance stem?"

"What?"

"Your arrogance. If you are not conceited by reason of your appearance, then by what?"

"I am not arrogant."

Anne clucked her tongue. "I shall remind you, then, of what you said to me in the lane but two days past: 'You may tell your friends you have been kissed by none other than Staverton.' "

"Oh, that," he murmured, a frown splitting his brow. He sighed deeply. "I spoke out of disrespect for your sex in general and because most women are impressed when a man has a handle to his name, with a fair amount of wealth attached to it."

"I see. Then you are just cynical."

He sighed once more. "I suppose you are right. However, you have given me something to ponder."

"Good. Now tell me what is in this missive, for I am become greatly curious."

He settled his glass of sherry on the dining table, broke the seal and read the contents silently. "Good God, it is from Bertaud!"

"Indeed? What does it say?" She felt a prickling of fear work its way over her neck and shoulders.

"Only that he has a matter of some import to discuss with me and that he desires to meet me at the churchyard in Mildenhall."

"May I see it?" When Staverton extended the note to her, she read it with a quick sweep of her eyes. "At midnight!" she cried. "The man must take you for a fool!"

She handed the letter back to him and saw that his expression had grown contemplative. "Staverton," she said. "Surely, you do not mean to go?"

"I have no choice," he responded quietly. "Bertaud must

have a reason, and an important one at that, for risking such a meeting as this."

"It is a trick, only," she responded earnestly. "And how, precisely, did he know you were here?"

At that moment, a servant entered the parlor, bearing a lit branch of candles which he placed on the table already laid with covers for two. He bowed politely and announced that dinner would be served directly if they should care to seat themselves at the table.

"I do not think you should go," she said, lowering her voice even though the servant had already quit the chamber.

He took up her arm and began guiding her to the table. "For the present, I suggest we simply enjoy our meal. Perhaps the evening will give counsel before the midnight hour arrives."

Anne was not in the least content with such a polite answer. She had not been in his company for two days without learning something of the workings of his mind. She could easily see by the stubborn set of his jaw that he had no such belief and that come midnight, he would be on his way to Mildenhall.

NINE

When the clock on the mantel struck eleven, Anne watched Staverton throw his caped greatcoat over his shoulders. She had waited with him for some time now, in his bedchamber, for the proper time to leave on his mission. He was armed with one pistol, loaded and primed.

"At least take a horse," she pleaded. She had been attempting to dissuade him from going on what she believed was a fool's errand. The lateness of the hour alone indicated foul play.

"No, I mean to walk. A horse, at such a quiet hour, might be heard for miles, and I hope to catch Bertaud unawares."

Anne could see the sense in this, but felt he could hardly escape quickly on foot if the meeting proved to be a trap.

She was about to try one last time to argue with him, but he took her chin in hand and shook his head teasingly at her. "Enough, Anne! I am going."

"Oh, very well," she muttered.

When the door closed behind him, she sat down on the edge of his bed and pouted for the longest time. After a quarter of an hour, she finally grew weary of brooding over his safety, and took up a vigil by the window.

The chamber was small and clean but must have seemed rather plain to Staverton in contrast to the rooms in any of his several homes. A scarlet velvet bedcover drew the eye away from four stark-white walls. The curtains were of a fine grade of muslin which she gently pushed back in order to observe the street below.

At so late an hour, there was scarcely any traffic. However, at twenty minutes before midnight, she noted a cart, drawn by a single swaybacked horse, progressing rapidly down the street. A large man, vaguely familiar in bulk, was driving, while two smaller men were hunched in the cart bed behind him. A moment later, and the creaking vehicle disappeared altogether, heading east toward Mildenhall.

She continued by the window for some time, the ticking of the clock on the mantel sounding loud in the silent room. Her mind drifted back to their arrival in Marlborough, how a sudden shower had drenched the countryside so thoroughly that when their coach had drawn into the inn yard, she had opened the door to a deep puddle.

She sighed, thinking how readily Staverton had simply carried her to the door. For a long moment, she was caught up in the memory, how easily he had lifted her as though she had been but a feather, and how powerful his arms had felt, surrounding her as they were.

After a time, she ordered her thoughts, for she was feeling uncommonly languid and knew she had become inattentive to the street below. To no avail, however. She was once more in his arms, he was transporting her to the door, her arm was about his neck.

In her mind, the images sharpened tightly as the door to the inn opened. She realized why her thoughts had taken her back to this precise moment, for she suddenly recognized the man who had just departed the inn.

The bulky figure in the cart!

She stood up, her heart suddenly in her throat, her mouth dry. She felt it too strong a coincidence that the same man she had witnessed earlier that day would be in a cart, *heading east,* with two other men, at the same hour Staverton was making his way to an arranged meeting with Bertaud. What was it Staverton had told her, that coincidences were always suspect. Where would these men be going, in the middle of the night, in a vehicle hardly designed for traveling long distances, though of sufficient size to make the trip to a church in Mildenhall with ease?

A sense of panic coursed through her. She left Staverton's chamber and returned to her room. She quickly changed her silk gown for her black velvet riding habit, donned a hooded cloak and, retrieving the case containing her pistols, decided it would best be carried in a cloak bag slung over the pommel of the saddle.

She hurried to the stables where a sleepy-eyed stable boy saddled a horse for her. Within a scant few minutes, she was urging her horse quickly along the moonlit lane toward the old Norman church at Mildenhall. She felt ill, so certain was she that Staverton, even now, was confronting not one, but four men, Bertaud along with his hirelings.

When she arrived at the outskirts of the church property, she dismounted, tied her horse to a nearby yew shrub and began the process of loading and priming her pistols. From some thirty feet away a pistol shot rent the air, after which Anne heard loud murmurings and a scuffling sound, all of which alarmed her.

What if Staverton had been shot? When her hands began to shake, she set the pistols on the ground and strove to calm herself. She could be of no service to the earl were her hands trembling like leaves in a breeze.

Ordering her sensibilities to a deadly calm, she completed the priming of the pistols and gathered them up, one in each now steady hand. She made her way stealthily around the side of the churchyard, inching her way toward what now sounded like a brawl.

Through a narrow space in the hedge, her worst fears were realized—Staverton had been overpowered by three rough-looking men. Bertaud, however, was nowhere to be seen. There was sufficient moonlight to reveal that at least one of the men was, as she had suspected, the large man she had seen leaving the Castle Inn earlier that afternoon when

Staverton had carried her in his arms. It appeared to her that Bertaud had, indeed, hired the three men to do his work. What an odious man!

By the bloodied faces of the men, it was clear to her that Staverton had not succumbed without inflicting a great deal of punishment of his own. However, the men were enraged and were even now raining flush hits on the earl's body, locked as he was in a strong hold by the burly man.

Anne did not allow herself to be overwhelmed by the situation before her. She moved swiftly toward the break in the hedge and stepped abruptly into their presence, aiming both pistols at the brutes. They paused, almost as one, expressions first of surprise, then amusement, passing from one face to the other.

"No, Anne," Staverton gasped, obviously struggling to breathe.

Anne ignored his strangled plea. She understood precisely in this moment of what she was capable, and that knowledge flooded her with a sensation of power.

"Don't move," she commanded, "if you value your lives!"

"Lookee 'ere!" the smallest of the men cried. "A lady wat thinks she can take three grown men."

"I can shoot the eye out of a sparrow at thirty yards," she said quietly. "However, if you do not believe me, I beg you will try my mettle for I am more than willing to prove myself to any one of you. Although I should perhaps inform you that my father presently holds the record at Manton's in London and he has had the complete training of his daughter. I know how to aim for the heart. Perhaps one of you could overpower me, but two of you would be dead before the deed was done!"

The men stared at her uncertainly, taking turns gazing at her pistols, then at each other.

She felt the indecision among them and took a bold step forward. "Release the earl of Staverton at once!" she cried.

"Staverton?" the thin man spoke up. "Eh? What's this? Ye said naught about him bein' an earl!"

The large man's arms grew slack and Staverton fell to the ground.

Anne gestured to the man. "Take your lackeys and leave on the instant. If I see any of you again, at Marlborough or Chiltenham, Bath or Bristol, I shall summon the constabulary and see that you are brought up on charges of treason, or did you not know that your employer is a Frenchman?"

These last words startled the hirelings. "A Frenchman? The guv wat we met at Thatcham is a Frenchy?"

The large man said nothing but took off at a run down the gravel path leading through the graveyard. The two smaller men followed quickly in his wake. Anne did not go to Staverton at once but followed the men at a careful distance to see what their intentions were. She had no confidence whatsoever that their purpose was to leave as she had bid them. She held to the shadows and moved silently.

Beyond the graveyard, Anne watched them board the cart she had witnessed from the window of Staverton's bedchamber. Once the vehicle was in motion, she finally breathed a sigh of relief. The creak and groan of the cart against the stillness of the countryside would permit her to know their whereabouts for some time. Even so, her cautious nature would not allow her to return to the earl until she had watched the cart become smaller and smaller on the ancient track as it headed farther east in the direction of Ramsbury.

Only then did she return to Staverton, whom she found sitting up and pressing his kerchief against his cheekbone. She stood over him, her pistols still armed and pointed toward the ground. "Can you walk?" she asked quietly. He nodded, struggling to his feet.

"Where is your pistol? Were you unable to make use of it?"

"Not in the manner I had hoped," he said. He turned around, and from the base of the hedge retrieved his weapon. "I had confronted two of the men with my pistol in hand, but a third, concealed in the shrubbery, attacked me from behind, knocking the pistol from my hand. It discharged by itself, firing without effect into the gravel."

She turned away from him and examined the shadows carefully. "Was Bertaud ever here?" she asked.

"No," he responded hoarsely. "Only those three ruffians. Bertaud must have paid them for their services."

She had no confidence in their present vulnerable position. "We must leave, immediately," she whispered. "I cannot feel we are at all safe. Any one of these rascals might return to try to do us harm." She held her pistols steadily, keeping them aimed at the depths of the shadows about her.

"You are right," he murmured. He moved slowly in her direction, holding his left side and wincing, stopping only once to stoop over and pick up his greatcoat. "I will need to be leeched once we return to the inn or these bruises will keep me in bed for a sennight."

"I shall send for the surgeon as soon as I see you to your room."

Anne led the way to her horse, listening carefully to the sounds of the night. Staverton stayed close beside her.

Reaching the horse, she turned to him. "Do you think we are safe? I do not know if I should disarm my pistols." Though her weapons enjoyed the finest craftsmanship, the process of loading and priming a pistol was never instantaneous.

Staverton, however, did not answer her. Instead, he leaned his head against the horse's side, which caused the buckskin to shift a curious head back to look at him. "I am so dizzy," he murmured.

Anne realized the decision was hers alone to make. She had watched the ruffians head away from the churchyard, the night had remained peaceful and her hope must be that the men would leave them in peace. Her foremost concern of the present had to be getting Staverton back to the Castle Inn.

She made her decision therefore, and disarmed one of the

pistols, returning it to the case inside the cloak bag that was still hooked to the pommel of the saddle. The other pistol she would carry until the safety of Marlborough had been reached. Staverton's pistol she also slid inside the cloak bag.

For the present, she set the primed pistol on the ground. She withdrew the earl's greatcoat from over his arm and slung it snugly over his back and shoulders, buttoning the top button.

"Come," she said, placing one hand on his back, the other tugging gently on his arm. "Mount the horse. I intend to lead you back to the inn."

"I could not possibly allow you to walk," he whispered, grimacing. "That would be unthinkable."

"Good God, Staverton!" she cried. "We are speaking of one mile, not forty. Now, pray, do as you are bid! This is no time for chivalry." She had spoken more sharply than perhaps she ought have, but the effect was a happy one since the earl made no further protests and moved immediately, if slowly, toward the proper side of the horse. After three failed attempts, he finally achieved the saddle.

Retrieving her loaded pistol, she guided the horse back in the direction of the town. She kept an alert watch the entire time, stopping only to shift reins and pistol from one hand to the other for comfort.

A half hour later, she entered the inn yard and found the stable boy awaiting her. He took one look at her bruised companion and whispered, "I'll fetch the surgeon."

"First, help his lordship down. Yes, that's it. Careful." Before he left, she gave him strict instructions. "You are to speak of this to no one," she whispered. "Do you understand?"

He nodded, his eyes wide.

"There will be a sovereign for you when you return," she said, disarming her pistol. "Now, do be quick about it! Oh, and tell the doctor to be sure and bring his jar of leeches."

"Aye, miss!"

Anne took the cloak bag from off the pommel, slid her

pistol within and then slipped her arm about Staverton's waist, bidding him to hold onto her. When she entered the inn, a concerned landlord emerged sleepily from his rooms, his expression growing quite shocked as he stared at the earl. She smiled at him and rolled her eyes. "A drunken tavern brawl," she explained. "My cousin is quite hopeless."

She thought she had managed the business handily when Staverton, upon climbing the stairs, chuckled.

"Why are you laughing?" she asked, keeping her voice to a whisper.

"I saw his face, poor fellow," Staverton said, his voice also quite low.

"You do not think he believed me?"

"I think he only wondered what you were doing at the tavern."

"Oh, dear," Anne murmured. "I had not thought of that and he is already suspicious of us, for I daresay no one believes we are cousins."

"No, they do not." He laughed again and then groaned. "I pray to God I have not broken a rib."

"Do you mean to begin complaining now?" she asked provokingly.

"Of course. If I do not exaggerate my injuries I shall never be able to explain how it came about I had to be rescued by the merest chit of a girl."

"Not the merest chit," she returned. "I am tall for a female and fully three and twenty."

"Ah," he murmured appreciatively. "But I think this is worse. Now I shall have to explain how it was I had to be rescued by a confirmed ape-leader."

"Oh, do hush. You will awaken the other guests and set everyone to gabblemongering about your terrible appearance."

Once the stairs had been mounted, she saw that he was moving with a much greater ease. She was about to release him, when he said, "I beg you will help me at least to my door. I am still frightfully dizzy."

She glanced up at him and knew at once he was attempting to bamboozle her. "You seem a great deal stronger to me. I doubt you are in the least dizzy."

"You are mistaken."

"Your color is much better."

"It is the bruising, I am sure. My head feels as if it is full of nothing but air."

Anne could only smile. Whether he was humbugging her or speaking the truth, she did not care. She could just as easily hold him about the waist as not. He felt solid and warm to the touch, and the truth was, it was rather pleasant to be hugging him in such a fashion.

He began to slow. "I am feeling faint," he explained in perfectly lucid accents.

"I can see that you are," she responded facetiously.

He chuckled. "All right, so I have achieved an excuse for getting you to embrace me, but I have excellent cause, do you not agree?"

"You are incorrigible," she stated. "However, I am relieved to see that you are feeling better. You have no notion." Her thoughts reverted suddenly to the moment she had confronted the earl's assailants. "Your attackers, one and all, will be very unhappy come morning, I am sure of it. The small man's face was nearly swollen from forehead to chin, and did you see the tall one? His lip was split badly."

By now, they were standing in front of the earl's door. He pushed it open with a shove and a rush of cool air flowed over them.

Once inside the darkened room, Anne released him, settling her cloak bag against the wall. She closed the door, and with the use of the tinderbox, lit a candle on his bedside table.

When she turned back to him, she saw that he had shrugged off his greatcoat but remained standing by the foot of the four-poster bed. A half-smile was on his lips and there was an odd look in his eye.

"I suppose I must bid you good night," she said, strangely

unwilling to leave him just yet. "The surgeon will be here soon."

Staverton looked down at the golden-haired beauty who had stumbled so swiftly into his life. Was it truly only two days ago that he had found her covered in raspberries and, believing her injured by Bertaud, attempted to thrust her against her will into his curricle? He felt as though he had lived an entire lifetime with her since then.

"Anne," he began quietly. "There is something I feel I must say to you."

"Yes?" she inquired softly.

He moved toward her and took her hands in his. How small they were, delicate lady's hands, which had so recently held a pair of heavy pistols. "You just might have saved my life tonight, you know that, do you not?"

He watched her glance down at their joined hands and wondered what she might be thinking. Her complexion had grown pale. "Surely you are mistaken, Staverton," she said. "I prevented further injury, but you do not truly believe they would have killed you?"

"I thank God that we will never know," he responded. "As for you, my dear Lady Valiant, I thank you a hundred-fold for coming to my aid as you did. You were . . . you were magnificent."

She lifted her gaze at that and caught her breath. "So were you," she replied.

"Whatever do you mean? You found me completely undone by three madmen."

She was all earnestness in the sparkle of her eyes and the urgency of her manner as she squeezed his fingers. "I saw the appearance of each of them. You obviously gave them a ferocious battle before finding yourself pinned by that horrible man. I only wish I could have seen you landing a flush hit or two."

He could not help but smile, though, at the same time his chest felt powerfully tight with all manner of sentiment. "I cannot answer for what actually happened since I recall little of it except that I became enraged and exchanged blow for blow at a rather fevered pitch."

"And so you must have!" she cried emphatically.

"I have never known a lady like yourself," he said truthfully. "I only wish I had met you sooner."

Her expression grew thoughtful. "And I, too, Staverton, for I should have liked nothing better than to have had a companion in adventure. I daresay you would have entered into all my schemes had we met as children."

When had he released her hands and taken her shoulders in a gentle clasp? "Anne," he murmured, "I was not at all referring to either my childhood or yours." He leaned forward, and without really thinking about what he was doing, settled a gentle kiss on her lips.

"Oh," she breathed against his mouth. "You must not."

"But I must," he responded, and with much delight kissed her again.

After a moment, she drew back. "You are to wed my cousin."

"All that must remain in the future, Anne," he murmured against her cheek. "The present belongs to us."

When he settled his lips on hers again, she whimpered slightly as though wrestling with her conscience. However, she did not pull away from him again, but rather slid her arms about his waist.

He embraced her fully, deepening the kiss, which seemed a most natural conclusion to such an evening as they had just shared. He wondered languidly whether it was possible he was actually falling in love with Anne Delamere.

Anne could not believe anything could be so pleasurable as feeling the softness of Staverton's lips on hers or the sensual delight of his tongue exploring her mouth. She felt utterly captivated by the sensations that held her good intentions entirely in check. She had never meant to permit him to kiss her. Indeed, she had promised herself she would never allow such an intimacy between them again.

However, when he had spoken of her as his dear Lady

Valiant and referred to her conduct earlier at the churchyard as *magnificent*, she had from that moment become enrapt by his compliments. In addition, there was just such a look in his eye which spoke to her heart as clearly as his words had spoken to her head. Even though she tried to stay the passion growing between them by referring to his forthcoming marriage to Cassie, she could no more have refused his kisses than she would have turned away a cloak on a cold windy day.

So it was that she held him closely and had all the pleasure of feeling his embrace tighten and his lips move over hers in waves of tender assault. Her mind filled with images of a flower-strewn wedding bed and Staverton covering her. She felt a weakening of her knees at such thoughts, as though she might faint. Was that peculiar warbling sound she heard coming from her throat?

"Anne, Anne," he murmured against her cheek.

She kissed him quickly in response. His lips parted and she drifted hers over them so that they were barely touching. A resonant groan issued from his throat.

"My darling Anne." Once more he assaulted her, holding her fast and kissing her wildly.

She became lost in the wicked sensations that took hold of her. She felt the strangest impulse to beg him to make this bed their wedding bed, so impassioned was the moment. At the same time, however, a sudden fear rose up in her breast. Staverton could have died tonight. Even he had admitted as much. The thought of a world without this man who had wrapped her in his arms seemed wholly unacceptable to her. How dull such a world would be. Who would the current ministry find to chase after French spies were Staverton to disappear from the earth?

She shivered slightly, drawing back from him, lowering her gaze to the floor.

"What is the matter? Have I hurt you? Are you cold?"

She shook her head. "Just frightened."

"You?" he asked in disbelief. He laughed and took her

chin in hand in order to raise her face to his. "I vow you are frightened of nothing."

"What if you had perished?" she asked, gently touching his bruised cheek.

"But I did not. Nor did you, thank God. We are both safe."

"Yes, we are," she agreed.

He kissed her again, once more embracing her fully. This time, Anne did not permit her fears to intrude, but gave herself completely to the sensation of being lost in Staverton's arms. He settled a string of gentle kisses over her forehead and eyelids, her cheeks and nose. *We are both safe,* she thought.

When he stumbled slightly, she drew back again. "Are you all right?" she asked.

He sat down on the bed. "Dizzy," he murmured.

She chuckled. "I believe you this time," she said. "Ah. I hear footsteps in the hall. The surgeon perhaps."

Anne opened the door and saw that a gentleman quite unfamiliar to her but wearing a powdered wig was just arriving.

"I am Dr. Barnes," he stated. "You were in need of a physician?"

"Your patient is within," she said quietly.

The surgeon nodded, his case in hand, and entered the dimly lit chamber. He settled his direct, searching gaze upon the earl, taking in the swelling bruise on his cheekbone, the scrape at his temple and the blood splattered over his neckcloth. "Anything else I should know?" he asked. "Were pistols involved?"

"No," Staverton murmured. "There were three of them. The bruises on my ribs are my greatest concern. You do have the leeches?"

From his bag he withdrew a glass jar. Anne felt it proper to retire, but before leaving begged the surgeon to speak with her when he had finished with Staverton.

Anne picked up her cloak bag and returned to her bedchamber, changing her riding habit for a simple muslin gown, over which she draped a paisley shawl. She brushed out her hair, but had no intention of seeking her bed until after she had spoken with the doctor. She was utterly fatigued, yet at the same time her mind refused to rest. Her thoughts were a mixture of worries and guilt. She kept reviewing the attack at the church in Mildenhall. The future might have been so very different had she arrived even fifteen minutes later. Staverton would have been even more badly injured. Had she arrived an hour later, or two, or perhaps not until the next day, she strongly suspected he would not have survived the extended beating or a night of exposure.

She shuddered, taking all three pistols from the cloak bag, after which she set about cleaning them.

She pressed her fist against her forehead, trying to think as clearly as possible. If Staverton remained in bed well into the morning, perhaps through the afternoon, Bertaud could easily make his escape on his ship at Bristol, if that was his plan. Indeed, the more she thought about Bertaud having hired such a trio of devilish men to do injury to the earl, the more she came to believe he fully intended to make a quick escape from England, perhaps even tonight!

She had just completed polishing the weapons, when a scratching sounded on the door. Pulling her shawl about her shoulders, she admitted the surgeon into her chamber.

"How is he?" she asked urgently. "Will he be all right?"

"Yes, yes. No serious injuries. He feared one of his ribs might have been broken, but he is a powerful man and he suffers only from a severe bruising. The leeches will keep the swelling down on both his abdomen and on his cheek, just as he had hoped.

"However, the injury to his temple concerns me. I would suggest you or a servant remain with him through the night to keep an eye on his progress. Should his sleep become fretful and his ramblings delirious, I would advise a dose of laudanum, which I have laid out on the table at his bedside.

Send for me on the morrow if you desire another consultation. And now, I shall bid you good night."

Anne would not let him leave, however, without full payment for his services. Once he was gone, she realized she had but one recourse, to spend the remainder of the night with Staverton. Entering his bedchamber, she found he had already fallen into his slumber.

Settling his pistol into the case she discovered in one of his portmanteaus, Anne took up her vigil in a hard chair at the earl's bedside. She awoke sometime later only to find herself slumped over on the bed, her arms folded beneath her head. She was a little surprised that she had fallen asleep so easily, but soon became aware of what had awakened her. Staverton was tossing fitfully in his sleep and murmuring incomprehensible things. She sat back in her chair and watched him for a time, intending to avoid dosing him with even a small portion of the powerful drug unless it was absolutely necessary.

Fifteen minutes passed and it was obvious that his restlessness had increased instead of diminishing. She prepared the powder, stirring it into the glass of water. She gently began rubbing Staverton's hand and arm and speaking to him in a soothing yet firm voice until he awakened. He immediately complained of his head aching.

"The doctor left you something. You must drink now."

"Laudanum?" he murmured. "No, I should not. I must find Bertaud on the morrow."

"The doctor insisted. I did wait a quarter of an hour to see if the symptoms would abate, but indeed they have worsened. Staverton, your sleep has been very troubled and you will be of little use to anyone tomorrow if you do not find some rest."

He agreed reluctantly, but would take only half the dose.

"Very well," she murmured.

Staverton had been dreaming about being at a ball and having a dozen ladies pecking at him like hens after grain. One of the hens had been Cassaundra Bradley. Something sour had risen within him as he tried to leave the ballroom, a bitter resentment of his experiences in society. Then Anne had awakened him, but the desperate feeling of the dream remained, that though he had been searching for a truly honorable and selfless woman all these years, such a creature did not seem to exist in the realm of womanhood. Even Anne, whom he was coming to admire very much, had dubbed him the Infidel, besides having kidnapped him.

As the drug began weaving its way through his veins, he recalled how tender the kiss was he had shared with her but an hour or so ago. How unfortunate he had not met her before the kidnapping. Perhaps then he might even have come to love her. When these thoughts became entwined with images of sailing ships on a smooth ocean, of gulls wheeling over a blue-gray surf, of waves breaking against the shore, he let the laudanum simply carry him out to sea. If Anne went with him in his drugged state, holding his hand and smiling mischievously into his face, well, it was his dream, after all.

Anne wondered what the smile on his lips had meant, particularly since just a moment earlier he had been scowling. In her concern, she had taken his hand and stroked it very gently, after which he had begun to smile. His breathing quickly eased into a slow and steady rhythm. The laudanum had done its work.

She glanced down at his hand and felt odd tears burn her eyes, though why she was suddenly distressed she could not say.

The night had been difficult to say the least, but the attack at Mildenhall was not what was disturbing her. It was the earl's hand and the way she felt with her fingers overlaying his lightly that seemed to be working strongly on her heart, as though somehow he belonged to her and she to him.

She smiled and shook her head. She was being ridiculous and well she knew it. She drew her hand back from his and rose to her feet, afterward stretching her back. Crossing to the windows, she peered out over the silent street. The August moon, dipping toward the west, still cast a glow on the numerous red roofs of the ancient town.

When a faint moan sounded from the direction of the bed, Anne whirled about and retraced her steps swiftly. She lifted the candle on Staverton's bedside table and moved it closer to him in order that she might better see his face. His complexion was pale but not overly much, the bruising on his cheek had diminished considerably, and he seemed quite peaceful. A small piece of sticking-plaster had been placed over the cut at his temple.

"Why must you be so very handsome?" she whispered. He did not stir.

She settled the candle back on the table and returned to the windows once more. A faint gray tinge was now touching the horizon to the east. In August, dawn came early.

Her thoughts turned abruptly to Bertaud and his journey to Bristol. She was still afflicted with the fear that the spy meant to make a dash for the westerly seaport and escape England with the damaging papers in his possession.

The prior arrangement she had with her servants was to meet with Shaw at Beckhampton. Staverton unfortunately would sleep for hours, possibly all day, so it was up to her to do what needed to be done. At the very least, she must be at Beckhampton by nine.

She shivered slightly, drawing her shawl more closely about her shoulders. She contemplated the situation and after several minutes of deliberation, she quit Staverton's bedchamber and once more awoke the landlord from his slumber. That good man, sleepy-eyed, was happy to be of assistance to her, particularly when she produced two sovereigns for his trouble over the matter.

After fifteen minutes, she had arranged the situation to her satisfaction. A serving maid was to sit the remainder of the night—or morning, as it happened—with Staverton, while she slept for a few hours. Her intention was simple— at eight o'clock she would depart alone for Beckhampton unless the earl awakened, in good health, beforetimes.

TEN

Staverton awoke and squinted at the sheer muslin draperies covering the windows of his bedchamber. The morning light at half past eight o'clock was as bright as direct sunlight to his tired eyes. He rolled on his side and discovered that a serving maid, quite young, was sitting slumped in a chair, fast asleep, not far from his bedside.

"Good morning," he called to her, surprised to see a stranger in his room.

The young woman's eyes opened and she immediately straightened in her seat. "Yes, m'lord?" she queried, in a voice that sounded as though it belonged more to a child than to a young lady.

"Have you been there all night?" he inquired.

"Only a few hours."

Staverton frowned. "Is Miss Delamere still abed?"

"Nay. She has been gone this half hour and more."

"Gone?" he asked, a trifle bemused. "Where on earth did she go?"

"Beckhampton," she replied. "She said I were to tell you, m'lord, but not to worry."

At that, any sleep clinging to his mind darted away entirely, like startled trout in a shallow stream. "Oh, dear," he murmured.

"M'lord?"

"Nothing to signify," he said, gesturing dismissively.

He would have left his bed immediately, but he felt obliged, given his state of undress, to request that the serving maid leave his chamber. "Toast and coffee," he added as she entered the hall. "If you please."

"Yes, m'lord," she said, dipping a polite curtsy. "In a trice. Ye will not be needing the doctor then?"

"No," he responded. "Not in the least."

"Very good, m'lord. I will tell the landlord. He were anxious on yer behalf."

"Thank you."

The moment the latch clicked shut, he attempted to sit up but found the muscles of his abdomen were not so responsive as he had hoped. He groaned faintly, then hunched over sufficiently to come to a sitting position. He forced his legs over the side of the bed and let out a breath when his feet touched the floor. Regardless of the pain he was experiencing, he had but one concern, to join Anne as quickly as possible. Bertaud had already proved his intentions, and should Anne stumble upon him in Beckhampton by accident, Staverton had every certainty the spy would do her injury if he was at all able.

He stretched for a few minutes, encouraging his stiff muscles to begin responding, which they soon did. It was not long before he found he could move about with only a minimal amount of discomfort. He was soon dressed, at which time the maid arrived with his coffee and toast. When he began packing his belongings, he thought to check for the documents and found that they were gone.

"Oh, dear God, Anne," he murmured. "What are you about?" He came to a swift conclusion that she had believed him too ill to continue the mission and therefore meant to complete the exchange of documents herself.

He stuffed the remainder of his clothes into one of his portmanteaus. After gulping down his coffee and two bites of a slice of thick, fresh toast, he paid his shot and left the inn. He was not surprised to find that Anne had left Marlborough in the hired coach with her man driving. Speaking with the hostler, and offering a generous tip for his efforts in lending his assistance, Staverton was soon tooling swiftly west on the road to Bath in a curricle and four, his luggage strapped on behind.

The sun was warm on Anne's back as she peered around the corner of the inn. Bertaud was standing by his carriage, apparently perusing a map and discussing the route to Bath with the hostler. He was fortunately so intent on his business that he gave no indication of being aware of her presence. For herself, she was acutely cognizant of the fact that she was all that stood between the damaging documents in the spy's baggage and the safety of England's army in Spain.

She had arrived a half hour earlier and had discovered from Shaw—with Quince offering helpful additions to his recounting—that Bertaud, traveling under the inconspicuous name of John Smythe, was still abed, but had ordered his breakfast to be brought to his chamber at nine o'clock. They were expecting him to leave the inn at any moment, as was his habit once he had partaken of his first meal.

Conferring with her footmen, she had concluded that little could be done until Bertaud actually quit the inn. She therefore sent her servants ahead to the village of Cherhill to await the spy, where they were to continue following him discreetly. She then took up a vigilant watch for Bertaud's departure from the interior of her coach.

She had drawn the blinds and spent the next thirty minutes peeking through a small opening at the edge of the blind which, from her position, overlooked the entrance to the inn directly off the inn yard.

At first, she had meant to do nothing since Bertaud still gave no evidence of being in haste to reach Bristol. However, waiting inside her coach, she gradually realized that with a little push, she could make the exchange of documents herself, even this morning, with no one the wiser.

Her plan was simple. She meant to approach Bertaud in a hysterical manner, which she had begun practicing quietly while seated in the coach, for the purpose of accusing him of having tried to do her injury in Sulhurst. Her intention was to try to interest the local constable in detaining him until such time as she could search his baggage secretively and find and replace the documents. Once the switch had been effected, she would declare she might have been mistaken in Mr. Smythe, that he perhaps was not the man who had tried to harm her after all, and that she would feel terrible if she somehow sent an innocent man to prison. Bertaud would continue on his way, with the whole business settled tidily. Then she could return triumphantly to Marlborough and lay the documents on poor Staverton's bedcovers, the heroine yet again of her numerous adventures, only this time, a *real* one. He could be at ease and she would have concluded his mission in the most exciting and noble manner possible.

When five and forty minutes had passed within the confines of the coach, she knew the time was drawing near in which Bertaud would leave the inn. She had quit the safety of her coach and taken up her place at the side of the building. A moment more and he had emerged from the inn with a servant trailing behind him, carrying his baggage.

Presently, however, as she watched Bertaud fold up his map, her courage began to flag since she was painfully aware that he was the same man who had shot her two days past and who, only yesterday, had hired ruffians to beat Staverton senseless.

However, with so many lives at stake on the Iberian Peninsula, she drew in a deep breath and prepared herself to begin her theatrical attack on the spy.

As the hostler moved toward the stables, she watched Bertaud put his map away and reach for something within the same satchel. She readied herself to move. To her horror, however, she saw that the object emerging from the leather bag was a pistol. He began turning slowly in her direction. Had he known she was there all along?

Despite the firearm, she took a step in his direction, intent on executing her plan—surely he would not shoot at a lady in a public inn yard!—but just as she would have appeared in view, she found herself hooked at the elbow quite strongly from behind and drawn back to safety. At the very same moment, Bertaud fired his pistol and the accompanying pistol ball whirred past the corner of the building at the precise place she would have been standing had she been allowed to continue on her way.

Anne turned about in some shock, wondering who it was who had just saved her life and found herself staring into Staverton's eyes.

"Good God, how did you get here?" she cried. "Staverton, he . . . he shot at me . . . again! He would have killed me!"

"Come!" he whispered urgently. "He is not finished yet, if I know this man!"

She did not hesitate to be commanded by him. He gestured toward the highway and she ran beside him at breakneck speed, crossing the alley and rounding another corner where a low wall ranged alongside the road. Entirely without ceremony, he lifted her up and over the wall. Before she knew precisely what he was about, she found herself headlong in the dirt.

"Lie still!" he whispered.

A moment later, he was stretched out beside her, an arm slung protectively over her back. "Let us hope he has not seen where we went."

"I daresay he will leave Beckhampton with all good speed, firing his pistol as he did," she responded quietly. "He will not want to answer for having done so, particularly if anyone else saw that he had actually shot at me."

"You are right," he murmured. "Hush. I hear a carriage." Anne held her breath.

When a carriage could be heard leaving the inn yard rather slowly and a moment later passing beside the wall at the same frighteningly lethargic pace, Anne was in no doubt their quarry was hunting for her, a truth which caused her heart to beat erratically. As though sensing her distress, Staverton gently stroked her shoulder and squeezed her arm.

After what seemed an eternity, the coach wheels began gathering speed and finally could no longer be heard grinding against the crushed stones of the road.

"Thank God," she said, releasing her breath and sitting up, as did Staverton.

"Indeed, yes. For a moment, I thought we were done for."

"As did I." She glanced at him and shook her head. "I am grateful beyond words that you arrived as you did but, Staverton, whatever are you doing here?" Her gaze raked his face for signs of weariness, pain or further injury.

"The moment I learned you had gone, I made haste to follow after you. I have been in the worst agony. Anne, please do not ever do anything like this again, I beg of you. What if I had not come?"

"I believe I would be dead," she stated, her mind reeling at the thought.

"I believe it, too. But whatever possessed you to leave Marlborough?"

"You were very ill last night, and after I gave you the laudanum, I felt certain you would sleep most of the day. I feared that Bertaud would make a dash for Bristol. I couldn't let him leave, not with the fate of our army weighing in the balance."

He smiled at her and touched her cheek with the back of his hand. "Anne, dear, brave, foolish Anne. Whatever am I to do with you?"

His expression was warm and tender. She smiled in response. "You are to tell me that you would have done nothing less had you been in the same predicament."

"I cannot possibly say what I might have done," he responded. His hand found the back of her neck, a friendly gesture, a comforting touch. She stared into his gray eyes and felt all the compassion in his concern for her in this moment. His gaze drifted to her lips. He leaned toward her. She caught her breath. Did he mean to kiss her again?

She quickly placed a hand on his chest. "We should go," she said quietly.

His gaze flickered to her eyes. "I suppose you are right."

She gained her feet, as did he.

"Let me help you," he said, nodding in the direction of the stone wall.

Before she could tell him she was perfectly capable of scaling the stones herself, he had slid his hands about her waist and was lifting her easily to a sitting position atop the wall. "Thank you," she said. "But it wasn't necessary. Besides, I saw you wince."

"I did not," he countered.

"You did so, for I saw you, and pray do not pretend otherwise, for if you remember, I know how it was you received your bruises last night and you cannot possibly be completely healed of them after only a few hours of sleep."

She carefully shifted her legs to the opposite side of the wall and, tucking her skirts about her ankles, dropped to the grassy sward below. He followed after. "Well, as to that, I take it unkind in you that you must mention the matter at all. I was attempting to be gallant."

"You were not," she argued with an arch toss of her head. "You were trying to cuddle me again. You would have kissed me, too, if I had not stopped you."

"Must you be direct about everything?"

She turned toward him and smiled. "You know very well you cannot kiss me again," she responded, ignoring his query. "Even . . . even if I desire it, as well."

"I thought I did not mistake a flash of interest in your beautiful emerald eyes."

"Now you are flirting and I wish you will stop at once.

Tell me instead, truly, how you are feeling, that I might be at ease."

He gave her an honest report of the stiffness he had felt in arising that morning but that the leeches had indeed done their work. He was able to move about with an almost normal mobility.

"Then I was right," she stated, eying him wonderingly as she began walking back toward the inn.

"About what, precisely?" he asked.

"Only that I have come to believe you are a god. You must be. How else can you account for being able to walk about this morning, with scarcely a limp in your step after having been at the hard end of such a terrible beating last night."

He could only laugh. "I believe I shall let you continue in that deception, if for a time, since otherwise you tend to be quite rough with me."

Anne chuckled. "You are coming to understand me more and more," she said. "Oh, what a pretty arbor of red roses. Do but look. We must have passed by them while fleeing Bertaud."

Lord Staverton burst out laughing. "You have no great sensibility, do you?"

"Whatever do you mean? I have a great deal of aesthetic appreciation. Did I not just draw your eye to an exquisite waterfall of flowers?"

He slid his arm about hers in a sly movement that caught Anne quite off her guard.

"Yes," he agreed, "but at the very same moment you spoke of our recent encounter with Bertaud as though it had been no more significant than drinking a cup of tea."

She could only laugh. "I suppose you may be right." As they drew near the entrance to the inn, she queried, "Have you broken your fast yet?"

"Coffee and a bite or two of toast—hardly sufficient."

"I should say not. Shall we breakfast here, then? I have not had a single bite to eat since our dinner of last night."

"You will have to wipe the dust off your nose before we can sit down to dine."

"Your breeches are covered with dirt from top to bottom," she countered crisply.

"Your skirts are a disgrace and your bonnet is askew."

She laughed heartily as she removed her pretty white bonnet and began shaking the dust off it. She resettled it over her golden curls and had all the pleasure of having Staverton insist on tying the green ribbons into a jaunty bow beneath her left ear. Afterward, she began swiping the dirt off both the front and back of her walking dress. She had donned a playful summery gown of a white background printed overall with clusters of cherries. The light fabric, however, was tiresome, for the dirt from behind the stone wall tended to cling so that it was a full minute before she was in the least presentable.

As they turned to go into the inn, Staverton leaned close to her. "There is one thing I must know—where are the documents?"

"In my cloak bag, along with my pistols."

"When we have transferred my luggage to the coach, we can see the packet placed in my valise."

"Of course."

Before long, Anne was seated before a delightful meal of grilled kidneys, an omelet, wafer-thin slices of ham, poached eggs and fresh-baked bread. The effect of the sumptuous fare was a general mellowing that set Anne's thoughts in a more sober direction.

She found her mind caught up in many things, not least of which was the fact that Bertaud obviously had known she was watching him and had intended to fire his pistol at her probably the whole time he was reading his map. He was ruthless and cunning, and her fear of him was growing appreciably. She felt it necessary to fortify her opinions of him so that she might not underestimate his villainy in the future.

"You seem distressed," Staverton said, leaning back in his chair and holding his coffee cup with both hands.

"A little," she admitted. "I have been thinking of Bertaud."

Staverton took a sip and released a deep breath. "You must understand. He is as much a patriot as either you or myself, and I believe he is willing to die to achieve his ends. He cannot view his enemies as people with feelings or families or anything that would make them seem human and real, merely as obstacles that must be overcome, nothing more."

"Do you look at him in the same cold manner?"

"To a degree, I believe I must. I can appreciate his difficulties but I despise his loyalties. Bonaparte moved beyond the borders of France in order to achieve his thirst for what I understand he calls *glory*, and more than once he has threatened the shores of England. I have been given to understand that over the years he has formed a variety of plans by which he meant to invade our country."

"How could he possibly do so?" she inquired, almost laughing at the thought. "Nelson destroyed his fleet in 1805 at Trafalgar."

At that, Staverton smiled. "Would you believe an invasion of his army by the use of hot-air balloons?"

"What?" she cried, incredulous. "You cannot be serious."

"I am very serious," he replied. "Another notion was to dig a tunnel beneath the English Channel and march his armies straight through to our island."

Anne's mouth dropped agape. "How could any such thing ever be accomplished? It would be madness."

"Some believe Boney is mad."

"I begin to think so myself. A tunnel under the sea, indeed! What a ridiculous notion."

"Regardless how silly it might seem, the real point here is to always remember that it is the dedication of the individual that accomplishes so much, and Bertaud, like Napoleon, is quite dedicated in his service to his country."

"I am beginning to understand," she said, taking a sip of her coffee.

He settled his cup back on the table and leaned forward to cover her hand with his own. "But there is something more that worries you. I can see it in your eyes. Tell me, Anne. Let me offer you some relief if I am able."

Anne looked into his gray eyes, which were once more filled with compassion, and felt obliged to bring the matter forward. "You almost kissed me again," she stated.

"Yes," he agreed. "The moment seemed propitious. We were sitting in the dirt together."

She could not help but laugh. "You are being absurd."

"Of course I am. I do not like to see you so unhappy."

She drew a short breath. "Staverton, you must never kiss me again, even if . . . well, even if it appears to you that I might like for you to do so. Whatever your present interest in me, I beg you will remember that you are promised to Cassie, that you will be marrying her quite soon."

Staverton held her gaze steadily. He was recalling how it was he had felt just a little while past, behind the stone wall. "When we were sitting together by the wall, I was experiencing a profound relief that we had escaped Bertaud's notice," he said.

"And that is why you leaned forward to kiss me?" she asked.

"I do not know," he responded honestly. "I suppose in part." He realized he had many reasons for desiring to kiss her again, any of which would suffice to explain his conduct. He thought her pretty beyond words, he admired her bravery, and he had become entranced by her ability to make light of the most dire of circumstances; she had tended him last night when, apparently, he was in a delirious state, and she had risked her life for her country just a half hour past.

"Regardless," she said in the face of his silence. "I beg you will remember that you are in essence betrothed to my cousin."

There was so great a disparity between Anne and her cousin, that he could not help but say, "Will your cousin assist me in chasing after spies? Will she possess and keep a pair of pistols cleaned and primed so that when she is needed she will appear suddenly to vanquish those intent on murdering me? Will she be flung over a stone wall as though she were a bird in flight and not care that her gown of finely woven jaconet might be ruined?"

Tears welled up in Anne's eyes. "Do not make me think of such things," she whispered. "Our path must be one of honor and there is no honor in your kissing me when I have promised myself to bring to Cassie the man she loves."

Staverton could easily have told her he would never in a thousand years wed Cassaundra Bradley, but something within him kept the words in check. He sensed that Miss Bradley was only a small part of the difficulty before him. The greater trouble was that he did not know what exactly was happening between himself and Anne Delamere, nor why he could barely resist kissing her. The real question, for which he did not have an answer, was, what precisely was his interest in Anne?

Anne boarded the inelegant hired coach and watched Staverton arrange to have the curricle he had hired at Marlborough returned to the inn there. A few moments later, he took up his seat beside her.

"Did you transfer the documents to your valise?" she asked.

He patted the side of his rust-colored coat. "I decided to keep the packet closer at hand, at least for the present."

Anne smiled. "I suppose you have a secret pocket in your coat."

He smiled. "As it happens, I do."

Anne could only smile in return.

Once again on the road to Bath, Anne set aside her growing concern that Staverton might be developing an affection for her and that she, in turn, seemed to be responding in kind. She was so inexperienced in matters of the heart, that she chose to believe whatever attraction there was between herself and Staverton was merely a result of their having been thrown together on what was proving to be a rather dangerous mission. Anything beyond this she could not allow. The earl belonged to Cassie as surely as the wheels of her coach were meant for turning.

She concluded there was no true difficulty anyway, so long as Staverton ceased attempting to kiss her. She enjoyed a friendly camaraderie with the earl that seemed essentially to be quite platonic.

"We are not far from Somerset now," Staverton observed.

"No, not far," Anne agreed. In the distance, she could see a succession of hills, densely wooded, that indicated the nearness of the next county.

For the present, however, the village of Cherhill loomed close by, and as the coach rounded another bend a familiar sight appeared. "Do but look!" she called out. "My father calls it Alsop's Folly."

"Ah," Staverton murmured. "Cherhill's White Horse. I wonder how long it took him to carve the figure into the chalky hillside."

She knew that the horse was one hundred and sixty feet long, for her father had once climbed the hillside to observe the carving more closely and could not resist taking measurements. "I cannot say, but did you know the eyeball is made of glass bottles?"

Staverton laughed. "No, I did not. What an eccentric Dr. Alsop must have been."

"Indeed."

The coach moved past and the horse was left behind as the descent was made toward Cherhill.

"Are we still in Wiltshire?" Anne asked, as the first buildings came into view. When he nodded, she continued,

"Cherhill is a beautiful village. I know of no other hamlet with yellow and white thatched cottages, and I do believe the old tithe barn looks like a sailing vessel, it is so large."

"It is enormous," he agreed. "I am convinced it must be over a hundred feet long."

"Indeed." The coach began to slow and lumbered into the inn yard. Shaw was at the door immediately informing Anne that Bertaud had passed by both Cherhill and Calne, the latter of which was but two miles farther down the road. Quince was presently keeping pace with the spy.

Anne once more thanked him for his efforts. Shaw smiled broadly and wheeled his horse about. He was young and a bruising rider, and there was no mistaking that he thought the pursuit of Bertaud a complete lark. Anne laughed at his antics as he guided his mount in a complete circle. Then, in agreement with Staverton, she bid him continue on the road as he and Quince had done on the previous day. "We shall meet you at Chippenham," she said.

"Aye, miss," he responded, once more casting a beaming smile in her direction.

Just before he left, she called out, "Do you have sufficient funds?"

"Aye, miss!" He then spurred his horse onto the highway and was gone.

"You would think I had given him a holiday," she said, turning to Staverton.

"He certainly thinks as much."

Staverton ordered Jack Coachman to resume the journey, heading toward Calne. Once the ill-sprung vehicle was again marking its way in the direction of Bath, Anne said, "This entire stretch of road was a particular favorite of highwaymen many years ago."

"So it was," he said. "However, if you knew the password for that day you were safe enough. My father, as a young lad, was once stopped by two fellows who demanded a guinea from him, which they insisted they would repay once they were in funds. He took pity on them and gave each a guinea freely, stating they had no need to worry about repayment. In exchange for his kind words and generosity, and much to his surprise, he was then given the password of the day, which happened to be, 'Virgin Mary.' As it turned out, he found himself exceedingly grateful for the hint, since he was halted on his travels that day no less than three times by other, more sinister thieves. But on each occasion, when he gave the password, he was let go with a smile."

"I have often thought that only the most difficult of circumstances would drive someone to take up such an occupation, particularly when, if caught, the result could be a torturous death. I have read some of the accounts. They were truly abominable."

"Yes, they were," he agreed. "However, you and I shall not have to contend with highwaymen today."

"No, that much is true. But as a child, I can recall the bodies suspended from the gibbet between Beckhampton and Cherhill. Rather gruesome, I fear."

"You never longed for the life of a highwayman then?" he asked, a crooked smile on his lips.

She laughed. "Hardly, although I must say I have often envied the freedom of a highwayman's life."

He glanced at her. "I am curious, Miss Delamere. Did you truly never have a desire to be presented at court?"

"Never, although one of my aunts was most persistent, plaguing me nearly to death about the necessity of being properly introduced to society. Of course, she also believed that in doing so I would fulfill my primary duty, which was to find a husband."

"And she never could persuade you?"

"No," Anne responded definitively.

"You undoubtedly bowled her over with your superior strength of will."

"Hardly," she responded with a laugh. "The aunt to

whom I am referring is none other than the duchess of Alscroft. Are you acquainted with her?"

"Good God!" he cried. "Your aunt is Sally Alscroft? No, I should say nothing less than a bout of fisticuffs would have caused her to relinquish her designs for your future."

"We did not quite come to blows," she said, smiling. "But very nearly. Poor Aunt! She was so determined and I not less so in refusing her entreaties. She offered countless times, you can have no idea, to bring me into the first circles, and once she even threatened to abduct me from what she said was the nonsense of my existence. However, I made it abundantly clear that no one would ever force me into a white satin gown with hoops as large as a mail coach."

Staverton could not bring himself to close his mouth. He was utterly astonished. "So Her Grace, the duchess of Alscroft, is your aunt," he reiterated.

"Yes. My father's sister. I mentioned before that he came from a rather large family. In truth, he was one of twelve siblings. Cassie's mother was the oldest of the girls, but dear Aunt Sally eclipsed all her sisters by bringing Alscroft up to scratch. I have cousins scattered all about England. Several in York, the Whelford boys. Do you know them?"

"Good God!" he exclaimed. "I went to school with George."

"My mother was Lydia Whelford. Her brother, Lord Whelford, sired the boys—six of them and not one daughter. I am myself better acquainted with the youngest, Richard. George is nine years my senior."

"He came into the title last year, did he not?"

She nodded. "My uncle died of a putrid sore throat. We thought we might lose George, as well for he became ill shortly after, but he survived." The coach wheel hit an unexpected hole. Anne jumped in her seat and landed with a thud. "Oh, I detest this vehicle."

"On the return trip, I have every confidence we will be able to secure your coach. The wheelwright at Hungerford promised he would have the window repaired within a matter of two or three days, at the most."

"Thank God for that."

Staverton was silent apace, then continued, "And still, with such connections, you were never once tempted to come to London and make a brilliant match?"

"No, not by half," she said. "Love has not precisely pursued me and I shan't marry for any reason other than love. Besides, I am so much happier in the country, tending to the business of our village and county, seeing to my father's estate, which is a particular joy of mine, and riding my horses, of which I have three absolute beauties. London is a dirty city, full of very sad characters, and the life in Mayfair, about which my cousins kept me fully apprised season after season, seemed frivolous beyond permission. Admit it so. Admit that is why you chose to be a spy."

"Only a very small part of the reason, and you must remember, I am involved in matters of espionage only a portion of each year."

"Well, it seems to me you have chosen the better part, even if it is an intermittent occupation. However, you must be in London often."

"Yes, of course," he said. "I have my duties in the House of Lords, which I take quite seriously, and as a result I must spend the spring in the metropolis. Otherwise, as you already know, had I been a second, third, or fourth son, I should have joined the army, make no mistake."

"That's right," she mused, smiling. "That is one thing we do share in common. A pair of colors. Nothing would have stopped me."

"We are nearly at Calne now," he said.

"Such a pretty valley. I think I should enjoy a cup of tea at The Lansdowne Arms, if you have no objection."

"I have no wish to hurry to Chippenham, where I would not be surprised Bertaud will decide, if he has not already, to break for his nuncheon. Besides, I think I would be well-advised to walk about a bit, myself. I am feeling stiff again. Shall I inform your coachman we will tarry a while?"

"Yes, I believe it an excellent notion, if you please."

After a delightful cup of tea, Anne suggested a walk to the church to help loosen Staverton's sorely battered muscles. "For the lane is one of those beautiful, narrow, winding old streets, perfect for a stroll before resuming our journey."

"It will answer very well," he said.

The beauty of the day had an effect upon Anne. Her spirits had softened and warmed. She felt affection for everything and everyone she saw. "I am quite partial to August. I know some think it an abominably hot month, but I love how fall seems to be on every breeze, yet the land resists leaving summer and all its bounty behind."

He nodded. "I must agree with you. There is a lovely sort of tension in the air, a pull of one season upon another."

She glanced at Staverton who, at that moment, offered his arm to her. She took it gratefully. Perhaps a kiss was beyond permission, but accepting his arm during the course of a stroll was happily within the bounds of propriety.

"May I ask you a question?" she queried.

"Of course. You may ask me anything and I will vouchsafe as true an answer as I can."

"You are a good man, Staverton, and in this moment I am sorry I ever called you the Infidel."

He chuckled softly. "How angry I was with you when I learned you had been the one to have created such an odious epithet."

"I had reason, or at least I thought so at the time, which leads me to my question. Will you tell me of Molly Whitehaven? I have been given to understand you spent the night with her and afterward refused to marry her."

He chuckled. "I have spent the night with you, if you may recall, but a few hours ago. Why have you not insisted I take you to wife?"

"You know very well the circumstances are much different, so I take it unkindly in you that you must bring up such an absurd point, or do you not wish to discuss Miss Whitehaven?"

He sighed, not deeply, but audibly enough for Anne to hear his exasperation. "I pursued her for a time in Bath, some three years ago, during the summer. My interest, however, soon waned, and I broke with her, telling her that I had been called to London on some matter of business or other. She seemed resigned to my going without having offered for her. However, she begged tearfully that we drive out one last time in the countryside. The hour was late, I was reluctant to give her hope, but thought I might keep the excursion brief, particularly since the onset of rather dark clouds in the northwest gave every indication a downpour would soon be in order.

"We had not gone far, perhaps two miles out of the city, and I was preparing to turn back when the first drops fell. How was I to know the deluge which would soon follow and that well into the night? The streambeds were raging with muddy water and every route to Bath was blocked. You may believe me when I say I tried them all.

"However, I knew I had come to risk Miss Whitehaven's health, for in the unprotected curricle we were both soon soaked through. I took her to a cottage seeking shelter and found it deserted. I could not possibly take her farther, and led her inside. She was shivering with cold. I built up a fire, saw her clothes removed as discreetly as possible, having arranged for the small bed in the room to be surrounded with a blanket. There, she soon grew warm and fell into her slumber while I slept on the floor in front of the hearth throughout the night.

"In the morning, her expression was wholly triumphant. She seemed inordinately satisfied and when I returned her to her parents, she stated simply that I might call upon her father later that afternoon and offer for her. I was stunned, more by her hauteur than by her obvious belief we would soon be man and wife."

Anne contemplated the situation from his viewpoint. She knew little of Miss Whitehaven other than what she had observed when they were students together at Miss Mimm's Academy. "What did you do? Did you ever speak to her father?"

"Of course. I had kept his daughter out all night and by rights he could have demanded I wed her. I did as she required. I called on her father that afternoon but he was neither ambitious for his daughter, nor sympathetic with the situation that had aroused her expectations. I explained what had happened and how I had conducted myself, all borne out by Miss Whitehaven's explanation of her night's adventure. He asked me if I desired to wed his daughter. I spoke plainly and admitted that though I had initially formed an attachment to her, I found as the weeks progressed that we did not suit. He nodded and said, 'I thought as much. You were not precisely attentive at the last assembly.'

"I responded, 'I am certain she would make any gentleman an excellent wife, however—', but that was all I was able to say, for he interrupted me with a bark of laughter, saying, 'The devil she will. Spoiled, all three of my daughters.' He said he had no intention of holding me to a wedding I did not wish for, though he appreciated my willingness to do what was considered proper by most. All this was kindness enough, since I did not love his daughter, but he went even further, saying something to the effect, 'I shan't support any rumors that you jilted my daughter, but I warn you, her mother and sisters will spread it about that you used her abominably, so be warned.' He then told me the choice was mine, that he would be happy to welcome me as a son, but that he was perfectly willing to shake hands and let that be the end of it."

"What did you do?"

"I shook his hand. I did not love Miss Whitehaven nor was I convinced that she loved me. We truly did not suit. I am convinced we would have been at daggers drawn within the first twelvemonth."

Anne, standing at the portal of the church, said, "Did you not speak with Miss Whitehaven further, before leaving Bath?"

"No. Her father and I agreed that he would perform that office since he desired nothing more than to bring his daughter down a peg or two. I since learned that good Mr. Whitehaven had himself been trapped into a loveless marriage and had no intention of seeing the misdeed occur again."

Anne regarded him carefully. She had been with the earl now almost three days and had come to some understanding of his general character. She had spoken truly when she had called him a good man. However, the fate of Miss Whitehaven had been decided rather coldly by two gentlemen not disposed to thinking very highly of the lady's sensibilities. She recalled the gossip which rang across the entire island after that hapless night. Supported as it was by prior incidences of the earl's supposed misconduct with the fair sex, it landed at her front door by way of a letter from Miss Whitehaven herself, explaining in detail how badly she had been used by Staverton.

It now seemed to her, however, that the contents of the letter, initially read through her own prejudices concerning the earl, had had a second meaning which she had been unwilling at the time to even consider—that somehow Miss Whitehaven was hoping to force Staverton to marry her by garnering support from as many noble and genteel families as possible. Anne had always been surprised that the duchess of Alscroft had not been among those willing to take up her cause. Lady Alscroft had been a friend to Mrs. Whitehaven, or had been until this incident, and if anyone could have been expected to have become a staunch supporter of Miss Whitehaven's claims, it would have been her Aunt Alscroft.

Anne attempted to sort through the various aspects of the situation. "I knew Miss Whitehaven from having been at school with her many years ago, when I was sixteen. I recall her as having loved a good joke, of being entirely ingenuous in her relationships and being as pretty as a picture, all amber ringlets."

"I saw something of the young lady you have described and, indeed, I pursued just such a creature that summer in Bath. However, the level of her ambition soon made itself known to me and I grew cold toward her. The colder I grew, the more she drew forward every artifice imaginable in hopes of capturing her prize. I became disgusted. I have often wondered, if she had simply left me to my own devices, whether I might not have warmed toward her again."

"I suppose you will never know, but I will thank you for this one thing: you have been very forthcoming in your explanation. You could have told me to go to the devil."

He gestured toward the interior of the church. "At the doors of a church?" he queried. "I think not, Miss Delamere."

She could only laugh. "When did you decide you must be so formal with me?" she complained. "We have been getting on so nicely, or at least at times."

"Yes, we have, but then you seem to bring forward some female or other who has complained of my conduct and so you become *Miss Delamere* again, at least for a time."

"Your punishment then?" she asked, chuckling.

He smiled, but before she could enter the church, he stayed her. "Tell me, Anne, do you forgive me for having spurned Miss Whitehaven? Do you believe I was wrong in accepting Mr. Whitehaven's graciousness?"

Anne was thoughtful for a long moment. "I know that Miss Whitehaven suffered a severe disappointment, and because of my friendship with her, I must always honor her confidences. She wrote to me, you know. There were tear stains on the letter, making some of the words illegible."

"You believe her, then, and not me?"

"I will not choose, particularly since I am persuaded it is very difficult for a man to see from a woman's place and for a woman to possibly comprehend what it is to be a man. I would only say this to you: however much she might have been at fault in pursuing you when it was clear, probably even to her, that your affections had not been engaged, she did so out of the pressures of our society in general. Do you not see as much?"

"You forgive her conduct so readily? I have come to believe she planned the excursion."

"She could not have predicted the weather to have been so severe," she countered.

He sighed again. "I suppose you are right. I was so angry with her conduct the next day, her assumption I must now do that which it was clear to her I desired not to do, that I have never been sympathetic to her sufferings."

"Let me try to explain it this way. It is the very difference between myself and you on our journey." She lowered her voice to nearly a whisper. "I am here because I broke a very solemn rule of our society, that a single woman should never be in the sole company of a man. I did so because I wished to have the first of what I hope will be many adventures.

"However, in living this life that I have for three days, I know I must continue to break rule after rule, to give rise to every manner of gossip and slander to my good name and to my honor, if I hope to enjoy even a particle of the adventures I wish to enjoy. You, on the other hand, had but to offer your help to your friends in government and you are here, of service to your country in circumstances that are dangerous in the extreme. I could never have done so. I would have been mocked and sent home to work on my samplers and watercolors. The choices a woman may make in society versus the choices a man has laid before him are as different as night from day and wholly limiting to a woman. You must admit this is so."

"That much, yes, but what does Miss Whitehaven have to do with"—here, he, too, dropped his voice quite low—"with your kidnapping me and accompanying me across

England? I see no connection. There is too great a disparity in circumstance."

"I am trying to explain how different life is for a woman, any woman, than a man in any part of our society. You pursued Molly when it pleased you but the moment she set her cap at you, she was in your view entirely unworthy. A woman may not do as she pleases as men may do at every turn."

"You are speaking nonsensically."

"Am I? Let me ask you this. What would you do if you were a second son, but not just a second son, impoverished, as well? What would you do—I mean besides the purchasing of a pair of colors? What would your choices be?"

"I do not know, precisely. I suppose I would seek out a profession, try to earn my fortune as best I might, perhaps even emigrate to the Colonies."

"A sensible answer. Now, imagine yourself as a woman in similar circumstances. You are impoverished. You need not be second- or third-born, you may even be firstborn, but you have no dowry. What do you do?"

The expression on his face grew very still.

She smiled faintly. "You are beginning to understand. A lady of quality might become a governess or a companion to some infirmed person, but what fortune can she acquire earning sixty pounds a year? A woman's lot in our society is highly restrictive. I daresay Miss Whitehaven understood only too well what she was losing when she saw your interest vanish. The prize you represented was undoubtedly more than she could bear losing without putting up some manner of fight for it. She had only a thousand pounds for her dowry, scarcely anything by general standards. You did know as much?"

"Yes, of course, but you cannot mean to actually justify her conduct?"

"No," Anne cried. "Not by half. I am only trying to help you understand why she behaved as she did, that for most young ladies, you represent not just an agreeable suitor, but in your handsome face, your intelligence, your wealth and your title, besides the fact that you are a delightful companion, the epitome of every girl's daydream. You have been given so much, Staverton, except the ability to be truly compassionate, that I doubt there is a young lady in the kingdom whose head would not be turned by your mere appearance in a doorway. Therefore, I would suggest to you that the same rebuff, one dealt in kindness, the other in arrogance, can be construed in two entirely different ways."

He frowned slightly. "I believe you may be the first person to ever say such things to me," he responded. "I do not agree entirely with all you have said, however, I will think on it. For the present"—here he gestured to the door of the church—"shall we enjoy a stroll through the church for a few moments before taking up our places again in that horrible coach, which we ought to do very soon if I do not much mistake the matter?"

Anne acquiesced, wondering if she had gone beyond the pale. Regardless, she realized that in speaking of Miss Whitehaven she had herself finally come to understand the heart of the matter, particularly with regard to Staverton's conduct. Had the earl been truly compassionate in his dealings with any of these ladies—Georgina Patney, Prudence Marsh or Molly Whitehaven—she had no doubt the outcome would have been entirely different instead of his having earned the epithet the Infidel.

The subject was left far behind in view of the church's many attributes, the ancient nave, its interesting style of architecture known as Perpendicular, and a Gothic tower replacing one that fell in the seventeenth century.

Another half hour saw them once more on the road to Bath.

ELEVEN

As the rickety conveyance entered Chippenham, Anne surveyed the ancient stone town in which the old market was surrounded by coaching inns, the two most prominent being the Angel and the White Hart. The latter was arrayed with a lovely facade, and bow windows from which the hostlers and postillions could see the Bath or London coaches approach.

The coachman halted the equipage before the Angel. Shaw, as planned, bounded up to the coach, breathless. "He broke his journey at the White Hart. He is there even now."

Instinctively, Anne gripped Staverton's arm.

"Very well," the earl said, nodding to Shaw. To Anne, he said, "I believe it best we dine here, at the Angel, and await circumstances."

Shaw cleared his throat. He was frowning deeply.

"You do not approve?" Staverton asked of the servant.

Anne glanced at her footman, who seemed reluctant to speak. "Shaw, pray do not stand on ceremony in this instance. I—we—rely on you completely and most particularly upon your opinion. If you have a suggestion, we would like to hear it."

"Yes, Shaw," the earl added. "Do not hold anything back."

"He's a hard man, Bertaud is. I worry for Miss Anne, for her safety."

Anne met his gaze fondly. "I will be all right. Indeed, I

will, but if that is all . . . ?" She raised her brows questioningly.

"Yes, miss."

She smiled. "You may return to Quince. Once you have word of Bertaud's movements, you will find us here, hopefully in a private parlor."

"Very good, miss."

Anne watched him go, grateful to have such loyal and trusted servants. She was about to say as much when she watched Staverton descend the steps, wincing as he did so.

"Are your wounds giving you much pain?" she asked, following behind.

He turned to her and offered his hand. "Only what must be expected but nothing to signify. A little walking about shall soon set me to rights." When her feet were planted securely on the cobbles, he stretched his arms and worked his shoulder muscles a little.

Anne smiled, remembering how Harry Chamberlayne would set up a fierce caterwaul with the merest scratch or bump. At least Staverton was not so tender a creature. "I am longing for my nuncheon," she announced.

Staverton rounded on her, laughing. "And is that all the sympathy I am to receive?" he asked.

"As though you need any. You are made of stern stuff, Staverton, and for that I admire you prodigiously. Of the moment, however, I am more interested in my meal than in your sufferings. So, if you please, do come into the inn, or would you prefer to traipse about the town while I order a nuncheon for us?"

"The latter, if you do not mind." His expression was rather serious, which alerted her instantly.

"Of course I do not mind," she responded sincerely. However, when she reached the door she could not help but turn back to him. "You do mean to stay out of harm's way. Tell me you do not intend to do anything foolish."

He drew in a deep breath of summery air. "Lovely day

for a walk," was all he would say as he turned in the direction
of the White Hart.

She watched him go. She could see that he favored his
left side and yet, even with his usually brisk gait broken by
his discomfort, he still presented a formidable figure. He
wore a coat of Russian flame-twilled stuff cut in trim lines
across his broad shoulders. Because of his jaunt in the curricle, he had donned serviceable buckskin breeches and top
boots. With his top hat settled over his black locks at a
slightly rakish angle, he would surely draw the attentive eye
of every female from here to the White Hart.

Regardless of her admiration for him, Anne entered the
inn with her stomach having drawn itself into a knot. She
strongly suspected Staverton meant to spy upon his enemy.
What if Bertaud saw him? What act of madness would he
attempt in this town?

She shuddered at the thought until another intruded. Perhaps Staverton meant to switch the documents while Bertaud enjoyed his meal at the White Hart. He now carried the
packet secreted within his coat, so that if the proper occasion
arose he was certainly prepared to make the exchange. Of
course, if he succeeded, then there would be no reason to
continue on to Bath, no excuse to remain in his company
longer than necessary.

Anne was surprised at how much this particular avenue
of thought depressed her spirits. In truth, she did not want
her adventure to end. She wanted to continue on with Staverton, in just this manner, as companions and spies, for at least
another sennight or two, possibly a month or more. With
something of a sad smile, she realized that forever suddenly
did not seem so imposing a distance of time.

As she addressed the landlord, she was once more amused
to find how simple it was to secure a parlor when all she
had to do was mention the name Staverton. The man before
her in this instance bowed so many times, he turned a shade
of pink. He led her to the private chamber and begged to

know if she would like some sherry while she decided just what she and her cousin would enjoy consuming for their midday meal.

She thanked him for his kind attentions, agreeing readily to a glass of sherry. Once she had delivered her order to the landlord—for no mere serving maid would do in this instance—Anne sat back in her chair and sipped her wine. She was soon lost in thought, pondering how incredible her experiences had been thus far and how much she was truly enjoying herself, in great part because Staverton's company was precisely what she delighted in. He had no difficulty in remaining silent when she did not wish for conversation, nor was he unwilling to engage in even the smallest discourse should her inclination fall in that direction.

She wondered even now where he was and whether or not he had seen Bertaud for himself.

Staverton meandered along the alley behind the coaching inns. After passing under an archway, he found the stables of the White Hart. He was about to cross the inn yard when Bertaud suddenly appeared in the doorway, pulling on his gloves.

Staverton turned abruptly and slipped into the inn's old brewery. The heavy smell of ale surrounded him instantly, which in ordinary circumstances would have been a most delightful experience. Presently, however, he found the fumes to be an annoyance, straining as he was to see where it was Bertaud meant to go.

Having left the door open slightly, he was able to peer through the crack by the doorjamb. He watched Bertaud walk to the center of the inn yard behind a coach and four that had recently arrived quite dust-laden and was presently disgorging its passengers.

He was still pressing on his gloves when he turned toward the brewery and looked directly at the door. Staverton cursed beneath his breath. Bertaud was awake upon all suits, which made it deuced difficult to plan anything where the man was concerned.

A moment more, and Bertaud turned entirely in the other direction, toward the Angel, disappearing under the archway.

Staverton waited a few minutes, then slipped easily from his hiding place. He nearly collided with one of the inn's servants who held a cart by which it was evident he meant to transport another barrel of ale back to the taproom.

He went to the stables first and, giving the hostler a sovereign, queried to know if he had any idea how long "Mr. Smythe" meant to stay.

"He's ordered his horses put to in an hour," the man responded.

"And is his luggage strapped to his carriage?"

"Aye. That be his curricle at the far end."

"Thank you for your trouble."

The hostler moved away briskly, calling out orders to his stable boy to begin harnessing the horses for the mail coach, which was due to arrive shortly.

At that moment, another large coach rattled into the inn yard, the hostler called for a stable boy, and before long, what had been a fairly deserted yard was one now bustling with every manner of activity. There were fresh horses being exchanged for tired ones, people ascending and descending their coaches, and children racing toward the inn, making use of legs fatigued with traveling.

Staverton made his way to Bertaud's curricle and glanced at his baggage. His portmanteaus were strapped tightly onto the vehicle and the valise which might have held the documents was nowhere in sight, presumably buried within one of the spy's larger portmanteaus. He desired more than anything to rip open the bags and to perform even now the task of switching the documents, but it would be utterly impossible without removing every piece of luggage from its careful place on the back of the curricle, opening each one, and

hunting for the packet. Not only did he not have sufficient
time to do anything of the sort, for Bertaud could return at
any moment, but he would surely draw a great deal of unwanted attention to himself were he to be seen strewing another man's clothes about the cobbles of the inn yard. This
image was entirely laughable.

He decided there was nothing more he could do at present
and began his return to the Angel. Because there was a
strong possibility he would meet Bertaud coming out of one
of the shops, he chose to return to the inn by a circuitous
route behind the numerous shops lining the High Street.

The small portion of sherry Anne was sipping was having
a gentle effect on her nerves. In the past few minutes, she
had even found herself smiling a trifle now and then, particularly since her thoughts had become fixed on Staverton
and their journey together. She had already gleaned some
of his preferences generally. For instance, he was often silent
after a meal, and she suspected he would be the sort of man
when he grew quite old who would seek his comfortable
library after a hearty meal and fall sound asleep in his chair.
On the other hand, he was most animated an hour or so after
supper when the sun was beginning to set, as though the
approach of night brought an excitement he could not contain.

She was about to take another sip of her wine when movement in the doorway startled her. "It is you!" she cried.
Unable to think of anything more appropriate to say, she
added, "W-would you like a glass of sherry?"

Staverton breathed a sigh of relief when he finally
reached the Angel without once having met Bertaud along
the way. The landlord, bowing to him at least five times
when he made himself known to that good man, finally di-

rected him to the parlor. He made his way contentedly not only because he had escaped meeting Bertaud but because he was happy to be seeing Anne again. He realized there was one fortunate aspect of Bertaud's departure from Chippenham without the switched documents—he would be able to continue in Anne's company. He was wondering just what paths their conversation would take during the course of the forthcoming meal, when his thoughts were stopped abruptly by the sight of a man standing very near to Anne and taking a sip of sherry.

"Ah, here we are," the landlord said. "You, of course, know your good friend, Mr. Smythe."

"Yes, of course," he responded smoothly.

A glance at Anne's unusually pale complexion proved what it was he saw himself, that Bertaud was directly in front of him.

He thanked the landlord, who once more offered a string of obsequious bows before disappearing down the hall.

Staverton felt angry, suddenly, at the effrontery of a man known to be an avowed enemy of England, who would appear so unexpectedly, so threateningly, in the same parlor with the woman who was for the present his particular charge. "What are you doing here?" he snapped.

Bertaud tossed off the remainder of the sherry and settled the small glass on the table, at which Anne sat rather stiffly.

"Your, er, *cousin,* desired to share a glass of wine with me. You cannot possibly object, not after how many miles we have all traveled together. Why, it is almost as though the three of us have become fast friends. Indeed, without your presence these many miles, I vow I should have felt positively lonely." His thin features enhanced the sarcasm lacing his words. Everything in his demeanor spoke of hatred and purpose.

"I should have killed you in Dover last spring, when I had the chance," Staverton said.

"Yes, you should have, but, then, that would not have

served your government, would it? Ah, but I shall take my leave, for I can see that the lady is distressed and I would not for the world discompose your *cousin*. I am, after all, a gentleman, although I feel I ought to give you a small hint that you would be wise to take better care of Miss Delamere. We would not want anything untoward to happen to her *again,* would we, life being so very precious?"

Staverton moved to stand between Bertaud and Anne. "You dare to injure one hair on her head and I shall not give a damn what my government desires me to do. I shall most happily send you to your forefathers."

"Fine words," Bertaud responded. "Well, we shall see, shan't we?" With that, he turned on his booted heel and quit the parlor.

Anne found that she was trembling as she lifted her own glass of sherry to her lips and took an infinitesimally small sip. She worried that she would even be able to swallow that little bit.

She felt Staverton's hand on her shoulder and she covered it with her own. "I was never been more stunned," she said, "nor more frightened than when he simply walked in here. All I could think was that my pistols were still in the coach and that should he desire to do me harm, there was nothing I could do to save myself."

She looked up at him, the horror of the situation burrowing so deeply within her that she wondered if she would ever be the same again.

Staverton dropped to his heels beside her and took her hands forcibly in his. Squeezing them hard, almost painfully so, he looked fiercely into her eyes. "He would never have harmed you in so public a place. You must believe me in this. He knew better than to do so. His only purpose here was to frighten you in hopes that he might intimidate you to the point that you would give up your part in the chase— one foe being far easier to manage than two."

"Oh, Staverton, are you certain?" she asked earnestly.

"For in this moment, after all my protestations of desiring to have adventures"—and here her eyes suddenly filled with tears—"I wished myself anywhere but in this room. The only thing I could think to do—which was what I did—was to offer him a glass of sherry! How could I have done so! I might as well have offered the same to the devil!"

He chuckled and kissed her cheeks, each in turn. "Oh, my dear, dear Anne! What a precious thing you are. Who else would have thought to offer sherry. 'Oh, it is you, my good spy. Do you care for a little sherry?' Precious, precious Anne."

He cupped her face with his palms. Anne covered his hands again with her own. "You are so good to me," she said, "saying precisely what I need to hear. I feel as though I have failed you somehow, to be this frightened. Oh, Staverton, you must promise me that no matter how sadly I behave, how cowardly, that you will complete your mission despite my weaknesses."

"Your weaknesses!" he cried. "Do not speak such foolishness. If you found yourself afraid, good. Such fears keep us alive when we are doing that which is brave and good. You have nothing to be ashamed of and you have not failed me. If anything, in not falling into hysterics, you have given Bertaud pause for concern. Whatever he might have thought of you three days ago, when he tried to run you down, he will know now that you are strong and not to be in the least perturbed by such antics as he performed today in approaching a lone female in a secluded parlor. No, his presence proved only what I already know about you, that you are the bravest of women, strong and courageous and I . . . well, I esteem you greatly."

He again kissed her cheek. Without thinking, Anne turned her face just a little in order to find his lips with her own.

He was surprised, drawing back. His gaze met and held. Her lips parted. "Staverton," she murmured, her heart racing. "I should not have . . ."

He dragged her suddenly to her feet, pulled her forcefully into his arms, and slanted his lips over hers. Anne leaned into him, entirely willing to be embraced by him in this moment. The experience became magical, transporting her to another place entirely, a place of wonder and excitement, of tremblings of a different sort entirely. Forgotten were her promises to bring a husband to Cassie. Her only true thought was that she loved being with Staverton more than anything else in the world and that being caught up in his arms was like the sweetest rhapsody ever composed in the history of the world—particularly since he kissed first her lips, then the tip of her nose, her chin, her forehead just at the temples, then found her lips again.

He drew back. "Anne," he murmured. "My darling Anne."

The fears she had known but moments ago seemed to transform into a piercing desire to be kissed and touched and embraced by Staverton. His kiss deepened, and with the wild probing of his tongue came a wave of intense pleasure. She held him tightly about his neck and he pressed himself the full length against her so that the sinewy hardness of his thighs were connected to her own in an intimate manner.

Anne's thoughts drifted to a place where she began to contemplate sharing a bed with the man holding her so wickedly against himself. How much she desired such a bed, with this man, and a lifetime of love.

"Staverton," she whispered against his lips.

He spoke her name a dozen times, still holding her in a crushing embrace.

Tears began to seep from her eyes, inexplicable drops that trickled down her cheeks, and onto their joined lips. She knew something extraordinary, if not in her mind quite yet, then most assuredly in her soul. She enveloped him in these feelings, surrounding him with the knowledge that still had not made its way into her thoughts.

He groaned as her hands spread themselves over his face,

through his hair, along his broad shoulders and descended over his back. She whispered his name again and again.

Thoughts began to curl from deep within her heart, moving with her pulse, finally taking shape in images and words.

She loved him. With all her heart, *she loved him.* She was as certain of it as she was that the sun would rise each day, and the moon each night.

Staverton felt his own sentiments as a great swell, like an ocean wave, beginning far out at sea and moving with increasing speed toward the shore of his life. When it peaked and crashed, he felt as though in holding Anne in his arms, he was holding everything that was dear and wonderful to him.

When he had seen Bertaud standing in the parlor with her, the rage he had felt had stunned him in its intensity. Holding her now, kissing her, feeling her hands drift over his back, knowing she was safe, worked in him like a raging fire. He had never, in his entire existence, felt this way before. He understood with great clarity that *he loved her,* with all his heart, *he loved her.*

Anne drew back quite suddenly.

"Dearest," he murmured. "What is it?" Her beautiful green eyes were filled with fright anew.

"You belong to Cassie," she stated, pulling out of his arms as though in holding him she was touching something that burned.

He wanted to tell her it was not so, that she had been ridiculous from the first to believe he would ever acquiesce to marrying Miss Bradley. However, he knew her well enough to comprehend that whatever his opinion on the subject, she was convinced she was doing that which was right in attempting to force a marriage between himself and her cousin.

"Anne," he began quietly. *This is madness,* he wanted to say, but such words would be offensive to her. He sought about in his mind for something that might reveal the error of her thinking, but at that moment, a servant, bearing a large tray, arrived with their nuncheon.

He took a step away from her and watched her dab quickly at her tears as the servant settled the various dishes on the nearby sideboard. He took up his seat opposite her and quieted his thoughts. However was he going to persuade her she should relinquish the absurd notion that he should marry Cassaundra?

Another thought, more difficult than even the issue concerning her cousin, assailed him. Was he even worthy of the lady before him? A shot of fear struck him like a wave of cold air assaulting a warm room. He had no confidence that he was. She already disapproved of one aspect of his conduct. Were he to court her, would she grow to despise him the more she came to know him?

Taking a strong gulp of the claret the servant poured for him, he pondered a number of the ladies he had previously courted. He felt a nagging suspicion, perhaps because of all the things Anne had said to him at the church in Calne, that he had not been entirely without fault in his dealings with them. *The same rebuff, one dealt in kindness, the other in arrogance, can be construed in two entirely different ways.*

Still, he did not know how he could have conducted himself differently given each situation. This was perhaps more troubling than the rest. If Anne found fault with him, yet he could not see the defect himself, perhaps he was flawed in other ways as well, ways that would soon grow repugnant to her. Even Lady Katherine had intimated her poor opinion of his conduct toward Miss Bradley.

Anne nibbled at her meal, her heart and head still at war with one another. Somewhere in the middle of embracing Staverton, an image of Cassaundra, standing beside the raspberry vines and weeping into her lace kerchief, had vaulted into her head so suddenly, that she had all but gasped as she pulled away from the earl. How had it come about that she had, yet again, permitted herself to fall beneath his spell and once more allow him to kiss her? Certainly, she had been frightened by Bertaud's presence and by his words, but this could not entirely account for her sudden desire to be embraced by him yet again.

Worse, still, however, was the daunting realization that she had, indeed, tumbled in love with the very man destined to become Cassie's husband. How had such a terrible thing occurred? How had she been as foolish as so many of her friends? How had she permitted Staverton to so turn her head?

She lifted a fleeting glance to his face, then reverted to cutting a slice of her artichoke heart. He was devilishly handsome and she was a fool. That was all. She was not so different from all her friends after all. Cupid had pricked her with his golden-tipped arrow and she had succumbed, and that for no particular reason except that Staverton was handsome.

No particular reason. She dabbed the slice of artichoke into a light Benton sauce. No particular reason, only that he had been so concerned for her safety that he had sworn to kill Bertaud were he to ever touch her again. That, and at the very moment when she was flooded with self-doubts, he fairly ordered her not to be so nonsensical, praising her for her courage and admitting he esteemed her.

"Are you not hungry?" he asked.

She offered a half-smile. "Only a very little now."

"You are overset."

She sat back in her chair. "I suppose I am. Staverton, I am so sorry I kissed you. I beg you will forgive me. I do not know why I did so, especially when I have asked you not to kiss me. I must seem like a complete hypocrite to you."

"Hardly that," he said somberly. "You are an honorable woman. I have no doubt that you will keep your self-made promise to your cousin, only, will it make you happy?" His gray eyes fairly bored into her soul.

"How can you ask me such a question?" she responded

on a whisper. "My happiness is not even a consideration in such a situation as this."

"What of my happiness, then?" he asked.

She swallowed hard. "You relinquished the right to it when you flirted so strongly with my cousin without even a single thought to her feelings." She could see that her words had affected him deeply. "Do you still not see where you are responsible?"

He appeared further stunned, as though she had struck him a hard blow across the face. He directed his gaze to the windows, and for a long moment appeared to become lost in thought. Finally, he said, "I wonder if Bertaud actually left Chippenham?"

Anne took up his hint readily. "Shaw will advise us, of course."

"Yes, of course," he said, spearing a small portion of a lobster patty.

Anne felt very close to tears. So this was to be the end of it, then, a cold diversion to the activities of the day, to chasing a spy perfectly capable of taking either of their lives.

Conversation soon ceased altogether, which Anne felt was just as well. Of what possible use could it be to continue speaking on a subject that wounded both of them?

Much of the pleasure of the trip was lost to Anne. She could not even enjoy the descent by way of Rowden Hill leading to the village of Corsham, which was usually a great delight to her. Her mind was so full of misery, she could scarcely take in the beauties about her as the coach worked its way west toward Bath.

Even though she tried to keep her thoughts away from her cousin, images of a certain, forthcoming wedding would soon fill her mind and she would begin to review all of Cassie's faults, which she realized were more numerous than she had at first supposed. For one thing, Staverton would be plagued to death by her once they were married, for it was very true that Cassie was fond of society more than anything. Nor did Cassaundra have even the smallest inclination for adventure. Not once over the years had either she or Harry been able to persuade Cassie to accompany them on any of their larks. How could Staverton ever be happy with a creature who had never once heard the call of the road, or the mountains or the sea! He would be bored to death before the end of the first twelvemonth.

She would then chide herself for being so unfair to her cousin. Who would not be happy with such a loving creature as Cassie? Staverton would never want for even the smallest housekeeping comfort and his children would be doted upon at every turn. Surely Staverton, by virtue of his being the eldest and requiring an heir to which he might pass his rank, his lands and his fortune, would wish for a dozen babes to fill his nursery, and Cassie was just the lady to oblige him.

She sighed deeply, keeping her gaze pinned to the window. As the coach passed down Corsham's High Street, Staverton interrupted the unhappy train of her thoughts by remarking that the golden stone used to construct many of the buildings was quite beautiful. "Although I find this row of white-gabled houses to be very unusual. I wonder at their history."

Anne glanced out his window and espied the buildings. "Papa said they were built by Flemish Huguenot refugees in Queen Elizabeth's reign."

"Two hundred years ago," he murmured. "Imagine all that was happening so long ago."

Anne smiled, some of her sadness dissipating in the contemplative nature of his remarks. "Only think what the world will be in another two centuries. Do you suppose everyone will travel by hot-air balloon?"

He laughed. "I cannot imagine it being so, but some predict even the horse will cease to be of use before long. The steam engine can actually pull coaches on tracks at very high speeds."

"I think it all nonsense," she observed. "The horse has

been with us forever. Besides, I once saw a steam engine, or rather, heard it. I cannot imagine the noise that would fill our land with the advent of such a machine."

"Who can say," he responded diplomatically. "Were we to meet Shaw at the Methuen Arms?" he asked.

"Yes."

A few minutes later the coach drew into the quiet inn yard. Shaw, who had been awaiting them, emerged from the inn, calling to Jack Coachman. "Shall I ring the hostler's bell?" he asked.

"Nay," Jack replied. " 'Tis not so far to Bath and we may stop at Box if we need to change horses."

Shaw approached the door, which Staverton had swung open. "Bertaud paused neither here nor at Pickwick. Shall I wait for ye at Box?"

Anne glanced at Staverton, who assented with a nod. "Yes," she said, addressing her servant. "At Box."

"Very good, miss," he responded, tipping his hat and wheeling his horse about immediately. She noticed that the animal was fresh, no doubt hired at this very inn yard.

She gave Jack the office to start, and once more the creaking equipage set forth on the road to Bath.

After a few minutes, Staverton turned to Anne and said, "I have been thinking about our conversation at the Angel."

She could not help but wish that he had not brought forward what was becoming for her a very painful subject. However, his desire to discuss the matter must preclude her preference never to address it again. "Yes?" she queried politely.

"I believe you may be right on one score."

She waited expectantly since his expression appeared very solemn, a frown splitting his brow.

He continued quietly. "After my experiences with the three ladies we have discussed most particularly, I grew rather cynical toward young ladies of quality, believing that one and all were interested in me because of my rank and wealth. Somewhere, in the course of my years in London, I believe I lost the ability to discern between those of an avaricious nature and those whose interest, perhaps even affections, had been truly engaged. I cannot help but think that regarding these latter women, I am truly repentant. I believe your cousin to be among them."

At this juncture, he turned fully toward her. "I hope you will forgive me, Anne. Had I been more aware, more perceptive, I should have long since altered my conduct. I can only express a certain amount of gratitude in your having stumbled upon my path if for nothing more than to instruct me a trifle."

Anne was stunned. "I can see that you are entirely serious," she said.

"Very much so. Do you doubt me?"

"No, for I have come to comprehend your character in the three days we have been traveling together. It is just that I truly do not understand why a man of your intelligence did not heretofore recognize the flawed nature of his actions. Why now?"

He took her hand in his. "Because it has become of supreme importance to me that you esteem me and not think me a complete brute."

"I could never think you that."

"You did three days ago."

Anne chuckled. "Yes, I did, and to some degree you were. You have changed, Staverton."

"I am more myself with you than I have ever been before. I trusted no one, but I trust you, with all my heart."

Anne felt her chin wobble inexplicably and tears rushed to her eyes. "That is the sweetest thing you could have ever said to me."

"Then do you forgive me?"

She searched his gray eyes for a long moment. "Yes, of course I do." She tried to bring Cassie's image strongly to mind in order that she might keep from falling into the warmth and tenderness of his gaze, but she could not. Part of her knew that in but a few more days she would be separated forever from Staverton, but there was another part that understood, however wrongly, that for these days she was able to be with him and to savor the intimacy of his company, she must take advantage of them.

So, when he leaned toward her and placed a kiss on her lips, she did not draw back nor reprimand him in any way, but rather gave herself to the wonderful sensation of expressing her love silently through the kisses she returned to him.

Staverton felt the delicate response of her lips and took the liberty of removing her bonnet. When she drew close to him, he surrounded her with his arm, pulling her within the well of his shoulder. She nestled her golden curls against him and sighed contentedly as he continued gentling kisses over her waiting lips.

He was entirely sobered by the recent exchange. He realized he had undergone a dramatic change, that because of her efforts in helping him to see the truth, the anger he had been feeling toward the ladies of his acquaintance in this moment melted away.

After a long moment, he drew back, knowing how unwise it would be to continue kissing her, but reveled in the joy of feeling her remain closely beside him, nestling more deeply into his shoulder and slipping her hand into his.

He fell to contemplating their present dilemma. Whatever the sweet nature of Anne's present tenderness, he knew her well enough to understand that regardless of her feelings, she had in no manner relinquished the notion that he was yet obligated to marry her cousin. The situation was rather ticklish. After all, were he to refuse to marry Miss Bradley, Anne would think him a man without honor. Yet, the thought of marrying her cousin, of wedding anyone other than Anne Delamere, was so repugnant to him that it was not to be borne. He therefore felt as though he was teetering on a narrow, weak bridge over a deep abyss.

"Staverton," she said, lifting her face to his. He did not wait to hear what it was she meant to say to him, but covered her lips quickly with his own.

"My darling, my darling," he breathed against her mouth. He was rewarded with delightful coos and warbles. Her hand stole to his chest and slid upward to encircle his neck. He kissed her more deeply still and did not stop until the coach reached the top of the hill that would descend to the hamlet of Box. He could hardly continue assaulting her lips while the coach scraped its way to the base of the hill.

The pinnacle afforded an exquisite view of the valley below and of gently rising hills opposite. Around the village of Box were the quarries that created the lovely city of Bath.

When the road evened out at the bottom of the hill, he once more took Anne into his arms, this time settling kisses over every inch of her face, claiming his territory.

"Oh, Staverton," she murmured after a long moment. "Whatever are we to do?"

He took her chin in hand and forced her to meet his gaze. "Do not concern yourself about that," he said. "For the present, we shall enjoy the remainder of what I believe is about six or seven miles to Bath, during which time I intend to convince you that I have fallen deeply and irrevocably in love with you."

TWELVE

Anne stared at the man beside her who still held her in a strong embrace. She searched his gray eyes, scarcely able to credit what he had just told her. She knew that her own heart was entirely given to Staverton but somehow she had never quite supposed that he might feel precisely the same way.

"You love me?" she asked.

"Would I have been kissing you in this scandalous manner if I did not?" he countered, chuckling.

She caught her breath, realizing that for all the angry protestations of the women supposedly injured by Staverton's conduct, not one had mentioned having been wrapped up in his arms for hours at a time.

"Did you never kiss any of the ladies you pursued in this fashion?" she asked.

"Of course not," he murmured, stroking her face with the his fingers.

Since he could not seem to resist kissing her yet again, she gave herself once more to the incredible sensation of being lost in his embrace. Only this time, the knowledge that his heart was engaged as well somehow impassioned the moment. Her curls, caught up in a knot atop her head, became unpinned and drifted about her shoulders as he bruised her mouth quite wonderfully, and a strange ache afflicted her entire being.

On approaching the small hamlet of Box, Staverton released her with some reluctance. Anne picked up her bonnet and began cramming her locks under the well of the crown, an inelegant process which served sufficiently to allow her to tie her ribbons beneath her chin just as the coach drew into the inn yard.

Shaw came quickly to the window and proffered the most welcome information that Bertaud was settled in rooms at the White Hart in Bath. Anne sent him ahead to find Quince, with instructions to meet them at the Pump Room sometime within the next hour or so. She could not be more specific about the timing since she had no notion how long it would take the old coach to cover the last five miles of their journey. Once at the Pump Room, her servants would be informed as to where the entire party would rest for the night.

When the creaking conveyance was once more on the King's Highway, Staverton quickly removed her bonnet, and as before, Anne welcomed the comfort of his arms as he drew her again into a tight embrace. He resumed kissing her quite passionately, which soon had her mind drifting to a pretend future in which she would be with the earl always.

The jostling of the carriage, as it wended its way up and down the hilly landscape, finally took its toll, however, and when a particularly large dip in the road sent her chin hard against Staverton's cheek, she relinquished the delight of his kisses for the much safer activity of simply leaning her head into the curve of his shoulder and holding him tightly as he surrounded her with his arms. She was infinitely content in a way she would never have believed possible.

When the city of Bath finally came into view, set in the crescent of its vale beside the River Avon, Anne straightened in her seat and began tidying her hair. Staverton, in turn, conducted a search for the pins that had become dislodged, a circumstance which made her smile, for it seemed the silliest thing in the world that a peer of the realm would be hunting for hairpins in a rickety coach with a mere Miss Delamere of Berkshire for company.

Having resettled her bonnet on her head, and tied the green ribbons beneath her left ear once more, she considered the circumstance of Bertaud having situated himself so openly, perhaps even purposely, at the White Hart.

"Shall we search out a lesser inn?" she asked.

Staverton shook his head.

"No?" she queried, startled. "Do you then intend for us to pass through and make our way to Bristol?"

Again, he shook his head, appearing determined.

"Staverton, you are not thinking—"

"It is the only way."

"But it is so very dangerous."

"Yes, I know. However, Bertaud made his presence known to us at Chippenham, so I see no reason to further the pretense that we are not trailing him. The White Hart is a fine, comfortable establishment; we will enjoy the best of fare, and the proximity of our enemy will allow my task to be accomplished expeditiously."

"Bertaud will not take it kindly."

"Of course not, but I am somehow convinced he chose the White Hart purposefully. May I direct the coachman?"

She nodded, her stomach tensing with fear. She felt it as well, a certain knowledge that this was the very best opportunity for Staverton to accomplish his mission. After all, Bristol was not so very far from Bath, and Bertaud could slip from them in the middle of the night, never to be seen again.

The remainder of the journey to the inn was spent in discussing how the switch was to occur. Though Anne suggested the notion that she and possibly her servants could create a diversion for his benefit, Staverton came to insist that he would wait until Bertaud left his rooms and afterward simply steal within to switch the documents.

"I know it seems less than heroic," he said teasingly, "and certainly not adventurous in the least, but I believe it will serve."

The scheme seemed perfectly reasonable to Anne, yet she could not believe that Bertaud would be so stupid as to leave the documents unattended in his room. When she said as much to Staverton, he shrugged. "We shall see," was all he would say.

Once arrived at Bath, Staverton directed the coachman to the Pump Room, where Shaw and Quince were informed of the plans. Within the following hour, Staverton secured lodgings for all three servants as well as two rooms, one for himself and one for Anne.

By the time Anne reached her bedchamber, she realized she was exhausted both from traveling and from having gotten so little sleep the night before. She fell into a sound doze from which she did not awaken until Staverton sent a servant, at the seven o'clock hour, to inform her that dinner would be served shortly.

She joined him in his rooms as together they partook of a fine meal consisting of broiled fowl with mushrooms, fried sole, broccoli, stewed eels, and a delicate almond cheesecake, all enjoyed with a flavorful East India Madeira.

During the repast, Anne waited for a scratching on the door announcing her servant, Shaw. Presently, he was stationed in proximity to the stairs in order to ascertain the very moment Bertaud left his bedchamber.

As it was, the spy did not leave his room until eight that evening, at which time Staverton did not hesitate to steal into the empty bedchamber. He found the leather valise in which the document packet was secreted just as he had hoped, and quickly removed his own packet from within the pocket of his coat. He was about to make the exchange when something began to nag at him, causing him to pause. He could feel that all was not as it should be. He felt it in his bones, an instinct only, but a powerful one.

After a quick moment's deliberation, he returned the true documents to Bertaud's packet, closed the valise and quietly left the spy's bedchamber. This, of course, meant the journey must continue, but he felt he had no choice other than to abide by his belief that something was amiss and that he must let Bertaud keep the potentially damaging documents a little while longer.

If the image of Wellington's army in Spain sprang to mind, and that he might be jeopardizing the lives of thousands of Englishmen by failing to act tonight, he quickly turned the thought aside. Now was not the time for indecision. He knew Bertaud, and nothing about the position of the valise in the bedchamber or his ease of access spoke of the spy's usual care in ordering his affairs.

He returned to Anne's bedchamber feeling grim.

"Is it finished?" she asked quietly, when he closed the door.

He shook his head.

"Whyever not?" she cried, rising to her feet from her chair at the dining table, precisely where he had left her ten minutes prior. "Did something happen? Did he return unexpectedly?"

Staverton shook his head a second time. "No, he did not. All was where I expected it to be; I even found the documents I was seeking. However, I could not be at ease. I felt something was wrong and I could do nothing less than leave his packet as I found it. I am sorry for it, Anne, but it would seem we will need to follow Bertaud to Bristol after all."

Anne released a deep sigh. "I had thought all would be settled and . . . and I was fearing that you would insist we board our coach this very evening and even now begin our return to Berkshire. Oh, Staverton, I did not want to do so."

He laughed, then crossed the room to her. "My darling," he murmured, letting his hand drift over her blond curls, which hung in beautiful waves past her shoulders. "I had been so disturbed by the knowledge that we must continue on to Bristol, that the game with Bertaud is not yet finished, that I might even now be risking your life. In truth, I had not thought how the same decision would keep us together perhaps another day or even two."

Anne smiled up at him, catching his arm with her hand and squeezing it fiercely. "If you were of a mind," she said urgently, "we could follow Bertaud to France, even to Paris, even to the court of Napoleon, just so long as we did not have to return to Sulhurst."

"I would be forced to marry you, then," he said, a warm light in his eye. "I might be allowed the liberty of traveling with you from London to Bath, or even Bristol. However, anything farther, such as Paris, would be unthinkable. Your father would undoubtedly hold a pistol to my throat to make his point."

Anne touched his cheek and smiled fondly into his face. "So you would marry me?" she queried.

He searched her eyes for a long, long moment. "Without a moment's hesitation," he responded softly. "Would you have me?"

She thought of Cassie. "We should not speak of such things," she whispered.

He smiled. "We should not speak at all."

With that, he gathered her up in his arms and showered her face with a dozen kisses. Anne savored this forbidden time with him, knowing with all her heart that within a matter of days she would be required to give him up forever.

On the following morning, Shaw informed Anne that Bertaud had left the White Hart just a few minutes earlier and had taken the road to Bristol, as was expected. She went to Staverton's room herself and found the earl sporting a corbeau-colored coat of sturdy drugget, which seemed oddly bulky. Otherwise, he was dressed to perfection in gleaming Hessians, pantaloons in the fashionable biscuit shade, and a neckcloth tied in what she recognized as the *trone d'amour*. His expression seemed stiff to her, even anxious.

"What is it?" she asked, closing the door behind her.

"My concerns of yesterday have returned to me."

"I see. What do you wish to do?"

"Anne, you will not like it, but I feel I must leave you here in Bath and finish this matter with Bertaud myself in

Bristol. The whole situation is like nothing I have ever before experienced. Bertaud himself is a dozen times more blatant in his actions, more hostile than I have ever known him. I fear that he intends the worst."

"You are right, I do not like it at all."

He took her hands, his expression earnest. "I refuse to risk your life one mile more on this journey. You are become so infinitely precious to me. I could not bear it were anything to happen to you."

Anne squeezed his hands in response. "Do not say it, nor even think it. I must go with you. I shall go with you. What if you should need me to—"

He laughed and leaned down to take her brusquely in his arms. "Do not say it, nor even think it, my darling."

Anne felt deeply in her heart that Staverton had made up his mind, that regardless of all they had been through she would not be journeying to Bristol. "You have hired a coach, have you not?"

He nodded. "Yes."

"You are determined, then."

Another nod, and she pulled away from him. "Very well. Do you intend to leave immediately?"

He shook his head. "I do not wish to meet him anywhere between here and Bristol. I mean to wait at least two hours before departing."

Anne was already plotting in her mind just how she was to follow Staverton to Bristol. He might have decided not to include her in the remainder of the trip, but that did not mean she would wait meekly at the White Hart to learn he had been injured or killed by the French madman.

However, there was no reason to say anything of the like to Staverton. Instead, she smiled. "Very well," she said amicably. "I can see that everything is decided. Why do we not take a stroll? The day is beautiful. There is not a cloud in the sky. We can pretend all is well and that neither of us has a care in the world."

He nodded, offering a half-smile. "Just as you wish. I believe it an excellent notion."

"Have you broken your fast?"

"I have had my toast and coffee, which is all I desire. And yourself?"

She smiled. "Hot chocolate, sufficient to sustain me until you must leave."

"Where then would you like to go?"

"The Orange Grove is so beautiful this time of year and perfect for walking about. Would that suit you?"

"Yes."

A few minutes later, Anne boarded the curricle Staverton had hired for the remainder of his trip to the port of Bristol. The Orange Grove was not far distant from the White Hart, so it was that she was soon walking beside Staverton, her arm hooked snugly with his beneath the fully-leaved sycamore trees which kept the gardens in a lovely, dappled shade. "Papa said these trees were probably brought to Britain by the Romans."

"Indeed?" he queried, sounding bored. "I had no notion."

She squeezed his arm. "Yes, I am full of absolutely fascinating information which I expect you to ply from me at every turn," she said facetiously.

He chuckled. "I did not mean to sound disinterested. I am, however, a trifle distracted."

"Just as you should be. Now, have I told you about the obelisk?"

"No, but I have the strongest suspicion you mean to impart all manner of knowledge to me."

"Yes," she answered crisply. "If for no other reason than to keep you comfortable for a time." She then launched into the history of the grove itself. "It was formerly known as the Gravel Walks. Beau Nash undertook improvements to the area, planting a great many trees as well as erecting the obelisk in commemoration of the visit of the prince of Orange in 1734."

"Then there are no orange trees?" he asked with mock seriousness.

"Do not be ridiculous," she countered. "Although Papa has grown them successfully in our hothouses for several years." She then asked, "Do we have time to saunter along North Parade?"

He shook his head. "No," he responded quietly. "As it is, I feel we should begin our return to the inn."

"Very well," she murmured.

As he guided her back in the direction of Staverton's carriage, Anne noticed that another curricle was drawn up behind his and that the driver was standing with his back to them on the opposite side of his vehicle. The man's hair was long and rather stringy.

She gasped and gripped Staverton's arm.

"Yes, I see him," he whispered. "I had thought, wished, that he would have waited until Bristol. Damn."

"I am frightened." She was scarcely thirty feet from the spy and saw the hatred in his black eyes as he turned and offered her a mockingly low bow.

Staverton disengaged her arm. "You must wait here," he said gently. "Never fear. Everything will be all right, I promise you, only pray stay where you are until he leaves."

"Oh, God," she whispered, tears of fright suddenly darting to her eyes. She obeyed him, for she knew what Bertaud was.

Staverton moved swiftly away from her, and at the same time Bertaud rounded the rear of his carriage, where he awaited the earl's approach. From where she stood, she could see that the spy held a pistol in hand, covered only slightly by a cloak slung over his arm.

"Did you think I did not have your movements watched last night, you fool?" Bertaud asked, his words just reaching her ears.

"Unfortunately, not until I had returned to Miss Delamere's room."

"I will have the packet you presently carry with you, or were you again so foolish as to think I would not search your own room before I departed. I credit you, however, for having secreted the documents on your person."

She watched Staverton reach inside his coat and toss his parcel at Bertaud's feet, who in turn threw the one in his possession at Staverton, striking him in the chest. "You might as well have these, since they are worthless."

Staverton stooped to pick up the packet and tucked it once more inside his coat.

It is done, Anne thought, a rush of elation sweeping over her. Bertaud was clearly none the wiser. Staverton had been right not to replace the documents last night.

"How did you know my purpose was to switch the documents?" he asked.

"Let us just say that I have many friends in England."

"I met three of them in Mildenhall."

Bertaud smiled. "They were useful, though I daresay I have your paramour to thank that the job was not completed as I had specifically requested."

"She is a courageous woman," Staverton said.

Anne was a little startled to hear herself referred to as little better than a courtesan. She even felt a blush creep up her cheeks. She wondered if that was how she had been viewed at the various inns along the way and decided she most certainly had!

"Or perhaps she is merely foolhardy," Bertaud countered. "Now the only question is, what am I to do with you today? I cannot have you following after me to Bristol."

Before Staverton could speak, however, a shot ripped through the air and Anne watched in mute horror as the earl fell back into the grassy sward beside the lane.

Bertaud smiled in much satisfaction. He quickly climbed aboard his curricle and drove away.

Anne's feet had been frozen to the earth until she saw that Bertaud was truly gone. Only then, as if by some instinct, did she run to Staverton's prone, quiet figure and fall down on her knees beside him.

"Staverton, Staverton!" she cried, touching his arms and chest and shoulders. She could see that the front of his coat was charred. "Oh, dear God, you are killed. You are killed! Whatever am I to do without—" She watched his eyes open rather abruptly. "Staverton!" she cried again, taking his shoulders and shaking him gently. "Can you hear me? Speak to me, my darling!"

He blinked several times. "I believe I struck my head," he murmured, after a moment. "Is he gone?"

She nodded. "Yes, but you must lie still. You have been shot in the chest. Your coat is smoking." She pulled at the burnt fabric and burned the tips of her fingers on something hot that appeared to be lodged within the fabric of the earl's waistcoat.

Staverton reached over and grabbed her wrist. "You must show me the documents in the packet quickly." He winced. "Now, Anne! I must know if we have truly won the day."

She obeyed him unwillingly and secured the packet from inside his coat pocket. Her fingers were trembling and tears bit at her eyes as she removed the documents from the leather packet. She unfolded them swiftly and held them up for Staverton to see. His gaze scanned line after line and within but a few seconds he drew in a deep breath and once more rested his head on the grass.

"It is done," he murmured, smiling.

To Anne's amazement, he then sat up. "We must get to my curricle and leave before we can be questioned about this incident."

"Do you think you can stand?" she asked, stunned.

"Yes, yes, of course I can." He rose swiftly to his feet.

She moved away from him, throwing her arms wide, not knowing what to think of him. For a terrible moment she believed he was, indeed, a god from Olympus, that he was immortal and that the pistol ball which surely had struck him had had no effect. "I do not understand!" she cried.

"Come!" he shouted. "Before the others arrive."

She glanced over her shoulder and saw that a number of people, having heard the pistol shot from the distance of the Orange Grove as well as North Parade, were hurrying toward them.

He grasped her arm and without seeking her permission, rushed them both to his curricle. He assisted her in gaining her seat, untied the reins, then clambered aboard the carriage himself.

Anne watched his movements in utter shock.

A moment more and the vehicle was moving at a clipping pace down the street.

"Do you drive?" he asked Anne.

"What?"

"Do you drive? Are you skilled with the ribbons?"

She glanced at his hands. "Yes, of course," she said, utterly bewildered. Why was he not dead?

He thrust the reins at her, which she took, diverting her attention to the hazards of directing a pair of horses down a busy city street.

"Good God this is hot," he said, unbuttoning his coat and afterward his waistcoat.

She glanced at him. "Do you mean to undress in the middle of the street? Only . . . only, where is the blood?"

He glanced at her and winked. "Careful of that cart trying to pull out just now."

Anne once more attended to her team, coaxing them skillfully away from the cart, whose driver appeared, when she passed him, to have been drinking more ale than he ought to have that morning.

She turned back to Staverton still utterly bewildered by his inexplicable conduct. "You are not well," she stated at last. "I must get you to a surgeon at once. You must be delirious from your injuries."

He turned to stare at her and then began to laugh quite heartily, far more than he ought. She was now convinced he was as mad as Bedlam, that the recent experience of having been shot had altered his mind. He had been shot in the chest and should not even be able to sit, let alone laugh hysterically, which is what he seemed to be doing, and why did he continue to undress?

A glistening of red at his chest nearly set her swooning. Surely, the blood from his wound had now soaked his white shirt. Since by this time they were well away from North Parade, she decided to draw the curricle to the side of the street and pull her team to a stop.

She put her hand on his shoulder. "Dearest, you must calm yourself and cease laughing. It cannot be good for your wound; only tell me, are you not in some pain?" She had heard stories over the years of severely injured people performing remarkable acts of bravery for a brief time following their injury. However, she had never heard of someone laughing themselves into a delirium after having been shot full in the chest!

"I . . . I am sorry, Anne!" he cried. "Oh, pray do not look at me in that dreadfully serious manner." He went off again, doubling over in laughter, seemingly unable to stop.

She took up the reins once more, intending to drive him to the infirmary on the instant. Whatever the reason he had fallen into a fit of hysterics, she knew the euphoria of the moment could not last, particularly since he was bleeding into his shirt.

However, before she could move her horses but a few feet, he gripped her hands and forced them onto her lap. "Whoa!" he called to the team between whoops of laughter.

By now, the earl was wiping his eyes. "Do but wait, Anne," he said, out of breath. "No, no! Leave the reins alone. I am laughing because . . . because I said the very same things to you just a few days ago when your gown was covered with raspberries. Do but look." He spread apart his charred coat and waistcoat, revealing a breadth of equally charred, red shiny fabric. He removed the pistol ball, which had been embedded deeply within.

She stared at the now harmless bullet and could not credit

what she was seeing. "I do not understand!" she exclaimed, afterward probing the vest gently. "Good heavens! What is this? I remember thinking this morning that your coat was rather thick, but I never suspected that you might be wearing some sort of vest capable of protecting you from Bertaud's pistol. What is it made of?"

"Taffeta. At least twelve layers folded."

"And it truly stopped the bullet?"

He handed it to her.

"It is still warm." She fingered it for a moment, then looked up at him. "You are not dying?"

He shook his head. "Not even a little bit."

At that she fell against his shoulder and began to cry. "You might have been killed!"

"But I was not," he said, holding her tenderly.

After a moment she lifted her gaze to him. "What if he had shot you in the head?" she asked sensibly, sniffing away her tears.

Staverton laughed. "He most certainly would have missed for he is not a great shot. I was perfectly confident he would aim for my chest."

Anne suddenly laughed, but in a rather crazed manner. "Oh, dear God, when I saw him lift his pistol and watched it flame, I thought, no, *I knew*, you were dead!"

"But I am not dead," he whispered. "Anne, you must remember that my decision to be of service to my country, like the choice of any good soldier, always brings with it the risk of death, however unlikely in my situation. You must know that to be true. Had I perished today, then I would have expected you to have shipped my remains to my mother, how was it you phrased it? Oh yes, with a note pinned to my hat stating that I had died being very brave."

She nodded, smiling tenderly at the notion he would repeat something she had said to him not so long ago. "Of course I would have done so," she said. "It is just that, well, you have become particularly dear to me."

"As you have to me," he returned, smiling and petting

her face. He kissed her suddenly, which caused her to blush quite deeply.

"My lord," she said. "We are in the middle of the street!"

He took the reins from her. "You are right. I should wait until we are returned to the inn before taking you in my arms again."

Anne could not tear her gaze from his face. Essentially, she had lost him and he had returned to her all within the space of a few minutes. She was still reeling from the image of Bertaud tossing his packet at Staverton's chest, then firing his pistol. Another thought intruded. "I have just now realized that you have fulfilled your mission."

He nodded. "I have, indeed."

She narrowed her gaze at him for a moment. "Staverton, did you, even from last night, believe Bertaud meant to assault you at the Orange Grove?"

"Not hardly," he said. "In truth, I thought we would enact the scene you just witnessed, or something very much like it, at some point along the road to Bristol. I am still unsettled by the fact that you might have been injured today."

"He had but one pistol," she said, "and there were far too many people about to allow him to reload and shoot at me. I am become convinced I was in no particular danger today."

He smiled and shook his head.

"Why do you laugh at me?"

"Do you know what a mystery you are?"

"I cannot imagine what you mean," she responded.

"I do not know a single lady of my acquaintance, who upon seeing a man shot, would have done anything other than fall into a profound swoon. You, however, began searching my clothing for the pool of blood you certainly expected to find, and now this! Anne, how can you say you were not in the least amount of danger?"

"I did not say *the least amount of danger.* I said, *no particular danger.*"

He chuckled. "That is precisely what I am trying to say. I

cannot believe any of the ladies I know would have been so prosaic about Bertaud having shot at me."

"Perhaps not," she said, smiling gently. "But we shall never know, shall we? Only tell me, the packet Bertaud threw at your feet, did it truly contain the documents you needed to retrieve?"

"Yes, the very ones."

Anne settled back in her seat. For several minutes, as the earl weaved his way through the traffic on the return to the White Hart, she reviewed all that had happened and found herself deeply content. She was proud of Staverton and thought the vest a very clever notion, about which she inquired.

"I had my tailor create the vest, but the idea was not mine originally," he responded. "I had heard rumors that Marie Antoinette and Louis XVI purportedly wore them for protection during the Paris uprisings before their respective deaths."

"How interesting. Papa will be fascinated to learn of it." Thinking of her father lowered her spirits quite suddenly. "I have just realized that my first adventure is come to an end and we must now return to Berkshire."

She heard his sigh, a very deep one, and noted the perplexion on his face. She felt a lump in her throat and worked very hard to resist a new spate of tears, which she could feel even now forming at the back of her eyes in little pinpricks.

The remainder of the journey to the White Hart was a silent one. Parting with Staverton at her bedchamber door, Anne entered the chamber slowly, knowing that within the hour she would be leaving Bath and returning to Sulhurst, where she would surprise Cassie by bringing Staverton to kneel at her feet. Closing the door, she began slowly the process of packing her portmanteaus.

THIRTEEN

Once within the coach, Anne's dampened spirits rose as a wonderfully errant thought struck her. She turned toward Staverton and looked at him in a purposeful manner. "Is it so very far to Gretna Green from here?" she queried.

"No farther than from Berkshire, I daresay. A little perhaps, but not much."

"I should like to see Scotland," she hinted breathlessly. "I have always longed to see our wild, northern parts."

"I was there once when I was a lad," he confessed. His smile was crooked so that she could be in no doubt he understood her meaning.

She smiled in return and fingered the lapel of his coat. "Scotland must be absolutely lovely this time of year, do you not think so?"

"Undoubtedly," he murmured.

She frowned slightly, wondering why it was he did not take up her hint. She tried again. "If a person wished to go to Scotland, to direct Jack Coachman to take the road to Gloucestershire instead of Berkshire, another person would not refuse a sudden, unexpected trip. I promise you, she would not."

Hope pounded in her head.

He took up her hand and placed a kiss on her gloved fingers. "I have learned so much from you, Anne, in these four magical days. You have instructed me in matters of honor, of duty, and of kindness. I have been your student."

She felt she understood precisely what it was he was saying and a terrible panic assailed her. "Teachers are frequently found to be wrong, you know." She averted her gaze, for she felt tears forming at the back of her eyes.

He caught her chin and turned her toward him. "Not this time. I must do my duty and speak to your cousin as quickly as I am able."

"Staverton, I was a fool to have kidnapped you in the first place. Why must you now listen to anything I have told you? I am merely a criminal who ought to be hanged for abducting you as I have."

"Anne, I love you so very dearly and I always shall, you must believe that."

"We could go to Scotland," she pleaded, taking firm hold of both his lapels. "I—I could explain to Cassie that—"

"Never," he stated, taking her hands off his coat and holding them firmly. "I have waited all my life to meet a woman of honor, and now that you have arrived I would not for the world sully your reputation or your spirit by being married to you out-of-hand and in the face of your cousin's heartbreak. I can think of nothing more despicable nor more unworthy of you than this. No, when you marry, you shall wear a cloud of lace and orange blossoms and have your vows sanctified by a man of the cloth. Nothing less will do for my Anne."

Her throat ached. She could not even speak. She turned her face away from his entirely, struggling to keep from bursting into a bout of tears. After a time, she withdrew her hands from his warm grasp and set her gaze resolutely out the window.

Staverton did not attempt to comfort her. Indeed, there was nothing more he could say. Packing for the return trip to Sulhurst had given him sufficient time to consider the unhappy nature of their circumstances. He had concluded that he could never marry Anne until he had addressed Cassaundra Bradley and discerned the nature of her sentiments toward him. If she truly loved him, he would have to do that which was honorable given his hapless conduct in Brighton only a fortnight past, and offer for her as was only right. Indeed, regardless of how Anne essentially had begged him to elope with her to Gretna Green, he knew her sufficiently to suppose that even had they embarked on the journey, her own conscience would have prevented the coach from proceeding much beyond Shropshire. Not even to the lakes, he mused sadly, and yet how much he would have enjoyed simply carting her off to Gretna Green.

The journey to Berkshire was broken at Marlborough. Anne retired for the night immediately after dinner, having no desire to suffer further the supreme torture of being in such close proximity with Staverton yet knowing she could never possess him. He, in turn, relinquished her to her bed without the smallest protest, a circumstance which caused her heart to shrivel. Already, he was forgetting her, just as he ought, of course, but he might have spared her pride a little and waited until he had returned her to her father before evincing so little interest in her.

As she climbed between the sheets, she found sleep eluding her. Even though she was exhausted from traveling and wearied from trying to envision a happy life without Staverton, she tossed and turned upon her bed hour after hour. One moment she would be mentally praising his lordship for his honor and determination to do what was right, but with the very next thought would come an irritation that he had dismissed her after dinner with but a careless, "Good night, Anne." Why had he felt obliged to be so considerate, so gentlemanly, when what she really wanted was to find herself locked in his arms once more? Cruel, cruel man!

Yet not cruel, for he was going to marry her cousin, which was just as he should.

What an odious man not to have kissed her. A devil, surely!

Oh, but Cassie would be so happy.

Yet, she would be so miserable. She would not attend their wedding. She had rather die! It was all Staverton's fault. Why had he seen fit to flirt with Cassie in Brighton? Yet, if he had not done so, she would never have kidnapped him nor come to know the truth about who he really was.

She flopped onto her stomach and pressed her pillow over the back of her head. Cursed journey to Bath! Cursed, cursed journey back to Berkshire! If only she could sleep!

By the time the morning arrived, Anne felt as though her mattress had been the worst-sprung coach in the world and that she had been traveling on ill-paved roads at a breakneck speed hour upon hour, all the while attempting to sleep.

She arose from her bed, therefore, with every muscle aching and her nerves in shreds. If once or twice she spoke rather sharply to Staverton, she quickly apologized. However, the third time she snapped at him, this time for not opening the door to the coach quickly enough, she met his concerned gaze and promptly burst into tears.

"Anne," he murmured, taking her in his arms once they were both inside the coach.

She held him tightly. "My heart is breaking and now I have taken to wounding you, and what is worse—I am become a watering pot!"

He chuckled, which only served to deepen her sobs and cause her tears to flow in a veritable flood.

After a time, her sadness lessened and she disengaged herself from the comfort of his arms. However, from that moment until they reached Hungerford, she dabbed at her eyes intermittently.

"You should never have kidnapped me," he stated sternly

as the coach slowed in its approach to the village, where hopefully her own coach awaited her.

"Of course I should not have," she returned curtly, her nerves still seriously frayed.

"You needn't come the crab. This is your fault, after all."

Anne turned to stare at him, wondering why he should suddenly become accusing and mean-spirited. She noted a certain devilment in his eyes and felt her heart quail. Did he mean to bamboozle her somehow, for he was not behaving at all like himself.

Staverton sat upright, his spirits soaring quite suddenly for he had finally achieved a plan which would hopefully bring their disastrous situation to an end.

He had been sorely distressed from the moment the coach quit the inn yard at the White Hart in Bath at the mere thought of having to live without Anne for the rest of his life. Yet he knew he had an important duty to fulfill where Miss Bradley was concerned. The real question was, how was he to accomplish the latter without actually marrying the chit?

"So tell me," he probed as the rickety coach drew into the inn yard. "Is your cousin fair-minded?"

"If you mean my cousin, Miss Bradley, yes, she is entirely selfless and worthy of you in every particular."

"I can tell by your tone you are yet in a sad temper. I hope you do not mean to continue so, for we are still many miles from Sulhurst." He knew he was pressing her, even taunting her, but he wished no more tears from her. Besides, it was far more enjoyable to see her lovely green eyes flashing sparks of anger at him than seeping with sadness.

Good God. What she could not understand and what he was wholly unwilling to explain to her was that his own heart was as near to breaking as her own. So much so, that he feared were he to continue comforting her, he would lose his courage entirely. He might just be persuaded to take the

North Road and see for himself what it was to be married
over the anvil.

His curtness had its effect. Anne's tears dried and in its
place was a determination to ignore him. *Just as well,*
Staverton thought, as together they descended the coach in
order to examine the repairs which had been made to the
shattered window of her far more elegant and comfortable
conveyance. When the new window was pronounced accept-
able, Shaw and Quince, now sporting her father's livery once
more, made the exchange of luggage from the creaking ill-
sprung vehicle to Anne's restored coach.

Staverton watched Anne smile as she climbed aboard her
coach. Such a beautiful smile! His thoughts skipped forward. In such a vehicle, a trip to Scotland would be a delight.
But what was he thinking! As he took up his seat next to
her, he steeled his heart. When she exclaimed over her gratitude that her coach had been repaired so tidily, he merely
murmured something incoherent, lowered his hat over his
eyes and after slumping in his seat, pretended to fall asleep.
However, because her coach was so delightfully sprung, he
actually did drift off in his slumber somewhere between
Newbury and Thatcham.

When he awoke, the hostler at Thatcham was bringing
round two fresh pairs and Anne was nowhere to be seen. He
descended the coach himself and stretched his neck, back
and legs. A tankard of ale suddenly seemed precisely what
he desired and he ventured into the taproom where the landlord was more than happy to oblige him.

He learned Anne was in the parlor enjoying a cup of tea
and a fine lemon cake his wife had made only that morning.
He debated joining her, but for the present decided that the
sight of her would only serve to tear at his heart further. He
had every hope he could win the day, however there was
still a chance Miss Bradley would prove only too eager to
keep the prize Anne would soon be laying at her feet.

When Anne emerged from the parlor, he had long since

drained his tankard and was now exchanging hunting anecdotes with the local vicar.

Anne saw his face lit with laughter, something it had rarely been since leaving Bath, and her heart simply turned over in her breast. He was inordinately handsome, particularly when his features were filled with amusement. She loved him so very dearly.

She had been grateful he had fallen into a doze just past Newbury and that she had been able to sit and enjoy a cup of tea—well, three to be precise—alone in the parlor. She had needed the time apart from Staverton to adjust her thoughts, and certainly her attitude, which had become wretched, indeed, full of self-pity and even hostility.

She approached him now with a half-smile. He turned and she watched as the laughter stilled on his face. She would not allow him to become unhappy again in her company. "Come," she said. "We have but a few miles and then we are home."

He smiled in response, following her lead. He offered his arm and escorted her back to the coach. She did not apologize for her former conduct since she had apologized far too many times already without having been able to effect a change in her conduct. Instead, she proved her intent of behaving more appropriately and certainly with greater decorum by entering into a lively discussion with him of estate husbandry. Her father's property was quite large and she had been in the habit since times out of mind of listening to his discussions with his bailiff and even traversing his estate on horseback whenever a major change in the landscape had been presented.

As the coach pulled once more onto the highway, she began, "Papa had at one time considered draining the marshy lands in some of the acreage north of the house. I enjoyed becoming informed concerning every aspect of the proposed project, from how much gravel and earth would be required to build up the low areas and drain the land to the effect such drastic changes would have on the wildlife in the region since the marshes are a wonderful resource for fowl."

"Stewardship of the land, even if it is merely a plot outside one's kitchen door, is a marvelous thing," he said. "What was decided?"

"To keep the marsh. There were a variety of birds which lived there and would perhaps disappear entirely from that part of Berkshire were we to drain the land and turn it into another field of wheat."

She asked about his estates of which he was in possession of no less than three fine properties, not including a hunting lodge in Leicestershire, nor his town house in Grosvenor Square.

"So, once you return to Sweetwater Lodge," he queried, "what do you mean to do?"

She smiled. "I happened to be thinking of the very thing," she said, "while I was sipping my tea at Thatcham. I believe I shall take a journey around the world. I certainly have sufficient funds to make such a trip and mean to hire for myself a very fine ship and an excellent crew, which I understand is most important, besides a notable captain. I shall become an explorer, perhaps even discover an island or two."

"Anne Island," he mused. "I think it will serve."

"Oh, no," she remarked, smiling. "Lydia, after my mother."

His expression grew very gentle, even loving, and Anne felt herself tumbling once more into the vast tenderness of his gaze.

She looked away hastily and countered the strong feelings which had swelled within her by remarking on the weather. "I believe it shall rain before long."

He said nothing more, but quietly took hold of her hand and did not release it until they had actually arrived at the Grey Castle Inn at Sulhurst.

Jack Coachman called for Mr. Delamere's horses, which

Anne had seen stabled at the inn for the purpose of awaiting her return to Sulhurst. She could not believe they had finally arrived and that very soon, Staverton would simply slip from her life forever.

When the horses were nearly in harness, he said, "I believe I would like to call upon your cousin before we complete the remainder of the journey to your house. Would that be agreeable to you?"

The notion was so horrific and unexpected, that she turned to stare at him in utter astonishment. "Y-you want me to come with you?"

"Well, yes," he stated. "There is much we both must answer for to your cousin. I believe she is entitled to know that we have been traveling together, without benefit of a chaperon, for the last six days. If she has questions of one or either of us before I lay my proposal before her, she ought to be permitted to ask them."

"You are right," she agreed, her heart sinking clear to her toes. "Of course, you are right."

"Does she reside far from the village?"

"No. One mile only, to the west."

The longest mile in Anne's entire existence. She suffered acute feelings of anxiety and a lowness of spirit which she had never before known. She hoped with all her heart that dear Cassie had perhaps fallen into a decline since she last saw her then chided herself under a desperate weight of guilt for harboring such a wretched thought as wishing her cousin dead!

I am a horrible person, she thought.

"Are you feeling well, Anne?" he asked. "You are become quite pale."

"Pay no heed to me, Staverton." She straightened her shoulders and forced herself to count the number of birds in the hedges as the coach moved toward her doom.

* * *

Once at Cassaundra's, Anne learned that her parents were not at home. However, Cassie knew well how to entertain her guests, even a man who had spurned her affections in Brighton. She ordered refreshments to be brought to the terrace, which overlooked a duck pond happily alive with at least a dozen quacking birds. The garden sparkled in the sun and had not the purpose of the visit been so disastrous to Anne's happiness, she rather thought the setting could not have been more idyllic.

"How did you enjoy your raspberries, Anne?" Cassie asked, sipping her ratafia.

Anne stared at her for a long moment. Of course her cousin could not have known what had happened six days past in the lane just beyond Sulhurst. "I lost them all," she said. "I, er, tripped, the basket flew into the air, the raspberries went everywhere and I landed squarely upon the majority of them. The housekeeper was quite upset because if you recall—"

Cassie laughed suddenly. "Because you were wearing your *white* muslin! Oh, dear. She must have been in hysterics." She turned to Staverton. "For if you must know, Mr. Delamere's housekeeper is meticulous where the laundry is concerned."

Anne began to relax. Cassie appeared to excellent advantage in a gown of a light-blue patterned silk and several fresh white rosebuds tucked into her brown curls, which had been drawn into a lovely knot atop her head. She was utterly fetching, her round blue eyes seeming to glow with happiness. And why shouldn't they, since she must know by now that Anne had brought Staverton to become her bridegroom.

Cassie would make a charming countess, Anne thought, and an excellent wife.

At that moment, Staverton rose to his feet. "Might I beg a word in private with you, Miss Bradley? There is something most particular I wish to say to you."

Cassie seemed quite surprised. "I shouldn't, that is, I—" She broke off and stared at Anne, appearing bewildered.

Anne nodded encouragingly.

"Yes, of course," Cassie murmured.

"The rose garden is not far," Staverton suggested. He offered his arm to her.

Cassie took it, lifting her sweet gaze to his face and smiling warmly upon him. "I am very glad you came today," she said, "for there is something I would say to you as well."

As they moved down the steps, Anne felt a coldness drift over her heart like nothing she had ever experienced before. Tears brimmed in her eyes. Here was the result of her plan of just a few days past, that she would bring the Infidel back to her cousin and insist he wed her. How wonderfully she had succeeded in her object! How infinitely sad she was that she had been able to do so. She remembered her father's admonitions that she refrain from meddling. How wise her papa seemed in this moment!

She wished that she could look away from Staverton and Cassie, for she could scarcely bear to watch what she was certain would be her cousin's exhilaration and triumph. However, she could no more avert her gaze than she could stop breathing. She had to watch, to learn what the result of her efforts had truly been. She could not hear what they said to one another, but she could see their expressions, which of the moment were quite serious.

Staverton looked into Cassaundra's sweet face and felt all the weight of his ridiculous conduct toward her. "Will you ever forgive me for my conduct in Brighton?" he asked sincerely.

"Wh-what?" she asked softly. "Forgive you? I do not understand."

"Your cousin has helped me to comprehend how badly I behaved toward you. I held an unjustified belief that you had set your cap at me, that your affections were not engaged, just your firm desire of becoming my countess, and therefore—"

She lowered her gaze. "You have spoken truly," she said, interrupting him.

"What?" he queried, stunned. "But I thought—?"

"You have spoken truly. I—I did set my cap at you, though I convinced myself I had not. I believed I loved you when in truth, I wished merely to be your wife. Of course you are remarkably handsome, which made it easier to persuade my conscience that I was in love with you when I was not." She looked up at him, her eyes full of regret. "So you see, you need not beg for my forgiveness. Indeed, I feel it is I who must beg for yours. Will you forgive me for not being more sensible and certainly for not being more honorable?"

"Good God," he murmured.

"Am I beyond forgiveness?" she asked anxiously.

"I had not expected this. Indeed, you must hear me out. When I suspected your affections were not engaged, I behaved abominably, pursuing you with the sole intention of wounding you, which I know I did."

She smiled faintly. "Only my pride. Don't you see?"

"Even so, that cannot excuse my conduct."

"Nor mine," she returned boldly. "Shall we perhaps both admit we were at fault and let the matter rest there?"

He was so taken aback, he did not know what to say, except, "Yes, I suppose we should."

"So tell me, have you tumbled in love with my cousin?"

His mouth fell agape and he could do little more than nod dumbly. "She kidnapped me and I suppose I was done for even at that very moment."

"She kidnapped you?" Miss Bradley asked, obviously dumbfounded.

"Yes, for when she learned of your sufferings and therefore came to believe your heart had been wounded without cause, she became your champion. She did not tell you the whole story of the raspberries. You see . . ." He proceeded to give as many of the details of the kidnapping as he could without actually speaking of Bertaud, ending with, "I decided to stay the night at the Grey Castle secretly hoping to see her again, and it was the next morning she arrived with pistols and rope in hand, her finely sprung carriage and her avowed intention of kidnapping me for the purpose of marrying you."

Miss Bradley covered her lips, hiding her smile. "Oh, dear. How very much like Anne to do something so ridiculous. But why were you then gone from Sulhurst for so long a time?"

He hesitated, not knowing precisely what to say. "We were on a sort of adventure which involved the friend with whom I was racing. We finally concluded the adventure in Bath and then returned here."

Miss Bradley narrowed her eyes. "I perceive there is something you cannot tell me. However, do you not see that you have compromised my cousin terribly?"

"It was she who kidnapped me, Miss Bradley, and though I mentioned the danger her reputation might suffer were we seen together in this manner, she said she did not give a fig for it."

"That is my dear Anne," she stated again, smiling. "Well, in all of this I have but one thing to say. When you wed her, you will have many difficulties. She is wholly spoiled and intent on having her way in everything."

"You have guessed at my intentions even though I came here today prepared to offer for you."

"I would have had to reject your proposal regardless," she said. "I am already betrothed. Harry Chamberlayne and I are to be married in a month's time."

"That's wonderful!" he cried.

She laughed. "Thank you, but somehow I am convinced you are expressing more relief for yourself than happiness for me."

"I am also horridly spoiled as well, and also intent on my own way in everything."

"Then I predict you and Anne will deal famously so long as you give her many adventures, or do you know that already? She will not be content to be a London hostess. She will chafe at having such a bit in her mouth and will likely plague you to death."

He dismissed this easily. "I believe our first adventure will be aboard a sailing vessel."

"You will be very happy together."

"I believe so," he responded. How happy he was! However, a truly reprehensible notion came into his mind. "Would you engage in a little playacting, Miss Bradley? You see, I have never quite known just how to punish your cousin for having kidnapped me in the first place, but I think I do now."

"There is such a devil's glint in your eye," she said, "and I know I should refuse you but, in truth, I should be delighted. When I was fifteen and quite enamored of one of my own footmen, I was preening by the duck pond, hoping to gain his attention, when Anne pushed me in. I was never more mortified and have been waiting for just such a moment as this to repay her."

"Give me both your hands then."

Anne watched Cassaundra place her hands in Staverton's and all her hope faded to nothing, particularly when, after a minute more of conversation, her cousin flung her arms about the earl's neck. Her throat hurt so severely from suppressed tears that it was all she could do to keep her countenance. However, when the pair turned toward her with linked arms and began their approach, she forced herself to dwell on the happiness now shrouding her dear Cassaundra. She would think only of Cassie's happiness, nothing more. She would not think about how Cassie would likely bore the earl to tears within a fortnight of their wedding, or how she would never be content with his being a spy, or how her greatest ambition was to create a new species of rose for her rose garden. No, she would think of none of these things, only how happy her cousin looked in this moment.

"It is all settled!" Cassie cried. She turned to Staverton. "But now you must take Anne home and do come tomorrow evening to meet my father. He will wish to speak with you, of course."

He took her hand in his and kissed her fingers. "Until tomorrow evening," he murmured.

Anne rose to her feet and attempted a smile. She heard a choking sound as Cassaundra suddenly caught her up in a warm embrace. "How happy you have made me today," she cried. Anne felt her cousin begin to sob and was not surprised when Cassie disappeared suddenly into the house.

Anne glanced up at Staverton, whose expression was inscrutable. "Sh-she often cries when she is happy."

"I see," he murmured. "Well, I suppose I must see you home then."

"Or if you wish, since your curricle is at the Grey Castle, I could return you there."

"On no account," he responded sternly. "I feel I must speak with your father if nothing more than to explain your absence. It is the only honorable thing to be done, although if he desired to force a marriage, there is nothing he could do now."

She shook her head. "No, since you are betrothed to Cassie."

Staverton gave no other response than to suggest they leave at once for Sweetwater Lodge.

FOURTEEN

By the time the coach turned onto the long avenue of beeches leading to Sweetwater Lodge, Anne felt so lost she could hardly breathe.

"I wish you to know," Staverton said, taking hold of her hand, "that I believe with all my heart that everything has turned out for the best."

She glanced sharply toward him. "You do?" she asked in a small voice.

How was this possible, she wondered. Was Staverton of such a quixotic nature that he could have professed his love for her in one moment then, upon offering for Cassie, have decided she would do as well? Anne was hurt and utterly mystified. And why on earth must the man seem so at his ease and so contented of the moment? It was not right!

"I have learned so much from you," he continued softly. "I only wish that I had been under your tutelage sooner so that I might not have wounded Miss Bradley, that is, *Cassaundra,* as I did."

"But everything is settled between you. Surely, she can have no regrets. Surely, after having received your proposal, she did not accuse you of your former, inconsiderate treatment of her? Surely she is not something other than *aux anges!*"

"Why, my dear, you sound a trifle peevish, although perhaps you will not be so when you learn that she apologized to me."

"Indeed?" Anne queried, stunned. "Whatever for?"

"Well, she admitted to having set her cap at me."

"She did?" Anne was utterly dumbfounded. "And you did not find this repugnant?"

"Of course I did, but her countenance was so humble, so abject, that I found myself appreciative and forgiving."

"How noble of you," she said, dampeningly.

"I must sound like a coxcomb."

"Yes, you do," she agreed repressively.

"Well, I suppose I am not completely cured of all my flaws. However, I daresay a few years of matrimony will work them out sufficiently."

Anne caught her breath. She did not know what to say, particularly since Staverton seemed so flippant, so careless in everything he was saying to her. She averted her gaze and stared out the window. She desperately wanted the conversation to end.

However, as the coach drew before the front door, he queried, "Is there no apology you wish to make to me, Anne?"

She cast him a scathing glance. "For what?" she asked.

Shaw jumped down from his place at the back of the coach, which set the vehicle to rocking slightly. As he opened the door, Staverton leaned close to her and whispered, "Why, for kidnapping me, of course."

Anne was irritated by the entire exchange and refused to answer him. Instead, she quit the carriage and immediately began issuing orders to her footmen and coachman. "No, keep his lordship's baggage aboard, he will be staying at the Grey Castle Inn."

"On the contrary!" he proclaimed as he jumped down quite merrily from the coach to land beside her. "I hope to spend the night here, provided Mr. Delamere will agree to it."

"And to what am I to agree?" a masculine voice sounded from the doorway.

Anne glanced toward the house and saw that her father had just arrived on the threshold. "Papa," she cried, experiencing a profound sense of relief at the sight of him as well as a rush of affection. She found she was anxious to be rid of Staverton, particularly since he was behaving so oddly. Her only present desire was to have her father comfort her in her profound misery.

However, it would seem she must first make a proper introduction of her traveling companion before she could send him away. "Papa, I wish to make you known to the earl of Staverton."

"Staverton!" he cried, stepping forward to offer his hand to the earl. "Of course I know who you are. I've seen you box at Jackson's a dozen times! Hah! I broke your record at Manton's, though. Did you know of it?"

"Indeed, sir, I did."

"How is it you know my Anne?" He gestured from one to the other.

"I nearly ran her down in the lane a half mile or so from Sulhurst."

"Ah, so you are the fellow! She told me about it at dinner, what was it, a sennight past? Well, this is serendipitous, what?" He turned toward Anne. "And you were a sly boots, my sweet. So it was Staverton, after all, and I see you've brought him home."

"No, Papa, he was just leaving," she said firmly, glaring at the earl. "He means to stay at the Grey Castle."

"Nonsense. I insist he stay here, if it is what he wishes."

"It is," Staverton said. "This was precisely what I had been hoping you would agree to when you appeared in the doorway. Unfortunately, I have the distinct impression your daughter wishes me anywhere but at Sweetwater."

"Pay no heed to her," he said, patting the earl on the shoulder. "I can see she's taken a pet, probably over some trifle. But never mind that. You know, my Anne is a great heiress. You would do well to marry her. Have you thought about it, my lord?"

"Actually . . ." Staverton began.

"He is betrothed to Cassie," Anne interjected hastily.

"Indeed?" her father cried, turning to look at each of them in turn as they moved into the entrance hall. "But I thought—well! This is interesting news. Cassie's a good sort. I daresay you will be very happy. My offer still stands, however. You may stay under my roof if you wish for it."

"Yes, I do," he stated irrevocably. "Anne has told me a great deal about your estate and I have a few questions about the marshes you decided not to drain. One of my properties has a similar lowland and we have been in a quandary as to what . . ."

Anne stayed by the door and watched as the two men put their heads together and meandered in the direction of her father's study. Before she could protest even in the slightest, the door closed and she was left standing in the entrance hall among a pile of luggage.

Sometime later, Anne viewed her elegantly piled blond tresses in the looking glass of her dressing table. She was fully dressed for dinner in a gown of white figured silk. A few minutes earlier, she had sent her maid to discover if the gentlemen had yet descended the stairs to the drawing room in preparation for dinner, and she had just returned.

"What do you mean they are still closeted in my father's study?" she asked, meeting her maid's gaze in the mirror. "But it has been three hours! Is not dinner ready to be served?"

"Very nearly so," her maid responded. "Oh, I hear the men now. They are just mounting the stairs."

"Quickly, Marie!" Anne cried, whirling around. "Close

the door! I will not be seen to be waiting for them, for either of them!"

"What do ye think is afoot, miss?" her longtime maid—and at times, confidante—queried. "Shaw thinks his lordship means to offer for ye. Would not that be wonderful?"

"He cannot," she said, shaking her head sadly. "He has already offered for and been accepted by my cousin." Glancing at her maid, she realized the young woman was staring at her in some perplexion. "What is it?"

"By your cousin, do ye perchance mean Miss Bradley?"

"Of course."

"This is very odd, miss."

"What?"

"I was given to understand by Cook, who had it by the milliner's wife, who is sister to one of the upper maids at yer cousin's house, that she is to be leg-shackled to Mr. Chamberlayne."

"To Harry?" she asked. "No, that is impossible. There must be some mistake."

"Harry Chamberlayne, it is," Marie reiterated. "The milliner's wife is never wrong about gossip. Well, hardly never."

"I do not understand," Anne murmured. "Cassie told me that Harry had proposed to her in Brighton and she had refused him."

"Cook said it was all settled three days past. Miss Bradley came across him sudden-like while walking near his property, they fell into conversation, and the deed was done, quick-like."

"Then . . . oh, she cannot be so bad as to be engaged to two men at the same moment!"

"Beg pardon, miss?"

"Never mind," she responded.

Anne thought back to the events earlier that afternoon while Staverton and Cassaundra were conversing in the rose garden. She had watched her cousin, as well as Lord Staverton, carefully. She was certain there was a point when he mouthed the words, *will you marry me,* and he was accepted. She was certain of it, particularly since her cousin had actually embraced him and later returned to the terrace beaming with joy. *All is settled,* she had cried. She could not have been mistaken in that. No, they were betrothed. Unless . . . unless Cassie wished to play a trick on her for all the times she had used her so badly as children. Indeed, she had used her sorely a dozen times, a hundred times, but would Cassie be so vindictive?

She simply did not know. She must speak with Staverton. "You may go now."

"Aye, miss."

After a few minutes of more useless conjecturing on her part, she quit her room. She knew the gentlemen would require at least a half hour to dress for dinner so she made her way to the drawing room and poured herself a sherry. She sat beside the window, which overlooked a fine vista of woodland, and sipped the nut-flavored wine.

Would that it were true, she thought, that Staverton was not to marry Cassie, but it seemed so improbable. Still, what if instead of merely discussing marshes and the like, the earl and her father had been settling matters of a betrothal?

She felt as though she would go mad. She sipped her sherry a little more and watched as the late afternoon sun began to slip behind the hills. Would Cassie have actually permitted herself to accept of Staverton all the while being betrothed to Harry?

This was utterly unthinkable, as were a dozen other thoughts that ran haphazardly through her mind. She took the last few sips of her wine and watched the sun sink lower and lower.

"Faith, but you are remarkably beautiful."

Anne whirled in her chair. Had she not already finished her sherry, she would certainly have sloshed it on her white gown. "Th-thank you, Staverton. How quickly you dressed!" Oh, dear, what a ridiculous thing to say to him.

"I did, did I not? A habit, I suppose, from traipsing after French spies and the like."

How irritating that he must be so calm and the subject must turn to spies instead of betrothals. "So, everything is indeed settled between you and Cassaundra?" she asked, unwilling to delay the point even a trice.

"Yes, very tidily I might I add."

She began to believe he was speaking in riddles. She narrowed her eyes suspiciously. "What did you and my father discuss for so long a time in his study?"

"I do not like to mention it," he said. "It was a matter best left between men."

She could see that there was a taunting glint in his gray eyes. "I begin to think you ought to mention it to me," she countered sternly. She had begun to feel decidedly annoyed.

"If you insist. As it happens, we were discussing your many flaws."

"My flaws?" she exclaimed. "My *many* flaws?"

"There, I knew I should not have mentioned it. Now you will fly into the boughs."

"Only if you were the one to list all of them first."

"No, your father did that."

"And I suppose you agreed with him."

"Not on all counts, but certainly on your impetuous nature."

She paused at this. "I will admit I am a trifle impetuous."

"A trifle?" he queried innocently. "Anne, you kidnapped me and then you helped me chase a spy. Were these long-deliberated notions?"

"I have already admitted to a degree of impetuosity."

"You said you were a *trifle* impetuous. There is a difference."

She sighed impatiently. It appeared he meant to be difficult and she sensed there was little she could do about it. "Why don't you have a glass of sherry."

"Thank you, I shall."

How confident he seemed, a confidence that caused hope to blossom within her. "Do you intend to call upon Mr. and Mrs. Bradley tomorrow?"

"I certainly should," he responded ambiguously.

A moment later, her father entered the chamber. "I met Hanning in the hall. It would seem dinner is served."

Staverton tossed off his sherry and offered his arm to Anne. Grudgingly, she took it.

Dinner was a trying affair. The gentlemen excluded her from nearly every subject. She did not understand what was happening until late in the meal when her father turned to her and said, "Anne, I truly wish you had not kidnapped Staverton. Bad form, quite beyond the pale."

She merely glanced from one countenance to the next and saw within their faces a conspiracy. She had had enough. "I find I am not hungry. I shall retire to the drawing room and leave you men to complete your meal and your conversation without my presence."

They both rose but said nothing to her, which only further exacerbated her mounting temper.

Once within the drawing room, she paced the long chamber for a full quarter of an hour. She intended to give each man a dressing down when they finally deigned to attend her in the drawing room. Their respective conduct had been rude and unkind.

One more pass, and the door opened. She turned, tossing her head, only to find that just her father had entered the chamber. "Where is Staverton?" she asked haughtily.

"Enjoying his port. I thought it time you and I had a word. Will you sit down, Anne, and talk with me?"

Anne stared at him for a long moment. Though her pride was still prickling, there was something in his demeanor which arrested her sense of injury.

He spoke first. "Yes, yes, we were both having sport at your expense, but only because I insisted on it. Anne, how could you have actually kidnapped him and trussed him like a Christmas goose? Really, he should bring charges against you instead of asking for your hand in marriage."

There it was, just like that, the truth of the situation flung at her like a bone to a starving dog. "H-he asked for my hand in marriage?" Tears filled her eyes.

"Yes." Her father approached her, took her hands and bade her sit on the sofa beside him. "I wanted to speak with you alone before giving you my blessing. Though the particulars of such a marriage have all been arranged, I am not entirely satisfied. You have known him but a handful of days and prior to that you despised him. You are an impetuous child and I would hate to see you rush into a marriage only to find you despised your husband."

Anne listened to his concerns, wanting to reassure him, but first she had to make certain she understood exactly what was happening. "Then he is not betrothed to Cassie?"

"As it happens, that would be impossible since she is to marry Harry Chamberlayne in three or four weeks, once the banns have been posted properly. Staverton and Cassie were playing a trick on you earlier and I must agree, given your conduct of the past several days, such a trick was the least you deserved!"

Anne collapsed, weeping, against her father's shoulder. "Oh, Papa," she whimpered. "Are you absolutely certain Cassie and Harry are to wed? For I have the worst fear there has been some terrible mistake or that I am dreaming and will awaken only to find that I have been asleep all this time."

"Completely certain," he said, handing her his kerchief. "You love Staverton, then?"

She nodded, drawing back to blow her nose. "Ever so much. More than life itself. Do you remember the night before I left and that I had had an accident and ruined the raspberries we were to have had for our pie?"

He nodded. "When Bertaud tried to run you down."

She drew in a deep breath. "Yes. Well, Staverton thought

I had been injured and tried to lift me into his curricle, only I was barefoot and was able to plant my feet on the wheel so that he was unable to move me onto the seat. I was laughing so hard because I saw his error, for you must know he was adamant that I see a surgeon immediately."

Her father smiled. "I know. It would be just like you to find amusement in what had been a very dangerous situation, but I can see there is more. Do go on."

"Once I ceased laughing and he understood I was not hurt, I looked up at him, into his eyes. Dear Papa, in that moment I knew I had met the man I would marry."

Her father seemed greatly struck. "Just like my experience in Tunbridge Wells with your mother."

"Exactly! Imagine my chagrin when a few moments later I learned I had tumbled in love with the . . . the Infidel."

"I sense the gods at work."

"Yes, precisely. Now you begin to understand." She blew her nose again. "I love him, Papa, with all my heart. I believe I always shall, and we, well, we had such an extraordinary adventure and we talked and talked and I got shot and he was attacked by three horrible hirelings of Bertaud's, and later, only a protective vest prevented his death. He did tell you of that, of Bertaud shooting him?"

Her father nodded. "Yes, he did. He told me everything. So you are intent on marrying him if you can?"

Anne squeezed his hand. "I desire it above everything."

Her father appeared quite solemn. "He told me I could force the marriage since you had been in his company without benefit of a chaperon for the past five days. I told him I did not believe in marriages for such a reason. I made him explain his sentiments toward you, which he did. It would seem you are both hopelessly in love. I suppose I must allow it, then."

"Oh, dearest Papa!" She slung her arms about his neck and wept a little more fiercely into his neckcloth until he gently pushed her away.

"I believe I hear Staverton at the door," he said, kissing her forehead and gesturing for her to make use of his kerchief a little more.

A moment later, Staverton entered the drawing room. Anne sat profoundly straight as she watched him. He smiled at her, his expression knowing. "Would you like to go for a walk? The temperature this time of evening approaches the idyllic. And I understand that during the summer the dust in the lanes about Sweetwater becomes so fine, it feels like powder between one's toes."

"I should like nothing better," she returned, her gaze never once wavering from his face.

He extended his hand to her, which she accepted, her heart thudding in her chest.

Anne was determined to experience everything the moment would bring, the feel of his hand in hers, the strength of his arm as he lifted her to her feet, the wonderful disparity in their heights.

Once in the avenue, Staverton glanced around the property, then set off in the direction of the village. Anne was a little surprised and wondered what he was about since he seemed intent on some object or other.

Very soon, however, she forgot all about his purpose and became utterly engaged in conversing with him. Of course, every other sentence brought her the hope he would declare himself formally and offer for her. Instead, he began rambling about his properties, about the marshland he wished to drain and the conversation he had had with her father.

She grew impatient and wanted to bring forward the subject closest to her heart, yet she was unable to do so. Was it possible that when her father released him from marrying her he had decided against it after all?

A shiver went through her. Had she been through so much to now lose the only prize that mattered to her?

"Are you chilled, my dear?" he asked, gently hooking his

arm about hers. They had finally reached the old lane that led to the village.

"No, not at all," she responded.

"Do you wish to remove your sandals?" he asked.

"Whatever for?"

He chuckled. "Anne, if I am not much mistaken, you told me you adored walking about barefoot. As it happens—or have you forgotten—that is how I first met you?"

Anne glanced down at the heaps of dust in long ridges beside the hedges. "This is the very place!" she cried. She whirled around and pointed to the bend in the lane. "That is where I first saw Bertaud! Did you bring me here to a purpose?"

"Yes," he stated. "Now, give me your foot."

"What?"

"Your foot." He gestured with his hand toward her feet.

She laughed, then lifted a foot to him, which he settled on his knee. He carefully removed her sandal and with a thoroughly scandalous motion, slid his hands beneath the hem of her gown and untied her garter.

Anne thought she would simply perish with the delight of feeling him touch her as he was. She caught her breath. "Staverton, you should not be doing this."

"Oh, but I must," he countered, rolling the stocking slowly down her leg and sliding it off her foot. He tucked the silk ball into his coat pocket. "Now, the other leg."

"Oh," Anne murmured, wondering if she could bear such a simple, forbidden pleasure as Staverton removing her stockings.

His hands once more slipped beneath her gown and found the garter. She should tell him he was behaving most improperly, but she doubted such an admonition would have the least effect on him.

When the second stocking was off her foot and tucked into his pocket, he led her to a drift of powdery dust. "There. Now you may enjoy the rest of our walk down this lane."

Anne, holding her silk skirts away from the dirt, smiled up at him. "All this bother just so I might enjoy the dust between my toes?"

"Of course."

Anne sunk her toes deeply and laughed. When she looked up at him, he swept an arm about her waist and pulled her close. She let go of her gown, settling her hands lightly on his arms.

"I have thought about the odd circumstance of our meeting in this lane a hundred times," he said quietly. "Of you being barefoot, of how heartily you laughed when you understood the depths of my confusion about your supposed injuries, of how you first looked at me when I held you in my arms." His expression had grown very intense. "From the very beginning you were as no other lady I had ever known before. I wanted to see you this way just now." He smiled again. "Does the dust feel like powder?" His voice was barely a whisper.

"Yes," she whispered in return.

"My dearest Anne, my lady most valiant, will you do me the honor of becoming my wife?"

Anne stared into his eyes and became lost as she had so many times before. The Infidel was begging for her hand in marriage, the man whom she had previously regarded as a certain enemy just a few days past. She had known him only for a terribly brief time. Did she know him well enough and did he know her sufficiently to create a truly happy marriage?

"I am strong-willed and at times ill-tempered," she said, stroking his cheek with the backs of her fingers. "I have been known to prevaricate upon occasion, I have no patience with timidity, and," here she paused and drew a deep breath, "I am in possession of at least a hundred other faults which do not spring to mind of the moment. Staverton, are you certain you truly desire to marry me?"

He pulled her closer still so that his lips were but a breath away. "I have no doubt we shall brangle, perhaps every day, but there is this wicked part of me that looks forward to it. However, I also anticipate great joy and conversations that will last into the small hours of the morning, and a great deal of adventure. Will you have me with all my faults, as well? You are already acquainted with many of them quite intimately."

"You are proud, at times arrogant, you lack perception," she paused and searched in her mind, "and also—"

"Whoa!" he cried, laughing. "Why do we not make an agreement that we shall discuss the remainder of our respective flaws after the honeymoon."

Anne released a contented sigh. "An excellent notion and yes, I will marry you, for I desire it above all things."

He kissed her, sealing the agreement between them. Anne received his lips by leaning into him and allowing his already tight embrace to become a welcome vice. She trembled at the deepening of his kiss, at the wonder of such a joining, at the extraordinary knowledge that love had found her after all.

He drew back. "I was thinking we might journey to the Lavant, swim in the warm Mediterranean waters, and afterward have all the pleasure of being captured by a swift corsair."

"Oh, Staverton," she murmured, shivering in delight from head to foot, "Please tell me you are most serious, for I should like nothing better."

"What?" he asked facetiously. "Nothing better than being held for ransom by a Barbary Coast thief and murderer?"

"Oh, yes, if you please, my lord."

There was only one thing he could do, Staverton thought. He must kiss her until such foolish notions left her head entirely. He therefore slanted his lips across hers, gathering her into a rough embrace.

When she drew back, her eyes glittering, his thoughts swung back quickly to the image of chasing after a corsair in a swift yacht, a yacht perhaps of his own design, in possession of a cannon. Now *there* was something to ponder.

"Our ship must have weaponry," she stated decisively.

He was a little startled, for it was as though she had entered his own reverie. "Yes, I was thinking precisely the same thing."

She turned him back toward the house, slipping her arm about his. "Were you also thinking we might become negotiators on behalf of the Crown and those held captive in Tripoli, Tunis and Algiers?"

"I have already been approached by the regent himself."

"That's why you were in Brighton!" she cried. "Oh, Staverton, we must do it. We have enough money between us to build the finest yacht imaginable and to hire a crew worthy of her and to settle the cannon in just the right places, perhaps saving one or two for secret compartments in order to—"

"Yes, to surprise our enemy."

"We could also smuggle our spies out of Europe as occasion required."

He began to laugh. "Yes, of course."

She was silent for a very long moment so that Staverton glanced toward her, wondering what she was thinking, particularly since a frown furrowed her brow.

"What is it?" he queried gently. "A moment earlier your face was filled with excitement and now you seem troubled."

"Not troubled precisely, only, Staverton, I do not wish to wait a month before we are wed."

He chuckled. "But the posting of the banns requires four weeks and we do have obligations to our respective families. Your father will certainly wish to attend our wedding, as will my mother."

An image popped into Anne's mind and she began trying to determine just where she had put her rope. Her pistols were in prime order and ready for use again, and her servants, of course, would go with her anywhere.

"A-n-n-e," Staverton murmured, drawing out each letter.

"What?" she asked as innocently as possible, but even to her own ears her voice sounded false.

"We shall wait a month and no nonsense," he cried. "You might as well put Gretna Green out of your mind."

She released a deep sigh. "I suppose you are right. Papa has forever told me he hoped to live long enough to see me wed." She did not elaborate on this statement since a more precise version of his words were, "I wonder if you will be married before I stick my spoon in the wall." She suspected he did not give a fig concerning the actual wedding day. As for Staverton, even a nodcock could see he was unwilling to discuss the matter.

Now, where had she put that rope!

"Do but look," she said, gesturing to the left. "There is a particularly fine drift of dust." She happily sank her toes into the delicate powder and cooed her delight, after which Staverton once more drew her into his arms.

Author's Note

Of the numerous towns, villages and hamlets mentioned in this story, only Sulhurst exists solely in my imagination. The rest can be found along the old Bath Road from the starting point of Reading in the county of Berkshire to Bath itself.

—V. K.